SINS OF
OUR FATHERS

Visit us at www.boldstrokesbooks.com

SINS OF OUR FATHERS

by

A. Rose Mathieu

2017

ISBN 13: 978-1-62639-873-3

THIS TRADE PAPERBACK ORIGINAL IS PUBLISHED BY
BOLD STROKES BOOKS, INC.
P.O. BOX 249
VALLEY FALLS, NY 12185

FIRST EDITION: MARCH 2017

CREDITS
EDITOR: CINDY CRESAP
PRODUCTION DESIGN: STACIA SEAMAN
COVER DESIGN BY MELODY POND

Acknowledgments

I would like to thank my editor, Cindy Cresap, for guiding me through the process. I would also like to thank my spouse, Elizabeth Mathieu, for her keen proofreading skills and her inspiration to keep on writing. And my children, Jamus and Evan Mathieu, for giving me the biggest reason to work hard every day.

Dedicated to my mother, Mary,
for her love and support through my life.

PROLOGUE

April 1982

Death's blood stained the four boys who stood in a ring, dressed in jackets zipped to the top and hoods pulled around their faces, which served to thwart the moist night air and conceal their identity. Naked trees stretched out above their heads, with branches of bony fingers pointing down as though accusing. An oppressive stillness surrounded them, threatening to suffocate their labored breaths.

"Hurry up. I'm cold!" the first boy demanded.

"Shut up. I can't go any faster," snapped another.

The sound of a shovel scraping against small rocks as it dug into the soil produced an unnatural sound to accompany the dark setting.

"You do it." The boy passed the shovel to a third who stood holding a flashlight. The scuffing sound continued to fill the air until at the center of the boys' circle there was a shallow grave.

"Come on," said the first boy as he led the others to a piece of plastic sheeting and pulled. The others grabbed hold and helped pull, then the smallest of the boys let go and the weight of his corner dropped to the ground. The boy fell, scrambling backward until his back was against a tree.

"What the hell!" yelled the first boy.

The smaller boy hugged his knees to his chest. "It's moving."

The boys released their hold, letting the plastic fall to the ground, and fixed their eyes on the heap in the center. A small clawing sound came from inside the wrapped sheeting, and the first boy picked up the shovel and brought it down on the plastic, making a sickening thud. A soft whimpering came from inside, until repeated blows brought deafening silence and stillness again.

The first boy dropped the shovel. "Let's go." He resumed picking up the plastic, and the other two followed.

The smallest boy curled into a ball on the damp ground, and his body shook as he tried to conceal his weeping. "Shut up," hissed the first boy, and the smaller boy held his breath and pulled himself up, scraping his back against a tree. He placed his palm on the tree trunk to steady himself and felt a carving on the tree and looked down at it. Underneath his hand someone had crafted a heart with two sets of initials inside. It seemed misplaced.

As the smallest boy studied the tree, the other boys pulled the lifeless heap, and the plastic easily slipped into the grave. Without looking down, the second boy picked up the shovel and began redepositing the soil into the hole.

The morbid task complete, the boys mutely walked through the trees, but dead foliage cracking under their feet would not allow them to leave in peace. The boys flinched at the rustling of a small animal in the undergrowth, their only witness.

The boys retreated to a wooden structure obscured by trees that easily blended with a small stone mountain. The first boy reached for the handle on a fortified wooden door that marked the entry into a discarded mining tunnel and turned to the others before he let them pass. "We will never speak of this again."

CHAPTER ONE

Present Day

Dressed in her charcoal gray suit, her skirt respectfully at knee level, attorney Elizabeth Campbell sashayed down the sidewalk, keeping time with the Madonna song pumping in her ears, butchering the words as she sang. Song lyrics were never her strong suit. Before reaching the storefront of the legal clinic and transforming into a respectable attorney, she belted out one last lyric that made even the tone-deaf cringe.

Southern Indigent Legal Center, better known as SILC, was founded nearly fifty years ago by Joseph Manderson, whose vision was to offer competent legal services to the underserved of the city, the hardworking poor, the forgotten. Although its visionary founder passed on, SILC continued its noble service through grants and donations from larger, more prosperous law firms, whose donations relieved them of any guilt for overlooking pro bono services of their own.

With her morning savior in its Styrofoam cup in one hand, she hoisted her shoulder bag higher with the other and cautiously stepped over a sleeping bag occupied by one of the forgotten who made camp near the front door. She startled him awake, and the sleeping bag quickly rose, causing her to jostle her caffeine fix just enough to leave brown splatter across her crisp, formerly white blouse.

"Damn it."

She yanked open the glass door and entered, throwing the cup in a small metal trash can with more force than necessary, which caused it to ricochet and leave a spatter mark on the scuffed white wall behind the can. She stared at the pattern on the wall, noting how it resembled an old woman with a head scarf, and she considered cleaning it up, but was saved from her internal debate by the voice of an intern. "Oh good, you're here. Dan's looking for you."

"Thanks, Jeff." Elizabeth's office sat in the back corner of the clinic, not quite the corner office her parents had envisioned for her when they paid the hefty bill for her Ivy League law school. She crossed the threshold into her modest-size office and tossed her bag on a pile of folders sitting on a worn black chair across from her desk. Behind her scarred wooden desk sat a matching black chair on wheels that Elizabeth had nicknamed BD, short for Black Devil for its propensity to flip over its occupant who sat too far back. Only a person experienced with Black Devil dared approach it.

Behind her desk were two sets of windows that offered light in addition to the fluorescent bulbs that stretched across the ceiling. Black iron bars partially obstructed the view of the alley and the row of trash cans that seemed perpetually full and that were currently being scavenged by Fred, her pseudo pet rat. She knew it was Fred because he had part of his tail missing, which she learned was a result of an encounter with a sharp knife and the owner of the diner across the way. What she wasn't sure was whether the injury was a result of the proprietor chasing away the unwanted critter or whether Fred was meant to be dinner and made a timely escape, minus a full tail.

Unlike the offices of many of Elizabeth's law school friends that boasted contemporary and expensive artwork, her wall proudly displayed a large corkboard adorned with papers and a to-do list haphazardly fastened with multiple colored pins. Her right wall exhibited two inspirational posters, offering words of wisdom including, "Don't put off to tomorrow what you can do today because today is yesterday's tomorrow." This made her dizzy thinking about it. However, it was better than the second. "If at first you don't succeed, try, try again." Elizabeth's definition of insanity and contrary to her adage, "If at first you don't succeed, break it; it will make you feel better." She had little need for the posters' secrets of life but left them in place because they offered covering for a few holes from obvious mishaps of the past.

The walls were lined with file boxes with neat script on the outside indicating that they were organized in alphabetical order; filing cabinets were a rare commodity and never seemed to make it into the clinic's budget. She switched on her computer before exiting her office, allowing the computer to boot up in her absence.

In the center of the clinic, a series of gray cubicles stood side by side like a lineup, and small offices ringed the outside walls. She crossed the clinic to Dan's office, which sat in the opposite corner diagonal to her own, and gently knocked on the door frame before passing through and unceremoniously plopping herself on a worn leather chair. Dan, with a telephone to his ear, barely glanced up as he sat with his profile to her. She patiently studied a crack in the leather of the chair and noticed the yellow foam threatening to spill out. The decor of Dan's office was much like her own, mismatched furniture with a brown-and-gold plaid couch from an era past against the side wall. The only item out of place was the soft leather high-back chair that Dan occupied, which offered a seat warmer and vibrating motion. She briefly contemplated the chair but quickly shook off the thought and turned her attention from vibrating furniture to study Dan. He was an average-looking man, with salt-and-pepper hair that contained more salt than pepper. Slightly pudgy in the midsection, he depicted a well-fed, happily married man who didn't feel the need for a gym membership. Unlike her tailored suit, Dan's dark blue suit and matching blue and gray striped tie were probably purchased from the rack at a department store.

Dan Hastings had been the supervising attorney at SILC since she started four years ago, and she wasn't quite sure how long he had been with SILC or what compelled him to stay. Although he carried the title supervising attorney, it carried no tangible benefit that she could see. She knew with his experience he could earn a six-figure salary in a law firm of his choosing. Yet Dan seemed to find emotional prosperity in what he did that compensated for the lack of financial riches.

Elizabeth understood this all too well. She was drawn to SILC after a summer internship while awaiting her bar exam results. The people touched her and kept her coming back, much to her father's dismay. Charles Campbell, Elizabeth's father, corporate attorney and founding partner of Campbell, Roberts, Addelstein, and Krass, was the polar opposite of Dan Hastings. Charles Campbell was refined, with an office that oozed opulence and an assistant at his beck and call. Charles expected the same for his daughter, reserving an office for her down the hall from his own. Instead, she turned her back on CRAK, the nickname her father detested, but one that she threw out every chance she could. Her father continually reminded Elizabeth that her office awaited her when she was done "slumming it." At first, she tried to explain the importance of her work at SILC, but her father could never see beyond her five-figure salary. In the end, they agreed to disagree.

Elizabeth was a trust fund baby, and her modest salary from SILC was like a small bonus. The Campbell family came from old money. When she was young, Elizabeth's father liked to tell stories of how her great-grandfather built an empire from shining shoes on a street corner. In her later years, she realized that her family's early fortunes did come from boots, but more like the bootlegging kind.

Dan finally hung up the phone and blew out an exasperated breath. He turned to face Elizabeth and stared down at her blouse. "Tough morning?"

Glancing down at her chest, she remembered her morning mishap with her coffee. "It was the sleeping bag," she said as if that explained everything.

He scratched his head, and she sensed that he was warring with himself as to whether he should explore the sleeping bag comment or let it go, but he opted to let it pass.

Dan placed his arms on the desk and leaned forward. "Mayor Reynosa is running for the governor's seat. He has his agenda to sell. He promised the people a full review of convictions from the DA's major crimes division over the last five years because of the scandal over in Brewster."

"Brewster's three counties away. This means…what exactly?" she asked with suspicion.

"The mayor is reaching out, asking for assistance from clinics like ours to help because the PD's and DA's offices are overwhelmed."

"And we're not? Why are we even considering this?"

Dan leaned back in his chair, giving her a stern glance. "We're considering this because we're funded by grants and donations. If we don't play nice when they ask for help, they don't play nice when we ask for help."

She sank back in her chair. Brewster County had been rocked with scandal after an investigative reporter revealed a kickback system between the mayor, city officials, and the major crimes unit of the district attorney's and public defender's offices. Reynosa had been mayor as long as Elizabeth could remember, and she surmised that he and his people probably had plenty of closets full of skeletons scattered throughout the city. It made good political sense to open a few empty closets to give the appearance of transparency. For this reason, she knew the review would turn up no impropriety.

"Look," Dan said, "they're only asking us to review three cases. Look them over, give them your stamp of approval, and move on." He handed over a short stack of files. "It'll take two hours tops."

"Right," Elizabeth mumbled as she stood and grabbed the stack. "I serve at the pleasure of the mayor."

On the trip back to her office, she stopped in the communal kitchen, better described as the communal closet, for another try at a cup of coffee. A small counter space contained a brown microwave with twist dials with the numbers rubbed off, a toaster that had two settings—raw and burnt—and a new, state-of-the-art coffee machine, compliments of Elizabeth. The kitchen could fit one person comfortably, two people if they were well acquainted, and three if someone would risk being charged with lewd and lascivious behavior.

With a coffee mug that proudly announced "World's Best Dad" in one hand and the stack of files in the other, she carefully traversed back to her office, determined not to wear her second cup. After plopping the files on her desk, she scanned her emails and opened one from BestChef:

Hey Girl, we still on for tonight? I have perfected my sauce and you are my first ~~victim~~ customer.

She typed a quick affirmation and turned to her dreaded task, opening the file on top—Mark Waters, drug dealer, convicted of second-degree murder. It seemed he and his customer had a disagreement as to the quality of the product, and Mr. Waters decided to end the dispute in the most diplomatic way he knew and pulled out a semi-automatic weapon. Elizabeth reviewed the rest of the file and noted that Mr. Waters was convicted by a jury after three separate witnesses, who were in the park across the street, testified as to the exchange of words and shooting. Satisfied that the conviction was clean, she closed the file and reached for the second one.

Helen Akbajian, homemaker and part-time receptionist, was convicted of assault with a deadly weapon and mayhem. Mrs. Akbajian had learned of her husband's infidelity with the young clerk at his butcher's shop and decided to take matters into her own hands. She waited until he was sleeping, took a meat cleaver—apparently Mr. Akbajian's favorite, to add insult to injury—and removed his appendage. To ensure that Mr. Akbajian would have no chance of further indiscretions, she stuffed the appendage in the garbage disposal and turned it on.

"Ouch." Elizabeth giggled. "Hell hath no fury." As she scanned the crime photos, which included a close-up of the meat cleaver, the garbage disposal, and Mr. Akbajian's naked body, minus his private parts, she started humming Chuck Berry's novelty song "My Ding-A-Ling."

Comfortable that Mrs. Akbajian had been caught red-handed, literally, she closed the file. She was starting to enjoy her little assignment.

She opened her third and final file—Raymond Miller, unemployed, convicted of first-degree murder. Her jovial mood from the prior case quickly faded as she carefully read the file. Raymond Miller confessed to the killing of a Catholic priest.

The folder contained a manila envelope with the flap sealed by its metal clasps. Elizabeth lifted the envelope and bent up the metal prongs, releasing its hold on the flap, and removed a stack of photos. Father Francis Portillo was discovered naked with his bloody body left hanging on a large black metal gate on an abandoned property on the outskirts of the city. His body bore grotesque gashes, some deep enough to expose muscle and ligaments. His wrists and ankles were bound by rope and lashed to the gate, with his arms spread to the side, forming a sickening scarlet T. The ligature bruising around his wrists and ankles indicated that he had been tied up for an extended period, likely the full three days he had been missing. However, the evidence suggested that he was killed in a different location and left hanging on the gate for display.

There were a series of crime scene photos in both color and black and white, and as Elizabeth flipped through them, the photos almost seemed surreal. The wounds were so graphic, with flesh ripped apart, that it looked more like Halloween macabre created for thrill seekers than a true human body, but then she picked out a haunting black-and-white picture of the priest's face. A rope tied around Father Portillo's head held it up so that his vacant eyes stared back at her. A fly was perched on his cheek, feasting on an open wound. Those eyes did not find peace in the end.

Elizabeth placed the photo at the bottom of the pile, fearing his eyes would stay with her long after she closed the file. She selected another depicting the priest's lower abdomen, where the killer left a distinct mark. A circle containing three congruent triangles with their points joined at the center was deeply carved into the flesh. The triangles were formed by peeling back the skin, creating a stark color contrast. The circle remained flesh colored and the triangles a bloody red where the skin had been torn away. Elizabeth pulled out a sketch that she passed over earlier, now understanding its significance. It was a rendition of the carving on the father's body.

In other circumstances, the carving might have seemed creative and aesthetic, but on a human body, it was grotesque. She shoved the photographs back into their home inside the envelope and closed her eyes. She pressed the heels of her hands to her eyes and bowed her head. If there was ever a time that a prayer was needed, this was it. After a brief debate on whether to forge on, she sat up and picked up the file again.

The autopsy report indicated that the wounds were likely the result of a rawhide whip, with steel spikes strategically placed near the end. Fragments of the metal were still lodged beneath the priest's skin, and the spikes accounted for the particularly deep wounds and tearing of the flesh. The medical examiner believed that the carving on the abdomen was likely done postmortem due to the lack of blood compared to the other wounds, and the cause of death was substantial blood loss.

Unable to read on, Elizabeth dropped the documents on her desk and left her office. With no real destination in mind, she walked to the restroom and roughly pushed the door open with her shoulder. She grabbed the cold ceramic of the sink and stared into the mirror mounted on the wall. She barely recognized herself. Her eyes were streaked with red lines, her skin bore red blotches, and her bangs sported a cowlick. She could have gone a lifetime or two without seeing those images.

"Are you okay?" Elizabeth turned to see Amy, SILC's receptionist and resident mother, standing with the upper half of her body leaning inside the partially opened bathroom door.

"Yeah, thanks. Just looking at a tough case." She squirmed a bit under Amy's careful scrutiny.

"Well, Rosa Sanchez is here for you. Do you want to see if she can come back a bit later?"

"No, I'm good. I'll be right out."

Amy gave a sympathetic smile and backed out the door.

Elizabeth leveled a glare at her reflection. "Suck it up. It's not like your husband is beating you and threatening to have you deported."

❖

"I'm sorry to keep you waiting," Elizabeth said as she strode into the reception area.

Rosa Sanchez stood and pulled her eight-year-old son Hector up by the hand, which nearly caused him to drop his handheld Nintendo DS. "No problem, Attorney Campbell."

"Hi, Hector, how are you?"

"I'm good," Hector said with his eyes fixed on his coveted black device.

Rosa removed Hector's baseball cap from his head. "Hector, please put that away."

Elizabeth winked at him. "Have you ever played Pac-Man? It's my favorite."

"Pac what?" Hector asked, scrunching his nose.

"Oh come on, you know Pac-Man, where the mouth eats the balls."

Rosa's eyes grew wide, and Hector simply giggled.

"No, I mean little white balls." She gestured with her thumb and forefinger to demonstrate the size. She could see Amy with her head resting on the front desk and her shoulders moving up and down, trying to conceal her laughter.

"Oh, never mind," Elizabeth said as she turned and led the way back to her office. "Sorry, there never seems to be enough space," she said as she cleared a stack of files resting on her guest chair. "I'll be right back." She rolled a second chair in from outside that protested with a high-pitched squeak the entire journey.

Elizabeth pushed the Raymond Miller file to the side and stroked Black Devil as she cautiously sat. She ritualistically patted BD before she lowered herself to its clutches as an offering of goodwill.

"How's school going, Hector?"

"Good," came the simple reply.

She realized that her conversation with Hector would be one-sided and gave up. "Why don't you go back to playing your game while your mom and I talk?"

"Okay." Hector didn't have to be told twice and whipped the game out of his sweatshirt pocket.

"Rosa, have you thought of what we talked about?"

She started fretting with the hem of her shirt. "Sí, but it is very hard thing to do." Her accent became more pronounced.

Rosa had been on the receiving end of her husband's drunken fists more times than she would admit. She feared her husband Jacob's fury if she filed for a restraining order. She knew that Jacob didn't fear losing her. She was expendable. It was Hector he wanted. As cruel as he was to Rosa, he worshipped his son.

"He says he'll have me deported. I'll lose Hector."

Rosa's mistrust in the legal system was well founded. She'd fled Guatemala when she was seventeen after being raped by her drunken father. When the police brought her back to her father's home after the attack, she learned that women were merely property in Guatemala and fled, seeking asylum in the United States. Unfortunately, Rosa's asylum case was mishandled by an unscrupulous legal assistant, better known in the Latin American community as a "notario." The notario not only took Rosa's money, but more importantly, because of his incompetence, he took her only chance at an asylum hearing. She never got her day in court and was left with a deportation order. She'd been living under the radar ever since.

Elizabeth glanced at Hector, who was immersed in his electronic world, before she spoke. "I know you're scared, but he doesn't have that power over you anymore. You took control the day you walked out the door."

Rosa looked down at her hands tightly clasped in her lap. "Okay, I can do this."

"Great, I have the documents ready. I just need you to sign them." Elizabeth turned to her computer, clicked a few icons, and hit print. "I'll be right back." She exited the office and approached the central copy and printing machine, where her printer, along with everyone else's, was wirelessly connected. She found the intern, Jeff, with his head inside the open door at the center of the machine, pulling large wads of paper from its belly. The toner cartridge and other parts were strewn about the floor around Jeff's feet like spilled guts.

"This can't be good," she mumbled and returned to her office. "I'm sorry. We seem to be having some technical difficulties with our equipment." *That's an understatement. This place is going to hell in a handbasket.* "I can bring the documents by your home this evening when we have things up and running." *More like when I run to Kinko's and print it out.*

"I don't want to trouble you," Rosa said with a concerned look.

"It's no trouble. This way I can get the documents filed tomorrow as I planned."

"Thank you."

After escorting Rosa and Hector back to the reception area, Elizabeth proudly carried the "World's Best Dad" cup to the communal closet for a recharge before resuming the task of going through the Raymond Miller file. She passed Jeff as he continued his struggle with the copy machine, and a loud grinding noise burst from the machine as though the beast had been awoken. Elizabeth paused, unsure if she wanted to get involved.

"Come on, you piece of shit," Jeff yelled and shook it. The copy machine responded with a deep, angry growling noise, and he jumped back and turned to see Elizabeth watching the display. "That thing just growled at me."

Clearly not done with its rebellion, the machine started spewing black smoke from its back. "That's not all," Elizabeth said, pointing to the copier, and Jeff turned to witness the smoke rising. "Well, don't just stand there. Unplug it."

He yanked the power cord from the wall. "Do you want to tell Dan?" he asked hopefully.

"Not on your life," she said as she walked away.

Elizabeth resumed the task of the Raymond Miller file and reviewed a profile work-up that predicted that the killer was a Caucasian male between twenty-five to forty years of age with a deep hatred for organized religion. *Ya think?* She read on. The killer had likely been raised in a home that strictly observed Christian practices and harsh penances for any infraction.

Taking into consideration the victim, manner of death by whipping, and the display of his body in a cross formation, the carving was also believed to be religious in nature. A detailed report discussed the history of the triangle as a common Christian symbol of the Holy Trinity or triad of the Father, Son, and the Holy Ghost, and the number three a lesser-known symbol of the same.

Elizabeth found the profile unremarkable and moved on to the discussion specific to Raymond Miller. A psychological evaluation revealed that Raymond's IQ was well below normal. Although he was twenty-two when he was arrested, he had the intellect of a child.

Raymond lived in a shed converted to a living space behind his mother's home. He was unemployed but was known throughout the neighborhood as "the trash digger," as he supported himself by riffling through trash, looking for recyclables.

What was thought to be a routine call to chase off a vagrant Dumpster diving turned out to be an arrest of a lifetime for a rookie officer. When the officer searched Raymond, he had a set of black rosary beads with a large silver crucifix in his pocket. Testing of the beads revealed traces of blood from Father Francis Portillo.

A search warrant for Raymond's shed and his mother's home

was easily obtained, although probably not necessary. According to the notes of Detective Patrick Sullivan, Raymond's mother was more than happy to allow the police to search the premises. Raymond was the only child of Delores Miller, and his father was unknown. Delores relished the attention as the poor mother who had been carrying the burden of a defective son all alone for twenty-two years; however, the photos of the shed put into question how much caring she put into raising him.

The shed was nothing more than a wooden tool shack with weathered boards that offered little insulation. Inside, the shed was surprisingly tidy, with a mattress in one corner covered by stained floral sheets and a blue cotton blanket with cigarette burns throughout. Two wooden crates lined against the opposite wall and contained most of his worldly possessions—a pair of pants, three shirts, a sweatshirt, two pairs of mismatched socks, and three pairs of superhero underwear.

A wooden shelf above the crates held an assortment of Matchbox cars, a box of crayons, a Superman action figure, a small stack of comic books, and a blue toothbrush with a crumpled tube of toothpaste. The walls were decorated with colorful crayon pictures that depicted a life very different from Raymond's. There were plenty of trees filled with green leaves, neatly kept homes, and a bright yellow sun with a smiley face. In each picture, there were two smiling stick figures holding hands that, based on the height difference, appeared to be parent and child. Each picture was proudly signed by its artist, much like a child would, with uneven lettering and the second letter of his name written backward.

Despite Raymond's age, he still saw himself as a child. *Even with the squalor in which he lived, he held his mother in high regard, as if he were ignorant of his world.*

If she had stopped there, she would have been convinced that they had the wrong man. However, concealed under the clothing in one wooden crate was a rusted metal box with a broken latch. The box held a Bible belonging to the priest, another memento from his savagery.

A recorded confession, memorialized in a typed transcript, came shortly after the search of the shed. The confession was simple:

Detective Sullivan: Did you kill Father Francis Portillo?
Raymond Miller: Yes.
Detective Sullivan: Why?
Raymond Miller: To make God happy. Pappy is happy.

Detective Sullivan: What does that mean?
Detective Sullivan: This interview is recorded. Shrugging your
*   shoulders is useless. I'll ask again, what does that mean?*
*   What was that? Oh, never mind.*

Knowing that he would never really know why and possibly because he didn't care why, the detective ended the interview.

In exchange for his confession, the death penalty was taken off the table, and Raymond was now a permanent resident of the state penal institution for life.

With a flash drive containing the Rosa Sanchez documents packed into her leather bag, Elizabeth shut down her computer and headed for a gated parking lot a block down from SILC that offered security monitoring of her vehicle. The clinic offered parking for its employees adjacent to the building, but that wasn't good enough for her baby. She loved her red two-seater BMW Z4 Roadster. There were some definite perks to her trust fund. She loved cars, and in particular, fast cars, and was consequently on a first-name basis with the officers around her home.

After a brief visit to the local Kinko's, she drove her Roadster down a boulevard that was lined with storefronts much like her clinic. Metal gates were drawn closed for protection. The awnings on the buildings were faded and exhibited a few holes where the weather proved to be unkind. In time for its 100-year anniversary with its multitude of celebratory festivities, the city boasted of a financial revival, an economic boom. Although it was true for many, the inhabitants of this part of town had not fared so well under the economic revolution.

She turned onto a smaller street that contained residential structures where the apartment buildings had more dirt than lawn, and black metal bars were a common feature on the windows of the residences. A group of children played soccer in front of a two-story building, and an errant ball bounced into the street with a young boy closely behind it, causing Elizabeth to hit the brakes. She chose to keep her speed at a pace slightly above a crawl, an unfamiliar feeling to her. The slow speed allowed her to take in the neighborhood, which was a world away from her own community and not even in the same universe as her parents' home.

As she drove on, she recognized a street name and turned onto the block with rows of simple two-story homes that were likely built in the 40s. Many of the decaying homes had chipped and peeling paint with entire pieces of side paneling missing. She stopped in front of a now familiar address that contained a faded light blue home with a chain link fence surrounding the property and the gate to the walkway missing. The lawn was a sickly yellow with patches of dirt. She sat in her car and debated what to do. Were she religious, she would have deemed it divine intervention. She opened the car door. "To hell with it. Here goes nothing."

She ascended a set of wooden stairs that creaked to announce her arrival and rang the doorbell, but uncertain as to its working order, followed it with a knock on the door. A woman in a floral dress that hung loosely on her figure pulled open the door.

"Yes?" the woman asked in a curt tone.

"Ms. Miller?"

"Yes. Who are you?"

"I'm Elizabeth Campbell. I am an attorney with the Southern Indigent Legal Center. I've been asked to review your son Raymond's case."

"Why? What good does that do?"

Elizabeth hesitated a moment before responding. "I'm just ensuring that nothing was overlooked."

Ms. Miller crossed her arms and puffed out, "I've helped you people before, and I got nothing from it. They paid me nothing."

"Paid you nothing?" Elizabeth asked.

Ms. Miller jerked at a small gold cross hanging around her neck and held it between her fingers as she spoke. "I let them come through my home and search that godforsaken shed. What did I get for it? Nothing. That's what I got."

"Well, it's not customary for the police to pay to search a home, ma'am."

"I spent my best years raising that boy. He's been nothing but trouble since the day he was born. He's not right in the head." She let out a deep cough of a smoker and continued once she regained her breath. "I should have gotten something for spending all those years cleaning after him, dressing him. He couldn't even tie his own goddamn shoes. Now he's someone else's problem."

Elizabeth remembered the shed but held her tongue. "Do you believe your son killed that priest, Ms. Miller?"

"Who knows what that boy is capable of? Spending all his time by himself. Talking in riddles. If he said he did it, well then, he did it."

"Do you mind if I see the shed?" She was unsure what she expected to find, but figured she had come this far, she might as well go all the way.

"Well, I charge ten dollars for that."

"You charge?" Elizabeth asked incredulously.

"I have to make a living somehow. It was very popular after he was arrested. Not many people get to see firsthand where a killer lives."

Elizabeth stood staring with her mouth open. After a moment, she found her voice. "Did you let people in the shed before the police searched it?"

"Psshht, nah. I didn't know Raymond was a killer until the police came. I might have gotten more."

Exercising restraint she didn't know she had, Elizabeth remained silent. Her other option was to tackle the woman and shake her senseless.

"Do you want that tour?"

Elizabeth dug her hand into her bag for her wallet and, after handing over the bill, was led to the backyard. Ms. Miller entered a combination into a twist dial lock and opened the door, and a wave of stale air hit Elizabeth. It was obvious that Ms. Miller hadn't had a paying customer in a while.

The shed looked just as the pictures depicted, but the clothing items in the wooden crates appeared rifled through. The mattress still sat in the corner with the same blanket and sheets. Wrinkles in the covers indicated that a few of the voyeurs had lain on the bed to get the full experience. The toys remained on the shelf and the artwork still hung on the wall, but had faded with time. Elizabeth stopped in front of the picture with the two stick figures holding hands. As she stood in the middle of the shed, a deep sense of despair traveled through her. *Who is Raymond Miller?*

With nothing new learned from her visit to the shed, she turned to Ms. Miller, who stood guard at the door. "It seems that there's nothing for me to do here. Thank you for your time." She walked out of Raymond Miller's former home and waited as Ms. Miller secured the lock. She took several cleansing breaths as she retreated back to her car and drove on to Rosa Sanchez's apartment, which was only three short blocks from the Miller residence.

❖

After completing her task with Rosa Sanchez, Elizabeth headed home with a large glass of white wine in mind. She lived in a ranch-style, three-bedroom home with the proverbial white picket fence. A large willow tree proudly took center stage amongst a meticulously cut lawn and colorful flower beds that lined the walkway. She chose this quiet middle-class neighborhood because nothing about it reminded her of her childhood home with its protective gates, massive lawns, and marble columns. Her parents' disdain for Elizabeth's common home rivaled their disdain for her corner office. This was another perk, in her eyes—her parents never came to visit.

What really sold her on the home was the fully remodeled, state-of-the-art kitchen with professional-grade stainless steel appliances and a granite slab center island. Not that she enjoyed cooking. She was deemed culinarily challenged by her friends. In college, she was caught red-handed boiling a box of frozen vegetables, box and all. In her defense, the instructions never said to remove the vegetables from the box before boiling. That part was assumed, unless you were Elizabeth Campbell.

However, she enjoyed the culinary mastery of her former college roommate and closest confidant, Michael Chan, aka BestChef. Michael assumed control over her kitchen the day she signed the escrow papers, and he hosted legendary dinner parties, Elizabeth's presence being optional. Tonight was not a legendary dinner night, but a test run of Michael's latest creation.

As Elizabeth opened her front door, she was assaulted by Charlie, her large gray cat, who greeted her every evening without fail. He sat perched on the windowsill watching her stride up the walkway, waiting for the right moment to start his wailing of starvation. Charlie often told complete lies of never being fed, even though his bowl was filled to the brim with food; however, he scoffed at this inferior dry food. He only dined on the expensive wet food that came in the small square containers that had to be refrigerated. He knew when Elizabeth tried to substitute with a cheap imitation from a tin can and would repay her faux pas by regurgitating the food in her bed, so she could enjoy the scent of the food a second time.

As Elizabeth and Michael worked fluidly together in the kitchen moving past each other with comfortable ease, she recited a CliffsNotes version of her day, editing out the grisly details.

After a quick squeeze of her shoulder, Michael said, "You know, what you really need is a quick roll in the hay. That will fix things right up."

This earned him a playful slap on the arm.

"Seriously, how long has it been?"

She gave him a warning look, and Michael turned his back and resumed his chopping with curt but elegant movements. "Will you peel the carrots." It wasn't really a question.

Instead of tending to the carrots, she approached a pan of simmering sauce and lifted a wooden spoon. Michael turned on her, pointing his knife. "Step away from the sauce." She stopped with the spoon poised halfway to her open mouth and quickly debated whether to run her tongue up and down the front and back of the spoon, just to goad him. She realized that might be a bit immature and plopped the spoon back in the pan and sulked her way back to the sink to peel the carrots.

After successfully scalping the carrots to within an inch of their lives, she pushed the discarded peels into the drain and flipped the switch for the garbage disposal. As the grinding noise filled the kitchen, she unconsciously began to hum "My Ding-A-Ling."

"Damn it. You distracted me with your daily drama, and I forgot to start the roast. Can you tie the roast while I finish here?"

She measured out a sizeable piece of butcher's twine resting next to the small piece of meat and tied a bow around the roast like a Christmas present. "Now what?"

He looked over to inspect her work. "What is that!"

"What?"

"What do you mean WHAT? We aren't giving it away as a gift. It needs to hold the stuffing in." He stormed over and untied Elizabeth's bow and set about retying the roast. "You're hopeless."

"How was I supposed to know? You said tie the roast, so I tied—" She froze mid-sentence, her gesturing hand still suspended in midair.

"Forget it. No harm done." Michael's annoyance quickly faded.

"No, don't you see? His mother said he couldn't even tie his own shoes." Elizabeth recalled the reports in the file. "Then how could he have tied up his victim?"

Chapter Two

Elizabeth pushed open the glass door to the police station and briefly paused at the large sign that listed prohibited items. She studied the list—knives, firearms, explosives, dangerous chemicals, flammable liquids, brass knuckles... She observed the various pictures beside the list and tilted her head sideways when she came to a photo of a power saw. *Nope, I'm good.*

She stood in the queue waiting her turn, curious as to how so many people could have business at the police station. When she advanced to the front of the line, she was summoned to approach by an officer in a dark blue uniform. His stomach threatened to pop open a button as it strained against the shirt. She figured he didn't spend much time in the field, at least she hoped not.

"Morning, I'm Elizabeth Campbell. I'm an attorney. I'd like to speak to Detective Patrick Sullivan."

"Who?" the officer responded none too politely.

"Detective Patrick Sullivan. I've been asked to review an old case that was handled by the detective. I have a couple of questions." She briefly explained the mayor's request to review the Raymond Miller case.

"One second." The officer pushed himself off his swivel chair and disappeared through a side door. As the minutes passed, she felt the impatience of the others in line behind her mounting and felt responsible. Not wanting to face the crowd, she decided to commit to memory the mission statement that was boldly printed and framed on the wall behind the counter.

At long last, the portly officer returned. "Detective Sullivan's not here anymore. He's retired."

"Well, who else may I speak to, then?"

The officer huffed and again pushed himself up off his chair, shuffled toward the door, and disappeared.

Nope, definitely not in the field. She returned her attention to the mission statement. *Now, where was I?*

When the officer returned, she not only had the mission statement memorized, but also the officers' work schedules for the next two weeks, which was taped on the wall.

"Have a seat. Detective Donovan will be out in a bit to talk to you."

"Thank you." She finally turned to face the line and heard a not too faint "Finally" from the crowd.

She sank down into a hard plastic chair and squirmed a bit in an attempt to get more comfortable before she gave up, realizing it was useless. The chair didn't even offer armrests, so she leaned forward, resting her elbows on her knees. Out of the corner of her eye, she watched a wooden side door open and two figures emerge. A striking blond woman in a well-fitting gray suit walked beside a balding forty-something stout man with a suit that was not as complimentary. Fascinated, she discreetly watched the sleek woman who had her hair pulled into a loose ponytail accented with a few loose strands framing her soft oval face.

As they approached, Elizabeth stood and nonchalantly acknowledged the woman with a small smile before turning to the stocky man and thrusting out her hand. "I'm Elizabeth Campbell. Thank you, Detective Donovan, for taking the time to talk to me."

"My pleasure," answered the woman with her arms crossed and a smirk firmly on her face.

Flustered, Elizabeth turned to her. "Uh, I'm sorry, I—"

"I'll catch you later, Grace," the blonde's companion interrupted as he turned away and continued walking out the front door of the station.

"I'm Detective Grace Donovan. How may I help you?" she asked in a professional tone.

"I'm sorry about that," Elizabeth said and quickly debated whether to explain that her misjudgment was not because the detective was a woman, or better yet, an attractive woman, but simply because she was younger than most detectives. Elizabeth pegged her to be in her early thirties, only a few years older than herself. However, she missed any opportunity of redemption when Detective Donovan nodded with slight impatience, which Elizabeth took as a sign of accepting the apology and moving the conversation along.

Uncharacteristically flustered, but with no time to evaluate its meaning, she drew in a breath and straightened her shoulders. "I'm Elizabeth Campbell," she said, and with her usual confidence returning, proceeded with a quick rundown of her assignment with the Raymond Miller file.

"Why don't we step back to my desk?" Detective Donovan's tone remained neutral, and she turned to key in a code in a large oak door, clearly expecting Elizabeth to follow. She trailed behind the detective as they walked through a hallway, passing glass offices that Elizabeth feigned great interest in to avoid staring at the lean body confidently striding in front of her. She guessed Detective Donovan to be about two inches taller than her five foot seven. As she sized her up, she couldn't help but note that the suit jacket came only to the detective's waist, giving Elizabeth a full view of her backside in her tailored slacks. *Oh wow, look at that office.* Elizabeth mentally pulled herself away, hoping she wasn't sporting a blush. Elizabeth had always been able to appreciate the beauty of another woman, but somehow this felt different. The sensation was deeper and more primal.

When they reached a large open room that offered several desks neatly arranged in pairs, Elizabeth felt exhausted. She swore the walk down the hallway was more than a mile, but her watch told her it was under a minute. Detective Donovan gestured to a chair beside a metal desk near the corner, clearly unaware of Elizabeth's mental discourse on their journey. After seating herself in the designated chair, Elizabeth plopped her bag at her feet and rubbed a knot building in her shoulder. When she returned her eyes to Detective Donovan, she was startled to find the detective wordlessly watching her hand movement.

Having been caught staring, Detective Donovan returned her eyes to her desk and picked up a pencil with a set of teeth marks pressed into the yellow wood and began twisting it. Elizabeth tried to imagine her unconsciously biting down on the pencil, deep in thought.

"So, how may I help you?" Detective Donovan asked, breaking Elizabeth out of her thought.

"I was hoping to discuss the Raymond Miller case."

"I don't get the sudden interest in the Miller case," Detective Donovan said in a curt tone. "The guy had all of the victim's things. He confessed."

"You remember the case?" Elizabeth asked, pulling herself mentally back to where she needed to be.

"Not too many sadistic murder cases around here. Besides, I was the officer that arrested him."

"You were the rookie officer that arrested him after the vagrancy call?" she said, but it came out as a surprised statement more than a question.

"That arrest got me my gold shield early."

She realized that this would be a sensitive case for Detective Donovan and got to the point. "Well, there's just something that bothers me. I was hoping you could put it together for me."

"Go on. What is it?"

"I spoke with Raymond Miller's mother, and—"

Detective Donovan broke in. "You spoke to his mother? I thought your job was to review the file, not conduct an investigation and harass witnesses."

"I don't believe she was a witness, and I'm not conducting an investigation. I simply asked a few questions." Elizabeth took a calming breath. "Anyway, Raymond's mother mentioned that Raymond couldn't even tie his shoes."

"Yeah, so?"

"Well, if he can't tie his shoes, then how did he bind his victim with ropes?"

Detective Donovan tightened her grip on the pencil. "I don't know. But he is guilty as sin. Even he said so. Why don't you spend your time helping the people that say they're innocent?"

"Is it possible that he worked with someone else, an accomplice?"

"No! Miller didn't name an accomplice. He said he did it. I think we're done here."

Detective Donovan stood and started back for the doorway. Elizabeth rose and took one of the detective's business cards out of a neat stack resting in a holder at the edge of the desk and stuffed it into her bag, then quickly walked in her wake, attempting to catch up. When they reached the large oak door, Detective Donovan held it open and offered, "Have a good day," as her parting words.

Elizabeth watched the wooden door close. *Wow, what was that?*

❖

Grace held open the glass door. "Evening, Mrs. Correll. Heading for your evening stroll?"

"Gotta keep this body moving," Mrs. Correll responded as she attempted to move at a quickened pace with her walker.

"Well, you're looking great," she said as Mrs. Correll passed her.

Grace strolled into a bustling lobby that was made to resemble a living room with several couches strategically situated around a large fireplace that was glowing orange and radiating warmth throughout the room. She made small talk with two elderly men hunched over opposite sides of a checkerboard as she passed and then nodded to a trio of women who momentarily acknowledged her before they resumed their whispering gossip. Grace shook her head as she cleared the women. It never changed; there was always that one gossiping group, whether it was high school or Crestview Assisted Living. If anyone had business in this retirement community, these three women knew it.

Grace could hear the roar of the ballgame long before she reached the doorway of her father's room. "Evening, Pops," she shouted to compete with the noise as she entered.

"Gracie." George Donovan smiled as he looked up at her from his reclined position in his chair. "Let me turn this down," he said, pointing the black remote at the television and bringing the volume down to a more tolerable level. "How's my beautiful girl this evening?"

"I'm well, Pops. How are you feeling today?" She leaned over and kissed his forehead.

"Still here and causing trouble."

"I expect nothing less." Grace smiled, but it pained her to see how much her father had changed. He looked to be only a fraction of the man that filled her memories. Gone was the man that would toss her in the air and effortlessly catch her with his meaty hands, calloused by his years in construction work. Now he looked frail and vulnerable with hands that bore translucent skin and blue lines. She knew if she had to, she could carry him.

Her father had been a resident of Crestview for the last two years after suffering a moderate stroke. Although he regained much of his faculties, she felt better knowing that he was being looked after on a continual basis. The cost of the facility set her back, but she lived modestly to compensate. Knowing that her father was cared for was well worth the sacrifice.

Growing up, it had only been Grace and her father, as Grace's mother passed in childbirth. She only knew her mother through photographs that her father kept prominently displayed throughout their home, and although they never spoke of it, she knew how much he loved her and never fully overcame the heartbreak of her loss. It was Grace that gave him reason to keep moving on after she was gone. She envied the love that her parents shared, doubting that she would find something that pure and all-consuming.

"You got the goods?" her father asked, interrupting Grace's thoughts.

She opened her coat, pulled out a grease-stained brown paper bag, and held it out. He eagerly grabbed it and peered inside, inhaling deeply. "Now this is worth living for." He pulled out a chili-covered French fry and savored it. "Did those old biddies see you?"

She knew he was referring to the trio of gossipers. "No, our smuggling operation is still in business."

Grace pulled up a chair next to her father, reached into the bag, and snatched a fry. "So, who's winning?"

Chapter Three

W here are you going?" Dan asked as Elizabeth strode toward the reception area with her leather messenger bag perched on her shoulder.

"Road trip. I'm heading upstate to the penitentiary."

"I suppose it was only a matter of time before you ended up there."

She smiled, more for Dan's attempt at humor than the joke itself.

"So what's at the penitentiary?" he asked.

"I'm going to visit Raymond Miller."

"Who?"

"It's one of the cases you gave me as part of our PR for the mayor."

"A few days ago, you were protesting this. Now you're going on a two-hour drive? What gives?"

"Something doesn't quite fit, and I just need to check it out for my own peace of mind. Humor me."

He released a sigh like a man carrying a burden and couldn't be bothered with another. "Just don't forget that the motion is due in the Sheryl Davies case. The hearing is in less than two weeks."

"No worries. I have it covered."

"I hope so," Dan muttered as he walked away.

As Elizabeth settled into the Roadster and melted into the black and tan leather trim seats, she pushed the ignition and brought the beast to life. She navigated the congestion of the city with ease, earning a few fingers of disapproval as she maneuvered between cars. As the city faded into a two-lane highway, she keyed up a 70s mix from her MP3 player and sang at full volume.

An hour and a half and a close call with a speeding ticket later, she parked in the "employees only" lot of the penitentiary, snuggling her car in between two police cars for safekeeping. Elizabeth entered the small lobby area and signed in, passing over her identification and bar card, for which she was awarded a plastic visitor's badge that she clipped to the lapel of her red suit jacket. After being successfully scanned and prodded by security, she was escorted through a corridor to a heavy metal door. As the door ground open, she looked back to the world she would be leaving.

She followed her escort, who was armed with clubs and other nearly lethal devices on his belt, and rounded several corners before being led to the belly of the building. The echo of her clicking heels on the concrete ground filled the small space. She stared straight ahead to avoid watching the gray concrete brick walls pass, as they only reminded her that there were no windows or doors to the outside. The fluorescent lighting did nothing to dispel the sense of bleakness and desperation that blanketed the inside of the institution. The officer stopped at a steel door with a small viewing window made of thick glass and pulled a large key from a ring attached to his belt. She heard the click of the lock before the door was pulled open.

"Have a seat. The inmate will be here shortly." Those were the first words the officer spoke to her since they started their journey, and with that, the officer turned and closed the door. She sat in a green plastic chair behind a small round table that rocked when she rested her elbows on it and looked around, taking in the decor of the room, or lack thereof. The windowless room wasn't any larger than a prison cell and displayed the same concrete brick walls. A sign painted in red on the wall next to the door reminded the inmates that no contact was allowed; there was also a black button that was strategically placed by the door to alert the officer when she was ready to make her exit.

She sat back in the chair and took several shallow breaths to squash a bit of panic that was rising within her. She had never considered herself to be claustrophobic, but a mixture of the closed space combined with the despair that oozed from the pores of the structure unsettled her deeply.

As the officer promised, she heard the click of the lock, and the door was pulled open. The officer stood behind a man dressed in a matching orange pullover shirt and drawstring pants. Black lettering announcing the institution's name was printed on the pocket of the shirt, as if the owner would forget where he should return the clothes should he get the chance.

"Turn to me," the officer said. Raymond Miller complied, and the officer unshackled his wrists. He nudged Raymond toward a matching green chair across from Elizabeth. "Sit down." The officer kept his hand on Raymond's shoulder until he was fully seated. As the officer exited, he pointed to the black button. "Ring the bell if you need me," he said, and once again, she heard the click of the lock as she was being sealed in.

Raymond sat with his head bowed, rubbing his wrists where the cuffs had been removed, and Elizabeth briefly studied him. He had scruffy brown hair that stuck out in multiple directions. The back of his hair was long enough to touch the collar of his shirt, and his face, covered in stubble, was round with a small nose and red cheeks.

She broke the silence. "I'm Elizabeth Campbell. I'm an attorney. I was hoping I could talk to you about a few things. Is that okay?" She slowly slid a business card across the table.

Raymond followed her hand as it moved closer to him, and when she pulled her hand back, he picked up the card and stared at it with interest. It was then that she noticed the bruising on the left side of his face near his temple and under his eye. "What happened to your face, Raymond?" He shrugged and looked around the room. "Did someone hurt you?"

He settled his eyes on her. "Humpty Dumpty sat on a wall. Humpty Dumpty had a big fall."

"Did you fall down? Did someone push you?" she persisted, feeling a sense of protectiveness that she didn't understand. The man was a convicted killer.

He resumed staring at the wall behind her, and she recognized that he was ending the conversation on his bruises. "All right, Raymond, as I said, I'm an attorney, and I work with the Southern Indigent Legal Center. I've been asked to review your case. Is it okay if we talk about it a bit?"

She removed the photographs from the file and placed the picture of the rosary beads in front of him. "Raymond, do you recognize this?" He gave a nod. "Where did you get it?" He remained silent. "Raymond, where did you get it?" she repeated.

She then placed the photos taken of Raymond's shed in front of him. He focused on the picture of the Bible and placed his hand on top of it, as though he were ready to swear an oath. "Raymond, where did you get these things?" she asked, gesturing to the rosary beads and Bible. He stared at her. "Raymond, answer me. Where did you get these things? Did you find them somewhere, in the trash maybe?"

He shook his head. "They were a gift from God," he said without taking his eyes off the Bible.

"What do you mean? I don't understand."

He looked her in the eyes. "God led them to me. It's what God wanted. Pappy is happy."

"What does God want, Raymond? Tell me."

"He said he was a sinner."

"Who is a sinner?"

"Him." Raymond pointed to the rest of photographs that Elizabeth held back that depicted the body of Father Francis Portillo.

"Did you kill him, Raymond?"

"He said he was supposed to die. He said I could have an eternal life in His kingdom." His eyes glassed over, as though he were reliving the conversation in his head.

"Raymond, why this carving on his body?" She removed the sketch of the circle with the three triangles inside and placed it halfway between them.

Raymond reached for the sketch and began turning the paper in circles. He quickened his pace, and the circle appeared as though it were spinning. Elizabeth stared at it and, feeling dizzy, slapped her hand on the paper to stop its movement. "Enough, Raymond."

He withdrew and sat back in his chair. His fun had been ruined.

After a long silence, she repeated her question pointing to the circle. "Raymond, what is this?"

Instead of answering, he reached over and grabbed Elizabeth's pen resting on the table and looked at her to see if she would protest, but she nodded in approval. He flipped over the business card that she had given him and started drawing. Elizabeth waited patiently, and when he finished, he held up his creation for display. She took the card for a better view, but it was nothing more than a rendition of the circle with three triangles. "I see, Raymond, but what is it?"

"I gave you a falling star of your own." He looked at her, his eyes full of hope, waiting for praise for the gift.

Elizabeth jammed the card into an outside pocket of her leather bag, and Raymond sank back into his chair, bowed his head, and resumed rubbing his wrists. "I want to go home now." His voice was barely more than a whisper.

"Home? Where's that?"

"Where I sleep."

"Raymond, can we talk about your drawings on your wall? The

ones that you drew with the crayons. Do you remember those?" She pointed to the pictures from the shed.

He refused to look up and acknowledge her.

"Raymond, can you answer me?" The silence continued. "Raymond, will you talk to me?"

After several unresponsive requests, Elizabeth realized that he had shut down, so she gathered her documents and shoved them into the file. "Thank you for seeing me today, Raymond." And with that, she rose and pushed the black button.

CHAPTER FOUR

Mayor Anton Reynosa bent down to accept the crafted picture with sparkles and extra glue. "Thank you. What is it?"

"It's a picture of the city. See the buildings? I put pink glitter to make it sparkle." The girl beamed proudly.

"Oh yes, it's lovely."

Reynosa proceeded down the line of children, collecting their handcrafted gifts. The field trip to city hall was the highlight of the school year, and he did what he could to appear a gracious host. As the festivities came to an end, he bid his farewell and walked through the hall at a clipped pace, and his assistant, Simon Fisher, trailed behind, having to skip a few steps to keep up. Reynosa thrust out the pile of the children's pictures. "Take these damn things."

Simon reached for the stack, and Reynosa released them before he had a hold. Several pictures floated to the floor, and Simon quickly bent to scoop them up.

While looking down at his hands with disgust, Reynosa snapped, "I have glue on my hands," and without waiting for Simon, he moved down the hallway. "What's my next appointment?"

Simon ran to catch up. "Your advisors on the gubernatorial campaign are in the library. You have a meeting with the journalist from the *Times* in the South Room in twenty minutes."

"Oh yes," Reynosa responded, rubbing his hands.

Reynosa was in his fourth term as mayor. He rose from deputy mayor to the coveted seat when scandal forced Reynosa's predecessor from office. An anonymous source revealed the former mayor's long-term affair with a prostitute, and he stepped down shortly after taking office, citing the need to spend more time with his family. His abrupt departure vacated the seat for Reynosa.

As he strode through the door in the library, Reynosa began speaking. "Gentlemen, sorry to keep you waiting." He took a seat across from his two advisors, and he noted their nearly identical attire, dark suits, white shirts, and striped ties. "Nice suits. I see you got the memo."

With his feet propped on a low table that stood between him and his advisors, Reynosa asked, "What do you have for me?"

Both men straightened in their chairs, and Sam, his senior advisor, spoke up. "We've been through Senator Johan's financial records, interviewed former employees, college acquaintances, neighbors. We found nothing."

"That is not what I want to hear."

State Senator Johan's bid for the governor's seat threatened Reynosa's chances at the soon-to-be vacated position.

"Everyone has skeletons. Find his. Marijuana in college, a little piece on the side, ran over his neighbor's dog. I don't care how you find it, just find it." Reynosa slapped his hands on his knees and pushed himself up.

"There's one other thing." Sam spoke again.

Reynosa acknowledged him with a hand gesture encouraging him to continue.

"The investigation into the closed criminal cases."

"Yes, what of it?"

"Well, one of the cases has been..." Sam briefly paused, looking for the words, "getting attention lately."

"What case has been getting attention lately?" Reynosa asked slowly and deliberately.

Sam looked to the black leather folder in his lap and opened it. "It's, um, Raymond Miller, convicted of murdering a priest."

The muscle in Reynosa's jaw vibrated, and he spoke through clenched teeth. "You are mistaken. I know the name of every case that was sent out for review. I looked it over myself. That was not on the list."

Sam flinched. "Well, sir, a woman lawyer from one of the legal clinics has been looking into the case. She's talked to the police about the investigation, and she's gone to the prison to see him."

As Reynosa's senior advisor on the gubernatorial campaign, he had advised against the review of the criminal cases. He believed that it was an unwarranted risk because it couldn't be controlled and opened up the door for scrutiny, unnecessary scrutiny. However, Reynosa was not persuaded. He believed it showed candor at a time when confidence in elected officials had been waning, and with the cases handpicked by the mayor and the district attorney for review, the possibility of any negative outcome was eliminated.

"It was not on the fucking list!" Reynosa reached down and slapped the black folder from Sam's hands, sending it skittering across the floor. He turned and exited without another word.

Reynosa resumed his brisk walk down the hall, until he came to an abrupt stop in front of the double doors of the South Room and straightened his tie. He turned to Simon. "How do I look?"

"You look fine, sir."

Reynosa twitched his nose and scratched, removing a strip of pink glitter that was stretched across his nose, and glared at Simon.

"Pull me out of there in twenty minutes," he said and confidently strode into the room, extending his hand to the seated journalist who rose to greet him.

"Thank you for taking the time to meet with me, Mayor Reynosa."

"It's my pleasure, Ms…"

"Shepard, Kathleen Shepard."

"Please be seated, Ms. Shepard." He gestured to the seat behind the journalist that she just vacated.

He took the seat next to her and turned his body to face her in hopes of setting an inviting tone; a seat opposite her might appear confrontational. A positive profile from the *Times* would only boost his support.

"I don't want to take much of your time, so I'll jump right in." The journalist clicked on a small recorder. "The itinerary your office sent out to commemorate the city's one hundredth anniversary has been generating a lot of excitement."

Reynosa hid his disappointment with the lead-in question through a fictitious smile. "We have planned an array of events. Something for everyone, as they say. We anticipate an increase in tourism and advertising over the next year. It should prove to be a prosperous year for the city." He wanted to skip past the frivolities and get to the issues that would get him elected and did his best to turn his answer in that direction.

The journalist shuffled a few cards. "With the upcoming state elections, there's been a lot of concern about fraud and government kickbacks in light of the scandal in Brewster. If you were governor, how would you address this problem?"

"Transparency is the key. My office and this city are an open book. I encourage people to ask questions and conduct reviews. To prove this, our city, along with the help of private nonpartisan legal entities, are conducting a review of criminal convictions over the last several years to show our great citizens that our system is fair and just. If I were governor, I would do the same."

"In your time as mayor, the unemployment rate in this city has dropped nearly three percent, whereas the unemployment rate for the rest of the state has continued to rise. What's your secret?"

"Jobs. This great city of ours has a lot to offer companies, and I have worked hard to bring these companies to our city. If elected governor, I would continue to focus on incentives to bring companies to us."

"It seems you focus on smaller and start-up companies."

"I believe that these smaller companies are the backbone of our economy. By providing them financial incentives on city taxes and licenses, they will come. These incentives might seem inconsequential to larger companies, but to the smaller companies and the start-ups, it's what they need to get business growing. By growing their business in our city, we all reap the benefit."

"Like the start-up pharmaceutical company, IPR, which has now generated nearly one hundred new jobs?"

"Exactly."

Reynosa was pleased with how the interview proceeded. He was confident that he would get the positive coverage he was expecting and graciously answered the remaining questions, until Simon entered the room in twenty minutes on the dot to discreetly inform him of his next appointment.

The journalist understood the cue and stood, extended her hand in gratitude, and allowed him to make a speedy exit.

Reynosa walked toward his office. "Simon, where's the latest budget report?"

"It's on your desk, sir."

He took his seat behind a dark glossy desk and snatched up the bound report and flipped it open. "Christ, this is from last week. I want this week's, you moron."

Reynosa flung the bound report at Simon, bouncing it off his chest. Simon bent to retrieve the discarded report and quickly breathed out, "I'll get right on it," and nearly tripped going out the door.

Reynosa swiveled his chair and faced the picture window. He

glanced over his kingdom, contemplating his next conquest that would bring him more land over which to reign. *A simple retarded boy will not stand in my way.*

❖

Elizabeth sat at her desk eating a prepackaged salad from the corner market while staring at her computer screen to review her motion in the Sheryl Davies case. "Is it affect or effect? Damn, what's the rule? Affect is a verb. Effect is a noun. So am I using a noun or a verb? Eeny, meeny, miny, moe." After making her selection, she moved her mouth to the words as she silently read.

A knock on her slightly ajar door startled her, and she knocked the salad fork off her desk and onto her lap. "Ugggghhhh!" She frantically wiped at the ranch dressing on her slacks. Dan stepped inside and watched her with an amused look on his face. Elizabeth stopped her erratic hand movements, realizing that it looked more than PG-13, if one didn't know better.

"Sorry, did I startle you?" he asked sheepishly.

"Oh no, it's my lunchtime ritual to pour my salad dressing on myself. It helps release tension," she said with a straight face. "You know, you can use the intercom instead of creeping up on me. Oh wait, we don't have one of those. Never mind."

Dan ignored Elizabeth's sarcasm and seated himself across from her. "Sheryl Davies called asking about her case. So I thought I'd come by to see how it was going?"

"She called you instead of me because…?"

"She's a bit old-fashioned," he said while finding great interest in the inspirational posters hanging on the wall.

"Translation, women should be home baking cookies and not practicing law."

He unsuccessfully tried to hold back a giggle. "Something like that. So, how is it going?"

"It's done. I'm just proofreading it. I'll file it tomorrow morning."

"Excellent." He slapped his hands on his legs and lifted himself off the chair. "Well then, I'll just mosey on back to my office." As he reached the door, he turned. "Oh yeah, I forgot to ask, how was your visit to the prison?"

"I've had better experiences."

"Are you satisfied with the conviction?"

She moved her head side to side as she debated her answer. "It's just hard to believe that Raymond Miller killed a priest. He's so childlike, yet he doesn't deny it. He thinks it's what God wanted, so yeah, I'm satisfied. I'll type up a memo for each case and get you back the files."

"Sounds good. Thanks," Dan said as he made his exit.

Chapter Five

Perched above the courtroom, Judge Horace Bailey leaned forward on the bench and steepled his hands in front of him. "I understand that the plaintiff needs to collect rent, but cutting off the water supply to Ms. Davies's apartment is not only extreme, but runs afoul of the law."

The judge turned to Elizabeth. "Counsel's motion is granted. We'll set this for a status conference in about three weeks." He glanced at the court's large white calendar posted on the side wall. "Ms. Campbell, do you want a date?"

"Sure, dinner and a movie would be nice, Your Honor."

Judge Bailey chuckled. "I'm flattered, Ms. Campbell, but my wife might have an objection. How about we stick with a court date?"

"If you insist," she said.

After setting a date, she tucked her file into her bag and made her exit, powering up her cell phone. She noticed seven missed calls from an unknown number and hit the speed dial for her voice mail. A panicked message from Rosa Sanchez sent a chill down her spine, and she scrambled to pull out a legal pad to copy down the number that Rosa rattled off. She listened to the remainder of the messages, all from Rosa.

The phone was answered on the first ring. "Hello, this is Mary. May I help you?"

"Hi, my name is Elizabeth Campbell. I received a message from Rosa Sanchez to call her back at this number."

"Yes, of course, one moment please."

Elizabeth could hear a brief scuffing sound as the phone was set down, and moments later, the phone was picked up and a deep breath was exhaled directly into the receiver. "Ms. Campbell, this is Rosa. I'm so glad you got my message. I'm sorry to call you on your cell phone, but I didn't know what to do. I called your office, and they told me you were in court. I didn't know when you'd come back, so I called your cell phone." She finally took a breath.

"Rosa, slow down," Elizabeth said in a calm voice. "What happened?"

"Immigration, they came to my home. They're looking for me. Hector and me weren't home. They went to my neighbor and asked where I was. They said they didn't know. My neighbor called me at work when they left."

Keeping her voice controlled, she asked, "Rosa, where is Hector?"

"He's here with me. When I got the call, I ran out the door afraid that Immigration would come there. I ran to Hector's school and got him."

"Okay, where are you now?"

"I'm at St. Michael's Church. I couldn't go to your office. It was too far without taking a bus. I'm afraid to take the bus. They might be watching for me. The church is down the street from his school. We come here on Sundays. I didn't know where else to go."

"Where's the church? I'll meet you there." Rosa handed the phone back to Mary, who recited off the church address and directions.

❖

Elizabeth parked her Roadster next to a dark blue Toyota Camry near the side door of the church. She pulled on the church door but found it locked and circled around the front.

She entered the church and crossed through the vestibule passing a small marble sink set back in the recess of the wall. After entering the second set of doors, she noticed a small baptistery pool to her left. Large colorful stained glass windows were lined up on each side of the church, and each window contained a graphic picture from the Stations of the Cross. Streams of light filtered through the windows, leaving streaks of color on the floor and pews. The church was still and filled her with a peaceful feeling, but her peace was cut short when a door opened and clicked shut from the left side of pulpit. A man dressed in black slacks and a short-sleeved black button-down shirt came into her view. He bore a white collar at the neck of his shirt.

"Hi there, I'm Father James Parker. Please come in."

"Thank you, Father Parker." She walked down the center aisle. "I'm Elizabeth Campbell. I'm here to speak to Rosa Sanchez."

"Yes, I thought you might be. Thank you for coming. Please follow me. I'll take you to her."

The father turned and started back toward the side door from which he came, and she dutifully followed. The door led to a small hallway with a tan and blue linoleum floor, and after a short walk, he stopped at an entryway of a small office. The room was efficiently furnished with a computer, printer, fax, and copy machine, and Elizabeth looked around with office envy.

A robust woman sat behind a wooden desk typing on a keyboard, her painted nails making a rhythmic clicking noise. "Mary, this is Elizabeth Campbell," said the father. He turned back to Elizabeth. "I'll leave you to your business."

As the father exited, Mary stood and shook her hand. "It's a pleasure to meet you."

"Thank you. It's a pleasure to meet you as well." Elizabeth always thought that was an odd greeting to a complete stranger. For all she knew, the person could be on the FBI's most wanted list, or worse, the person that drives with the blinker perpetually flashing away, but never turns.

Mary's words broke her thoughts. "Rosa is in the back room lying down. I'll get her for you." She quickly exited, and Elizabeth was surprised at the speed in which she moved given her size. Elizabeth glanced down at Mary's shoes, taking in the beige nurse shoes, and figured that might have something to do with her agility. *Maybe I should give those a try*, she thought, as she glanced down at her black heels that were squishing her little toes. *Nah.*

Rosa entered the room, and the side of her hair stuck flat to her head, as testament to Mary's statement of her whereabouts. "Let me know if you need anything," Mary said as she closed the door behind Rosa, leaving them in privacy.

Rosa sat in a chair in front of the desk, and Elizabeth joined her in the matching chair beside it. "First off, how are you?"

"Scared," she replied without looking up from her lap.

"Do you have any idea how Immigration found out where you live? Your address was confidential in the court file."

Rosa nodded but didn't respond.

"How did they know?"

"I told him."

"You told who?"

"Hector was missing his father. He was crying. I thought if I let him talk to him, he would feel better. I called Jacob."

"Then what happened?" Elizabeth asked, as if questioning a witness on the stand.

"I called Jacob, and we started talking. He was being really nice, like when we first met. He said he was sorry. He said he knew we couldn't get back together because he messed up too bad, but he said he wanted to be friends, so we could work together with Hector. He said it was best for Hector."

Elizabeth sat in silence and waited for her to continue.

"We talked for a long time, and he was being real nice. He wasn't drunk. He said he didn't drink anymore and that he saw how bad he was when he drank and didn't want to be like that anymore. I believed him."

Elizabeth finished for her. "Then you told him where you lived."

"I'm sorry. I didn't plan to. It just came out. He said he wanted to visit Hector, but only if I was okay with it."

"Jacob must have contacted the immigration service. With your outstanding deportation order, they took notice," Elizabeth said. She felt equally responsible for Rosa's situation, as she encouraged her to file the restraining order. "Well, first things first. We need to find a safe place for you and Hector to stay. I'll be right back."

As soon as Elizabeth opened the door, Mary appeared in front of her. "Is Father Parker available?"

"I'll go fetch him," she said, and with her unusual speed, Mary was gone.

Elizabeth returned and found Rosa with her face buried in her hands, and she squeezed her shoulder. "We'll figure something out." She heard herself say it, but even she didn't believe it.

Father Parker entered, and Elizabeth rose. "Father."

"Please sit." The father rounded the desk and sat in a black leather chair. She observed how he didn't have to appease or make offerings to the chair.

"How may I assist?" the father asked.

"Well, we need to figure out a place for Rosa and Hector to stay where they'll be safe."

"They can stay here. The church has living quarters that are available. It's pretty basic and a bit small, but it has all the necessities. More important, it's safe."

Elizabeth looked over to Rosa, who no longer tried to hold back her tears. "Thank you," she choked out.

"That is very gracious of you, Father."

"The church is a sanctuary for those in need." He turned to Rosa. "Let me have Mary show you our supplies and clothing donations. I'm sure there's plenty there to keep both you and Hector going while you stay with us."

He summoned Mary on his phone, and as Elizabeth had come to expect, she promptly entered the room. After he passed on his instructions, Elizabeth was left alone in the room with the priest.

Father Parker had the trim build of someone who had a disciplined exercise regimen. His well-kept, short brown hair was slightly graying around the temples, and he was clean-shaven with smooth, clear skin. His green eyes seemed thoughtful and kind. A sense of serenity poured from him, and she couldn't help but contrast this meeting to that with Detective Grace Donovan, with all its frustration and fire. She had actually spent more time than she was willing to admit assessing her meeting with Grace and the tingling sensation that followed.

She's arrogant and stubborn, but God, does she have legs. I bet her breasts are— No, I will not think of Grace Donovan. Not of her hips. Not of her lips— Oh great, now I'm channeling Dr. Seuss. Oh Jesus, I'm sitting in a church. Oh God, am I going to hell for thinking this? Oh damn, I just used God's name in vain. I think I better get some holy water on my way out.

Father Parker sat and watched her as she went through her internal diatribe. "Is there something wrong, Father?"

"No, I just didn't want to disturb you. You seemed deep in thought."

"Thank you again, Father, for all you're doing for Rosa and Hector."

"I'm only happy that we're able to help. Will you be able to do anything to stop Immigration?"

She blew out a soft breath. "Honestly, I don't know." It felt strange to admit that out loud. She was used to being in control and having the solutions, but here, she felt stuck. It made her feel vulnerable.

"It's okay to not always have the answers," he replied. "Sometimes you have to have faith that things will work out as they should."

"Let go, let God?"

"Something like that." He smiled.

Elizabeth found it strangely comforting to talk to the father. She took in the warmth for a moment before she grabbed her bag and stood. "I should probably get going." She reached into her leather bag, and when she came up empty, searched the outside pocket before finding what she needed. "Here's my card. Please call me if you or Rosa need anything." On the bottom of her card, she jotted down her cell phone number.

Father Parker graciously accepted the card. "Thank you. I'll walk you out."

❖

Dan watched Elizabeth walk through the reception area of the clinic and stopped her before she reached her office. "How'd the Davies case go?"

"Fine. The motion was granted."

"Excellent." Confused by her solemn state, he asked, "What gives? You won."

She relayed the events of Rosa Sanchez. "I don't know what to do."

Dan was thoughtful for a moment. "I'm not sure anything can be done."

"I can't accept that. She and Hector are counting on me."

"Whoa, we're on the same side here."

"Sorry. It's just been a stressful afternoon."

"Why don't you go home and get some R and R?"

Amy broke into the conversation. "Dan, you have a call on line two."

"Who is it?"

"He didn't give a name. He just said that it was important."

"Fine, I'll take it in my office." He turned back to Elizabeth. "I'm serious, go home."

After returning to his office, he picked up the receiver. "Hi, this is Dan Hastings."

"Mr. Hastings, thank you for taking my call. I was hoping we could discuss some business that may benefit us both."

"Who is this?"

"That's not important."

"The hell it isn't. Who are you and what do you want?"

"We have a mutual friend—Mayor Reynosa. I understand that you've been given a little assignment as part of the mayor's campaign."

"What's it to you?"

"I can make it worth your while to close out all the cases you were asked to review without any further investigation."

"Why?"

"The justice system did its job. There's no need to dredge this up again."

"It's the Raymond Miller case that has you worried."

"Yes."

"Why do you want it closed? What do you know?"

"I know that justice was served, and it should be left alone."

"If justice was served, why are you so concerned by our review?"

"That was a painful time for the victim's family. Bringing it up again will only reopen those wounds and for what? Raymond Miller confessed."

"So you're just a concerned citizen?"

"I'm a concerned citizen who can ensure that your donation plate is full."

Dan stayed silent.

"Are you there?" the caller asked.

"Yes. How does this work?"

"You make sure all investigations in the case stop, and your clinic will receive a sizeable anonymous donation."

"How much?" Dan demanded.

"Straightforward, aren't you?"

"How much?" Dan repeated.

"Fifty thousand."

"One hundred," Dan countered.

The caller chuckled. "I see. Well, I'll see what can be done."

Dan heard a click and the line was dead. He set the receiver down with trembling hands. "Christ," he exhaled, running his hands through his hair, as he tried to reason with himself. *Elizabeth reviewed the case. She's satisfied. No harm, no foul.*

So why was there a knot in his gut?

❖

Naked and kneeling, Salvator sat motionless, bent over at his waist, his forehead resting on the cold concrete floor. He clutched his midsection, digging his fingers into his flesh, leaving bloody gouges in his sides. His body trembled not from the chill of the room, but from fear. Murmurs emanated from the rigid form.

A lantern hanging from a hook on the ceiling swayed back and forth, offering only a ring of light in the center of the room. The low mutterings formed into words. "I received the sign. I have come."

The room remained still but for his labored breathing. He raised his eyes to the ceiling and stretched up his arms. "You are still here. Guide me." He began humming "Twinkle, Twinkle Little Star."

"You dare come back here!" a voice exploded from the recesses of the shadow, causing him to flinch and cower.

"I-I—" he stammered.

"You are weak! You have forgotten our work."

"No, it was a mistake. I can't," he yelled, covering his ears.

A booming laugh thundered through the room. "You dare defy me?"

"No, it's just—"

"Just WHAT?"

"He was the wrong man. I don't know where to begin," he meekly confessed.

"Begin with the school," the voice commanded. "And this time, no mistakes."

"Yes," he sobbed and the room fell still again. Curled in a fetal position, he cried himself to sleep.

CHAPTER SIX

Father Samuel Rossi dug his aging hands into the soil. He loved the feel of the rich dirt between his fingers. It was like being a part of the earth. Over the last four years, Father Rossi converted an abandoned lot filled with the city's refuse into a thriving garden that came to represent life and hope in a city that had seen much depravity and desolation.

As Father Rossi retired from the day-to-day operations of the church, he found daily refuge amongst the vegetables that he tenderly cultivated. The garden offered a peaceful solitude beyond anything he found in prayer. His endeavor started as a small patch, but day after day, year after year, developed into a small farm that fed a significant part of the community that would otherwise have to do without.

He enjoyed the manual labor. However, as each year passed, he noticed that it was harder and harder to pull himself into a straight position after crouching over to care for his offspring. *The creaks are just getting louder.*

As he closed his eyes to soak up the warmth of the morning sun, he heard a voice. "I've been admiring your garden for quite some time. I was walking past and thought maybe I could offer some help."

Father Rossi opened his eyes and looked over his garden with pride. "Yes, she is something special." He started to rise, and the man gently grasped his bicep to help him stand. "Thank you. That seems to be getting more difficult. I'm actually done here for the day. If you don't mind, you can help me carry the tools to the shed."

"Absolutely." The man gathered the tools in his arms.

"Let me get some of those." He grabbed a trowel and small shovel that were threatning to fall from the man's hands.

"Thank you, Father."

The man trailed him to a metal shed in the far corner of the lot. Father Rossi opened the door and stepped inside, and the man followed. The inside of the shed smelled damp and musty and was considerably cooler than the garden. As Father Rossi laid the tools on a wooden workbench, the door of the shed closed. "Son, we'll need the door open for light."

When the light didn't come, Father Rossi turned and saw a face contorted with rage. The man bared his clenched teeth like an animal ready to attack. His eyes stood open wide with pupils dilated, and Father Rossi believed he was looking into the eyes of Lucifer himself. "Oh dear Lord, please help me," he whispered. The man swung a shovel down on top of Father Rossi, and he crumpled to the floor.

Elizabeth rushed into the clinic and offered a hurried greeting to Amy as she passed. After depositing her bag on the chair across from her desk, she walked to the communal closet and found Jeff making a cup of herbal tea.

"Herbal tea? I need the hard stuff," Elizabeth said as she watched Jeff's slow, methodical motions.

"That stuff will rot your stomach," he said without taking his eyes off his tea bag.

She debated whether to walk into the kitchen and start to brew some coffee. Not wanting to be that well acquainted with Jeff, she decided to wait impatiently, clasping her hands tightly in front of her until her fingers turned white.

"What has you so uptight?" he asked.

"Traffic was a nightmare this morning. I'm late. I missed my usual coffee stop."

"Ah, that explains it. This is Elizabeth without caffeine. I like the caffeinated Elizabeth better." Jeff continued his ministrations with his tea bag, as Elizabeth was ready to yank him out of the kitchen and drop-kick him back to his cubicle. She appreciated that it might be a legal nightmare for the clinic and tried to distract herself.

"So, what was up with all the traffic?" Elizabeth asked in the most conversational tone that she could muster.

"The mayor is holding a press conference on the steps of city hall. A bunch of the streets are blocked off."

"You mean campaigning on the steps of city hall," she said. "What's he selling now?"

"That fond of him, huh?"

"Never voted for him. Don't trust him," she said, crossing her arms.

"The mayor is launching the second phase of his economic revitalization campaign."

Jeff finished his tea ritual and stepped out, and before he crossed the threshold, Elizabeth was working the coffee machine. "Come on, come on, come on," she chanted.

"Mayor Reynosa, over here." A flash temporarily blinded him.

"Thank you for all coming this morning." Reynosa stood behind a podium at the top of the steps with a lineup of men to his left. "Today, I humbly stand here to honor some of the people that have helped guide this city onto a path of financial and moral prosperity. Our unemployment rate is down, our crime rate is down, our school test scores are up, as we invest our city's new financial success back into our youth. I am a product of this city, born and raised. I know the heart of this city. I know we'll continue to show others how we, as a community, can rise together."

He pointed to the men flanking him. "With me are some of our esteemed business and religious leaders who have come together to stand as a symbol of solidarity in support of our great city, as we mark this auspicious occasion." Applause erupted from the audience.

After concluding his political sermon, Reynosa escorted his honored guests to a private brunch inside a small but elegant dining room. In the center of the room, a large crystal chandelier hung over a round table with a pressed white tablecloth. The drapes were pulled open, allowing the sunlight to dance off the ceiling centerpiece. As the servers made the final preparations for the brunch, the guests clustered in small groups around the room immersed in conversations.

"I read the piece on you in the *Times*. Nice coverage," Seth Lowry said as he took a modest sip of champagne from his flute.

"I'm sure your favorite part was the mention of IPR's success," Reynosa countered good-naturedly to the pharmaceutical company's CEO.

"Yes, I was pleasantly surprised. I'm sure you somehow had a hand in guiding the reporter's research."

"Perhaps. No one appreciates unpleasant surprises," Reynosa responded while scanning the room, observing the guests. Confident that his guests were amiably chatting, he lowered his voice. "How are the clinical trials going?"

"Very well. By this time next year, IPR will be a household name," Lowry boasted. "And we will be fucking rich."

Reynosa clapped him on the shoulder approvingly.

"A toast," Lowry said as he raised his glass. "To even more profitable times."

"Hear, hear," Reynosa said as they joined glasses.

While the guests spoke in hushed tones around the room, Bishop Pallone stared out the top floor window and took in the view of the city that spread out below. Reynosa excused himself from his conversation and approached the bishop. "Bishop Pallone, thank you for being here today."

The bishop put out his hand and firmly gripped Reynosa's palm and placed his other hand on his shoulder in a warm greeting. "That was quite an inspiring speech."

Reynosa gave a slight bow of his head in acknowledgment of the compliment.

"Will you be able to remain after the other guests have left? It's been some time since my last confession."

"For an old friend, I can make time."

❖

Father Rossi slowly woke but had no strength to lift his head, not that he would were he able. A sharp pain radiated through his brain, and he drifted back into darkness.

The cold dampness on his naked skin once again pulled him from his dark refuge, and he floated back to consciousness. Pain in his wrists and ankles competed with the pain in his head. Disoriented, he slowly lifted his head and, with great effort, attempted to open his eyes. After several moments, he focused his vision on a gray concrete wall.

He pulled his right arm to rub it across his throbbing forehead, but found it pulled tight. His wrists and ankles were firmly held by metal cuffs connected to chains that dug deep into his skin. The taut chains were attached to large metal clasps anchored in the ceiling and floor, and he pulled his arms and legs apart like Da Vinci's *Vitruvian Man*.

He took in as much of the room as he could with his restrictions. The room was covered in concrete—walls, ceiling, and floor. A single lantern dangled from a hook at the center of the ceiling illuminating only the middle of the room, leaving the corners in shadow. The furnishings that he could see were sparse, with a small wooden table and single chair and a metal shelving unit holding nondescript cardboard boxes. Two concrete-covered doors that nearly blended into the wall sat opposite each other as though they were standing guard. The air was stale, and he wondered how safe the lantern was in such a confined space.

"I see you're finally awake. I was afraid I might have lost you."

Father Rossi turned his head, attempting to find the origin of the voice. "Where am I?"

A man mostly concealed in a dark cloak stepped forward and faced him. "A place where no one will ever find you. Screaming will be futile. No one will ever hear you. We are covered by concrete, but please feel free to try. I would quite enjoy it, actually."

"What kind of evil are you?" Father Rossi spat.

"Evil? Oh no, you are mistaken, Father. I am not evil, but merely your prodigy." Humming "Twinkle, Twinkle Little Star," the man glanced to the ceiling before he pulled a coiled rawhide whip hanging from a hook and ran his fingertips along the sharp thong of the whip. "It was a whip like this that was used on Jesus. Don't you think?"

"Who are you?"

"You may call me Salvator, a name I bestowed upon myself."

"What do you get from this?" Father Rossi asked, looking directly into the man's eyes.

The man stood motionless, contemplating his answer. "Joy."

"There is no joy in suffering," Father Rossi wheezed out.

"Oh, but there is. Hearing your plea for forgiveness is pure joy."

"I do not fear you. I'm old man. My time on this earth is near its end. You can batter my body, but my soul is with the Lord." Father Rossi spat at the man.

A maniacal laugh echoed through the bare, bleak space. "You're different from the other. He cowered, begged for mercy. You're a fighter."

The sneer on the cloaked man's face was quickly replaced by a startled look as he violently flinched, causing the whip to fall from his hands, and he turned to face to the corner. "You scared me. I didn't know you were there."

"Yes, yes. I'm sorry," the cloaked man stammered and hastily picked up the whip.

Father Rossi focused his eyes on the trembling man and looked around the room to see what scared him so. "You're lost, you're afraid. Don't turn your back on God. He is always there for you."

"Shut up!" screamed the cloaked man. A deafening crack reverberated through the solid room. Father Rossi felt rawhide rip into his flesh, and a shriek spilled from his mouth.

Elizabeth pulled on her long black wool coat. The weather was changing, and she enjoyed the opportunity to pull out some of her warmer clothes. As she turned off her office light and advanced toward the front door, Dan came up behind her.

"Pulling a late night? Hope you're not bucking for a raise."

"Nope, I'm gunning for your job."

Dan chuckled. "You only have to ask. So, what's got you here so late?"

"The Sanchez case."

"Tenacious, aren't you?" he said, laughing at his own humor, which was lost on Elizabeth. He pulled the front door shut behind them and reengaged the lock with his key.

"I'm going to file a motion to reopen with the immigration court based on ineffective assistance."

"Hmm, that's an idea. Well, go get 'em."

After a quick drive, Elizabeth strode up the walkway of her home, and the security light illuminated her way. She noted that it was getting darker earlier. As she opened her front door, Elizabeth was assaulted by Charlie.

"Hold on, my God."

She dropped her bag on the side table and hung her coat on a hook by the door. Charlie weaved in between her legs, impeding her progress. As Elizabeth walked to the kitchen, booting Charlie with her feet on the way, she glanced at the blinking red light on her home phone and hit the button for her voice mail as she passed.

"Two new messages," announced the automated voice.

"Hi, Ms. Campbell, this is Margaret from Dr. Bernstein's office.

You are due for a dental cleaning…" With cat food covering her fingers, Elizabeth punched the key to erase with her elbow.

"Elizabeth, this is your mother. Remember, you have one of those." Elizabeth sighed. She knew she was in for a long one.

"You could be lying unconscious under a bridge for all we know."

"Who are you talking to?" her father's voice interrupted.

"Our daughter. The one who never has any time for her parents."

"I had dinner at your house last weekend," Elizabeth argued back to the machine.

"Thomas Whittaker came by yesterday to review our stock portfolio. He's still single. He's a catch. You really should call him."

"He has wandering hands that are faster than the eyes, and he has a mole the shape of New Jersey on his forehead," Elizabeth countered. Over the years, she found it cathartic to argue back with her mother on the machine. In real time, she would never get a word in.

"When are you going to settle down and have kids?"

"When are you going to leave that flea-bit clinic and come practice some real law?" her father interjected.

"Call us, honey. We love you." The machine beeped, signaling the end.

"Oh yeah, I'll get right on that. Right after a long bath and a large glass of wine."

Chapter Seven

G race pulled up the collar of her jacket as she approached the dirt walkway to a flourishing community garden that stood in contrast to the concrete surrounding it. A silhouette of a cross stood against the garden as the early morning birds gathered around the vegetables looking for a morning meal. The air was brisk, and light dew dampened the ground. As the morning sun made its journey across the sky chasing away the cool moist air, the silhouette emerged into a form. Father Rossi's naked body hung on a wooden cross like a scarecrow, his hands and legs bound to the wooden posts. Parts of his skin were gouged and hanging loosely, with some pieces of his flesh ripped away. His left ear was dangling, barely attached. There was a savagery of deep gashes that left crevices across his body. A circle with three blood red triangles was carved deep into his stomach.

Grace stared at the grotesque figure hanging on the cross. "Damn it to hell," she muttered under her breath. A crew of criminal investigators efficiently worked around her processing the scene. A gaggle of reporters and onlookers were being held at bay behind the chain link fence that surrounded the garden. She could see the flashes of light as the photographers were snapping away, and she yanked at her phone clipped on her waist and viciously punched at the numbers. After a single ring, the phone was answered.

"Hello?"

"There's been another murder. What the hell is this!"

"I know. I can see."

"What?" Grace asked irritated.

"Look to your east. I live in the gray building. Nice containment of the crime scene, De-tec-tive. It's all over the news."

Grace turned to face the building. "Don't give me that crap. The reporters and looky-loos were here getting their fill before the first unit arrived. We need to talk. What number are you?"

"What?"

"What fucking unit number are you? I'm coming up."

Grace jabbed the end button and headed toward the gray building. She passed through the upscale lobby, and a sleek elevator ascended the floors. She found retired detective Patrick Sullivan leaning in the doorway of his apartment, and she moved past him, not waiting for an invitation. The apartment was well furnished. "This is a nice building for such a shitty neighborhood."

"Part of the economic revitalization. Move on or die out."

Grace crossed to the window that Sullivan previously occupied and stared down at the scene in the garden below. "What the hell is going on? This murder has Raymond Miller's markings all over it. At least I used to think it was Raymond Miller's markings. Now I'm thinking you screwed up."

Sullivan glared at her and crossed his arms defensively. "Don't forget who arrested Miller with the damn cross in his pocket. You got a nice fast track to the gold shield after that, didn't you."

A silent tension filled the space between them, and Sullivan backed off first. "Look, there's no need to get your panties into a bunch. There's an easy explanation."

Grace perched herself on the windowsill, waiting to be enlightened.

"Miller isn't the dumb fuck that he pretends to be. He knew the mayor's plan to have the cases reinvestigated. Hell, everyone knows. What better way to have his conviction overturned than by planning another murder and having it carried out by some ex-con lackey who he fucked up the ass? He has a solid alibi."

Grace didn't flinch at Sullivan's vulgar description. As a woman in a male-dominated world, she was often tested by her colleagues for her worthiness. Instead, she remained silent never taking her eyes off Sullivan, evaluating him for the veracity of his statements. She finally responded. "His confession was clean?"

"Yes, the confession was clean."

She pushed herself up from the window, putting her nearly at equal height to him. "All right then." She walked to the door and closed it behind her without saying another word.

❖

Elizabeth spotted Detective Donovan in the parking lot of the police station exiting her car. She had left her three messages that day, all unanswered, so she decided to pay her a visit. She spent much of her drive over counseling herself on staying mentally on task during her visit.

"Detective Donovan!" she shouted across the lot and waved her hand.

Elizabeth read her annoyed expression correctly and quickly walked to her before she decided to bolt. "I'm sorry to drop by unannounced, but I left you a few messages—"

"I'm a little busy right now. What is it you want?"

"I saw the news. You're investigating the killing of the priest."

"I can't talk about that case."

"That case," she said firmly, "is directly related to the Raymond Miller case. I watched the news reports from the crime scene. It has the same MO—a priest left naked and tied up with the carving in the stomach."

"Ah jeez, here we go."

"Don't tell me you haven't considered that."

"This case has nothing to do with the Raymond Miller case. Raymond Miller confessed. This is nothing more than a cheap copycat. End of story."

"A cheap copycat? How is that? In the first murder, the police never disclosed the carving on the victim's abdomen."

Grace's face flushed. "If you don't mind, I have a job to do."

"How are you going to do that with your head so far up your ass?"

Elizabeth turned back to her car before she could offer a response, and Grace watched her depart before she stomped into the police station.

Grace snatched the phone off her waist and tossed it on her desk with more force than necessary. After plopping herself in her chair, she rested her elbows on her desk and bowed her head, clasping her hands tightly. Those who didn't know better would probably mistake her for praying, but those that knew her well enough knew that was unlikely.

Although she was greatly disturbed by the discovery of another murdered priest, what seemed to bother her more was her contentious encounter with the strong-headed attorney. *Who the hell does she think she is?*

During their exchange, she did her best to keep her eyes trained on the soft aqua eyes, but she berated herself for allowing them to momentarily wander lower to the pink silk blouse where the top button was left undone, exposing just enough skin to tease.

"Focus, Donovan. Don't go there," she chastised herself.

She knew that any involvement with Elizabeth could unravel everything that she had worked so hard to achieve. She had unintentionally earned enemies as a result of her fast-track promotion, and as the only female detective in the unit, felt she had to prove herself worthy over and over. Despite her long hours and diligent work and dedication, there were plenty hoping to see her fall. There was no room for personal relationships, and in particular gay relationships. Despite the evolution in the rest of the country, "don't ask, don't tell" was alive and well in the department. She had not only herself to think of, but her father.

"Nope, not touching Elizabeth Campbell with a ten-foot pole," she mumbled and decided cool and aloof was the best approach, should there be future encounters. With her plan set, she turned to her computer to input her case notes.

Chapter Eight

Experienced in the protocol, Elizabeth passed through the security at the prison in half the time. She followed her armed escort down the passageways, keeping her eyes fixed to the floor. It was just easier that way. She was escorted to the same room and took her familiar seat.

While waiting for Raymond's arrival, she opened the file and sorted through the documents. "What am I missing here?" She reread the transcript of his confession. "Why, Raymond? Why did you confess?"

The door opened, and the officer uncuffed Raymond and led him to his seat. This guard was even less talkative than the last and didn't even advise her to ring the bell when her meeting was complete.

"Hi, Raymond, do you remember me? I'm Elizabeth Campbell."

He nodded, and she was pleased that he remembered her.

"Good, Raymond. Do you remember last time we were talking about this case?" She tapped the open file.

He nodded again. Encouraged by his responsiveness, she ventured on. "Raymond, I'm trying to figure a few things out. There was another killing. The man was also a priest." She lifted the photos of the first victim from her file. "He was killed the same way too. He even had this carving of the circle with the triangles on his stomach."

He sat silently and didn't look at the photos she held in her hands.

"Raymond, you didn't kill him." She shook her head as she spoke.

"He was supposed to die. It's what God wanted. Pappy is happy."

"Raymond, who told you that?"

He looked down at his clasped hands.

"Raymond, please talk to me. I'm here to help you. You confessed to killing this man, and I don't know why. Please help me understand."

He pulled his clasped hands to rest on top of the table but did not answer.

"Raymond, talk to me."

His silence stretched on.

"Damn it, Raymond." Elizabeth slammed her fist on the table, causing it to precariously tilt toward her before it settled itself again.

He jumped and then pulled his knees up tightly against his chest and buried his head.

"Raymond, I'm sorry," she said soothingly. "I shouldn't have done that. I didn't mean to scare you."

Despite her pleadings, he remained in his cocoon and refused to speak. Although he declined to help her, Elizabeth knew what she had to do. She gathered the documents in the file, shoved it in her bag, and headed for the door. After ringing the bell, she turned. "Raymond, we are going to see each other again."

As she handed over her plastic visitor's badge to the officer at the front desk, she turned and saw Father Parker enter through the double doors.

"Father, how are you?"

Clearly surprised to see Elizabeth, he stopped momentarily as though trying to place her. "Ms. Campbell, I didn't expect to find you here."

"I could say the same," she said with a smile.

"I try to come here as often as I can to offer spiritual guidance to these men. They're often forgotten and are reaching out for forgiveness and redemption."

"That's very noble of you, Father."

He blushed slightly, which she found endearing. "It's God's work, and I'm happy to do it."

"How are Rosa and Hector?" Elizabeth asked, changing the topic.

"They seem to be doing well. Rosa has been an invaluable help around the church, and Hector is a very pleasant young man. Smart too."

"That's a relief. I'll be stopping by the church tomorrow morning to go over Rosa's case."

"Well then, I shall see you tomorrow." The father bowed his head slightly, and Elizabeth bid him farewell.

CHAPTER NINE

Elizabeth parked her Roadster next to the same blue Camry and made her way to the front of the church. Mary was standing in the vestibule arranging pamphlets on a table by the door. After exchanging pleasantries, Mary said, "Rosa is in the office. She's helping out with the filing."

Elizabeth strode through the church, admiring the kaleidoscope of colors that were cast on the pews and walls by the stained glass windows. In the office, she found Rosa stooping in front of an open drawer of a filing cabinet.

"Morning, Rosa."

Rosa jumped slightly.

"Sorry. I didn't mean to scare you."

"No, that's okay. I was just so, what is the word, enthralled in my work."

"Enthralled, that's a great word."

"Sí, Father Parker is teaching me."

Elizabeth smiled at her. Rosa truly seemed happy.

"So how are you doing?"

"Very well considering."

"Do you have a few minutes to talk about your case?"

Rosa started fretting with the edges of the file she held in her hands, a nervous habit Elizabeth began to recognize. Elizabeth moved to one of the guest chairs and gestured for her to sit, and Rosa sat at the edge of the seat with the file clutched to her chest.

Elizabeth explained her plan to file a motion with the immigration court to reopen her asylum. "No promises, but I think we have a chance. We'll need to work together to prepare an affidavit. It will be your chance to tell the court your side of what happened."

"I like that," Rosa said hopefully.

"How about you come to my office tomorrow morning?"

A concerned look crossed Rosa's face, and Elizabeth realized that Rosa hadn't left the church since Immigration came to her apartment looking for her. She guessed that either Mary or the father saw Hector to school.

"You know what? How about I bring my laptop and we do it here? It's much quieter than my office."

"If you are sure?"

"Yes, I'm sure. I'll see you tomorrow."

Father Parker walked into the office as they finalized their plans. Rosa greeted the father and exited the office with the file still clutched to her body.

"Good morning, Ms. Campbell. It's good to see you again."

"Morning, Father. I was wondering if you had a few minutes."

The father took Rosa's vacated seat. "How may I help you?"

"Well, it's a case I am looking into. The man lived in this neighborhood. When I spoke with his mother, I noticed that she wore a gold cross. I thought maybe they came to this church?"

"What's this family's name?"

"The mother is Delores Miller. Her son is Raymond Miller."

His face remained neutral, and Elizabeth couldn't read whether either of the names registered with him.

"I don't know them well. I believe I've seen the mother in church a few times. The son is at the state prison where we met yesterday. I've met him a few times."

She sat up straight. "You have? What did he say?"

"I'm sorry to disappoint you, but he doesn't say much of anything. I've prayed with him, but he remains silent through the visit for the most part."

"Did he ever discuss why he's there?"

"No, I never discuss their cases. I'm not there to judge."

She sank back into her chair. "I appreciate your time, Father."

❖

Dan snatched up the phone while keeping his eyes trained on the documents in front of him. "This is Dan Hastings."

"You disappoint me," the caller growled.

Dan sat back in his chair and felt his pulse quicken. "What's this about?"

"You ridicule me? You received your generous donation," the caller spat out. "What do I get?"

Dan remained confused and hoped the caller's point would become clear.

"Your attorney filed a motion to vacate the guilty plea of Raymond Miller."

Dan took in an audible breath. "I-I didn't know that," he stuttered out.

"You-you didn't know," the caller mocked him. "What kind of poor excuse of a legal clinic do you run?"

"Elizabeth, Ms. Campbell, was supposed to close the case. I didn't know," Dan repeated in his defense.

"Now we know who has the balls in your clinic. This is not over." The caller disconnected, leaving him in a stunned silence.

❖

"What am I missing?" Elizabeth asked herself as she laid her head on top of the file and gently banged it a few times. She had spent most of the afternoon poring over the Raymond Miller case, and the photos were spread across her desk. She had stared at the photos long enough to become desensitized to the depravity of them, and she analyzed them like a seasoned investigator. The body hung like a gory scarecrow, and the iron gate that served as its prop displayed an artfully crafted cross and words forming a circle surrounded the cross. She couldn't read the lettering as the body partially obscured the view, but she guessed it was Latin.

Perhaps it was nothing more than a religious hate crime like the psychological profile suggested. She didn't know why, but she doubted that.

Elizabeth was startled out of her thoughts when Dan stormed into her office. "Who the hell do you think you are?"

She stared at him, waiting for the punch line.

"Who the fuck told you to file a motion to vacate in the Miller case? Who?" he demanded.

"Why are you so upset?"

"We agreed that the case was closed."

"*We* didn't agree. I said I was going to close it, but that was *before* there was another murder. What's the deal, Dan?"

"You're wasting the clinic's resources. Don't ever go rogue on me! I'm in charge, not you. You don't file anything without my knowledge. Now give me the goddamn file."

She held out her hand with the brown file, and he snatched it and exited, slamming Elizabeth's door on the way out. She opened the file drawer in her desk and pulled out a manila-colored file containing a copy of all the documents in the Miller case. She anticipated that someone would demand the file after she filed the motion, but she expected it to be from the government side, not Dan.

After a long and uncomfortable afternoon avoiding Dan, Elizabeth pulled into her driveway. She grabbed her bag on the passenger's seat and made her way up the walkway to her door. The exterior light didn't illuminate. She stumbled off the path into the flower bed, and the heel of her shoe imbedded itself into the soil.

"Damn it." She bent to pull her shoe out of the dirt, and the bag slipped from her shoulder, falling to the ground and spilling some of the contents. She bent to retrieve the rebellious bag and started shoving items back inside. She stumbled up the porch step in front of her door and addressed more curse words to the defective light.

Elizabeth fumbled with her keys, trying to make it fit into the keyhole. She pushed open the door, kicked off her shoes, and dropped her bag and keys inside, now not caring where the contents fled. She could hear the keys miss their mark on the table and clatter to the ground. She closed the door and switched on the entryway light, but the room remained dark. The hair on the back of her neck stood up as she realized Charlie hadn't come to greet her. She softly called out his name, but was greeted by silence, painfully quiet silence.

She crept forward, trying to make her footsteps as light as possible, and strained to look through the dark room while she debated her options. She knew it felt wrong. She knew she should turn and walk out the door, but instead she stood frozen, listening to absolute silence. She called out Charlie's name with more volume, and when she was greeted with only more silence, she turned and grabbed at the entry table for her keys. After remembering the clattering sound of the keys from moments earlier, she dropped to her knees and ran her hands along the floor. She came up with a tube of lipstick, an eyeliner, and her wallet, all escapees from her purse, but no keys. As Elizabeth ducked her head under the entryway table to search deeper, she heard a faint sound and lifted her head in response, slamming it against the underside of the table. She ignored the pain that radiated across the top of her head and pulled herself up, keeping her eyes and ears trained in the direction of the sound. Elizabeth cursed the beating of her heart, as she could hear it thumping in her ears.

There it was again. It was a definite sound coming from the direction of the hallway. Against her better judgment, she moved forward, drawn by the noise. She made stealth-like progress until she hit the one protesting floorboard in the house that squeaked in dissent at the weight put upon it. She flinched at what seemed to be a deafening sound in the stillness of the house.

Elizabeth held still, afraid to shift her weight, as it might bring a cascade of more squeaking protests, and waited for a reaction, any reaction, from inside the house. There was only more quiet. Emboldened by the lack of response to the cranky floorboard, she ventured on and reached the middle of the hallway when the sound came again, only louder and clearer. She was getting closer to the source. After turning to her bedroom and crossing the threshold, she settled her feet into the plush carpet, glad to be rid of the floorboards. She waited, and after several interminable moments, it sounded again. The closet. Elizabeth looked around for a weapon and looked down at her hands. She still clutched a lipstick tube and an eyeliner. *Oh great, I can give out beauty tips.*

She tossed the makeup on her bed and grabbed at the lamp on her bed stand, but it refused to come with her since it was still plugged in. *Seriously?* She set down the lamp and grabbed a heavy framed picture of her parents that rested next to the lamp. She looked at her mother in the photograph, who had a poised smile that told all that this was a woman in charge, and stripes were in fashion. *Maybe she'll scare them away. It works on me.*

Elizabeth's heart thundered in her ears as she raised the photo frame above her head and yanked open the closet door. Nothing. There was no boogeyman to be found. She lowered the picture frame and leaned against the closet door, waiting for the adrenaline rush to subside.

There it was again, the noise, this time right in front of her. Elizabeth peered into the closet, finding nothing out of the ordinary. Wait. At the bottom of the closet sat a cardboard box. That was new.

She crouched in front of it and set the photo on the ground. She ripped off the tape that sealed the top and pulled it open. Charlie reeled up, startling her and knocking her backward. She quickly sat up, reached into the box, and pulled him out. He was bound with masking tape, his legs held together and his mouth taped over.

❖

Elizabeth sat quietly stroking Charlie's back as he lay curled up in her lap. It took two cans of her best food to calm him, and an offering of leftovers before he allowed her to beg for forgiveness.

A team of police officers paraded through her home, but she ignored their presence. Nothing appeared to have been taken or disturbed, other than Charlie. The police dismissed the break-in as a juvenile prank; however, she knew it was a targeted act to scare her. It was the Raymond Miller case. She guessed someone other than Dan wanted her off the case, but why?

Elizabeth was broken from her deep thought when Michael set a cup of steaming tea on the table in front of her.

"For your nerves," Michael said, and she accepted without protesting, despite her preference for coffee.

"You can't stay here. It's not safe. I told you, you should have an alarm system, living alone and all."

She stroked Charlie and didn't respond to his lecture.

"You're scaring me. Say something. Tell me what's going on in your head."

"Sorry. I'm scared, but I'm more pissed off. I'm not backing down."

"Backing down?"

"It's the Raymond Miller case. Someone is trying to scare me away."

Michael digested this new information. "You can stay with me."

"I like you too much to live with you. We'd be at each other's throats in a week's time."

He raised his finger to protest but said nothing. They were best friends, but Elizabeth knew they were incompatible roommates. Michael had his rules and became very uptight when they were upset. She called them "anal retentive"; he called them "organized." Either way, they both silently agreed that they would not share a home together, even for the shortest amount of time.

"So where to then?" he asked.

"My parents', I guess."

"Seriously?" he said with his face scrunched in disbelief.

"Seriously."

Michael crossed himself.

"You're not Catholic," she reminded him.

"I figured it can't hurt. You're going to need all the help you can get."

Elizabeth offered no retort and instead gazed at the entryway where Grace Donovan stood conversing with one of the uniformed officers. "A new friend?" Michael asked, but Elizabeth didn't answer, and her eyes remained on Grace. "Have you slept with her yet?"

"What?" Elizabeth snapped back.

"Oh, *that* you heard."

Elizabeth turned back to Grace and watched her approach with confident strides.

"Are you all right?"

"Yes," Elizabeth responded softly. "What are you doing here?"

"I heard the call on the radio. I was nearby." She turned to Michael. "I'm Detective Grace Donovan."

"Michael Chan. It's a pleasure to meet you, Detective Donovan," he offered in a sickly sweet voice, causing Elizabeth to roll her eyes.

Grace trailed her eyes over Elizabeth, lingering for a moment on Charlie, who claimed proprietorship on her lap, causing Elizabeth to become conscious of her beleaguered state. She ran a hand through her tousled hair and adjusted her oversized sweater that was falling off her shoulder.

"Well, I won't keep the two of you. I just wanted to make sure you were all right. The officers are almost done, and you can get back to your evening."

She nodded to Michael before turning and walking back to the door, and Elizabeth watched her go in silence, too stunned by Grace's presence in her home to ask the question nagging at the corner of her brain. *Why are you really here?* Elizabeth wondered if Grace also saw a connection to the Miller case, or maybe it was more personal.

Grace reached her car in a quick retreat and hastily pulled away from the quaint home, pushing her foot heavily on the gas pedal and keeping her eyes trained ahead until she was several blocks away, a safe distance from Elizabeth's home, before she pulled over once again. "What the hell was I thinking going there! Cool and aloof, remember?"

Earlier on her drive home, she ignored the usual busy chatter on her radio, until she heard Elizabeth's name. Concern overruling reason, she pointed her car in the direction of the suspected break-in. It was only when she witnessed Elizabeth curled into a chair, looking rumpled and lost, that she realized her mistake.

❖

Elizabeth stood in the ornate entryway of her childhood home with a cat carrier in her hand. Charlie let out a few elongated meows of protest at his confinement, and Michael crouched behind Elizabeth.

"What are you doing?" she asked without turning around.

"Hiding. I'm hoping your mom won't see me. She scares me."

"There's no use. She has a sixth sense, and she sees through walls. Nowhere in the city is safe."

"Elizabeth, I thought that was you." Elizabeth's mother paused at the top of the stairs before she elegantly glided down the steps, a move straight out of a 1940s movie. Beatrice Campbell was a picture of refined elegance. She dressed as though she were going to an important outing every day because one never knew when unexpected company would arrive, like now for instance. As she descended the stairs, the pant legs of her tailored white suit flowed with ease in rhythm to her movements. Her highlighted brown hair was carefully cut and styled and her makeup artfully applied.

Elizabeth waited until her mother completed her traverse down the staircase before she spoke, afraid to upset her mother's entrance. "Hi, Mom. You remember Michael."

She turned halfway around to gesture to him, swinging the cat carrier. Charlie bellowed in response to the movement.

"What in God's name is that!" Elizabeth's mother exclaimed.

"It's Charlie," Elizabeth calmly responded.

Michael breathed a sigh of relief that attention was taken off him.

"You brought that beast in this house?"

"Yes, Mom. I can't very well just leave him behind. He'll be fine. He's housebroken."

Her mother visibly scoffed and turned away toward the library, no doubt to complain about the four-legged houseguest to Elizabeth's father.

Elizabeth stepped forward and looked around the room and knew she would be safe here. Not because of the fortified walls, iron gates, alarms, and security guards. It was her mother that would keep the boogeyman at bay.

"Come on, my room is upstairs," she said as she hefted a suitcase with her free hand. Michael lifted the remaining suitcase and garment bag and mutely followed behind.

Chapter Ten

W hat do we have here?" sneered a tattoo-laden inmate who kicked the back of the plastic chair where Raymond Miller sat.

Raymond, who had been sitting in the common room coloring, bowed his head, pulled his arms tightly around himself, and slowly rocked his body. He had learned that answering was futile.

"Ah, the retard is coloring." The inmate snatched up the paper and held it up for the fellow prisoners to see. "Isn't it pretty?" Several of the men laughed in response.

"Oops, I'm sorry. Did I ruin your pretty picture?" the inmate said as he ripped the paper into several pieces and allowed them to fall to the floor.

Raymond remained mute.

"You too good to talk to me?" asked the inmate as he slapped the back of Raymond's head, causing him to lunge forward and hit the table.

Tears streamed down Raymond's face.

"Ah, he's crying. The little bitty baby is crying."

Before Raymond could straighten himself back into the chair, the inmate struck him in the face with a closed fist, sending him sprawling to the floor. Raymond tucked himself into a ball, covering his head with his arms. A wall of bodies encircled them and the inmate knelt beside him and began delivering blows to Raymond's body. Raymond's body trembled uncontrollably, and his muffled wails of pain and fear were drowned out by the excitement of the men.

When the blows stopped, tears streamed down Raymond's face, but he tried to stay quiet out of fear that any sound would bring about a new fit of fury. He peeked through his arm and watched the inmate pull off his shoe and lift the inside sole. He removed a handcrafted metal shank and admired it for a moment. "They are very upset. You shouldn't have fucked with the way things are. Your friend, who is he? Huh, asshole, what's his name?"

Raymond remained tucked in a ball and buried his face again. "Don't feel like talking? No more pretty pictures for you, then," the inmate sneered.

"What the fuck is going on in here!" bellowed the guard from the doorway.

The inmates quickly dispersed while Raymond remained trembling and sobbing on the floor.

The guard knelt next to him and spoke into his radio. "We have an inmate down in the comm room."

"It's a good thing for you that you had a visitor," the guard whispered to Raymond as he waited beside him for the medical personnel.

Father Parker recited a prayer through the phone as a prisoner kept his head bowed, phone pressed to his ear, mouth moving with the words. Father Parker pushed his hand against the thick glass that separated them in an offering of a blessing. When he completed his task, the prisoner stood and gratefully thanked him.

"That's the last one, Father," announced the guard.

"Oh, but I thought there was one more," Father Parker responded.

The guard consulted his list. "Oh right, the last one went to the medical unit, so you're all done."

"Perhaps the one in the medical unit could use a blessing," he offered.

"No, he's not up to visitors. Perhaps another day."

CHAPTER ELEVEN

The courtroom bustled with activity as defense attorneys brokered deals with prosecutors, and the court personnel chatted amiably about their weekend. Elizabeth skipped the courtroom pleasantries and approached the court clerk and announced her case was ready. There would be no deal to be made in the Raymond Miller case. Elizabeth felt the eyes of one prosecutor boring through her as she moved to take her seat in the front row of the gallery. She ran her hand over the seat of the wooden bench that bore carvings of initials, gang insignias, and crude political statements about the justice system. She wondered how these wood-carving artists got away with it, sitting only a few feet away from the bailiff.

Elizabeth dismissed the thought and began taking in the room. She had never considered the similarities of the courtroom to the church. Change the cast and a different play formed—the court spectators as parishioners, the jury as the choir, and the judge as the preacher. The defendant would be cast as the sinner, but what about the attorneys? As she pondered that thought, she was startled back to her surroundings when the door behind the bench opened. Elizabeth rose with the masses as a sign of respect and waited for Judge Rose Walters to take her seat behind the altar. Before she had an opportunity to resettle, the clerk called her case.

She moved forward to the counsel table and did her best to hide her jittery nerves. She knew she was asking for a lot. Elizabeth wanted the court to vacate Raymond Miller's conviction on the ground that his plea wasn't considered "knowing and voluntary" under the law, given his mental status. She couldn't help but throw in the fact that a subsequent murder with the same marking occurred, casting serious doubt on the veracity of Raymond Miller's confession.

She felt the eyes of the prosecutor on her once again. Assistant District Attorney Robert Burke settled across from her, and a small smile formed on his face that resembled more of a sneer when he looked her way.

"Bailiff, please bring in the defendant," the judge instructed.

Elizabeth began unpacking her bag, preparing for a fight—a three-ring binder with case law cited in her brief, the criminal code, a legal pad, two pens (in case one ran out), and a highlighter. This process settled her nerves. By the time her unpacking was complete, she was ready both physically and mentally, so she thought anyway.

Elizabeth didn't hold back her gasp, neither did the judge, when Raymond came into the court. His face was badly bruised, and his left eye was nearly swollen shut. It was evident by his gait that walking, or any movement for that matter, caused great pain.

The bailiff gingerly led Raymond to the seat next to Elizabeth and uncuffed him.

"Bailiff, what happened to this man?" the judge asked.

"I'm sorry, Your Honor," the bailiff stuttered. "I don't know all the details. There was apparently an altercation in the prison. The defendant was attacked."

The judge stared at Raymond, distress apparent on her face. "Mr. Miller, are you all right to proceed?"

Raymond didn't answer, but only rocked in his chair, keeping his eyes trained on the table in front of him. Elizabeth leaned over to him and soothingly spoke in his ear and asked if he would like for them to continue. Raymond nodded, and Elizabeth wasn't sure he truly understood what she asked or only agreed because it seemed easier.

"Your Honor, the defendant wishes to proceed."

Satisfied with Elizabeth's statement, Judge Walters continued. "I've read both of your briefs, and I find both the confession and the guilty plea troubling. The court cannot ignore the defendant's IQ, nor can the court ignore the fact of the recent murder that has been published in the news. It seems that in the interest of justice, the court must vacate the defendant's conviction, set aside his plea, and reset this case for trial."

The sneer that once occupied the prosecutor's face turned to disbelief. "But, Your Honor, this is highly irregular. There's nothing in the record to indicate any impropriety."

Judge Walters raised her hand and cut him off. "I've made my ruling. This case will be set for a grand jury."

Feeling emboldened by the judge's ruling, Elizabeth ventured forward. "Your Honor, may we address the issue of bail?"

"You have got to be kidding me," the prosecutor nearly spit out.

"Mr. Burke, I assume that means you are opposing bail in this case?" Judge Walters asked, slightly annoyed at his tone.

"Absolutely, Your Honor. This man has been convicted of first degree murder."

"Correction, Mr. Burke, he has been charged with murder. I have vacated the conviction." Judge Walters looked at Raymond, who kept his head bent through the proceedings and nervously rocked himself.

"I have not seen any evidence yet to support the prosecution's case against the defendant, so I will presume he is innocent until proven otherwise. It is clear from the report in Ms. Campbell's brief that the defendant does not have the mental capacity of an adult, and it is clear that he does not have the mental capacity to care for himself in prison. It is also apparent that the prison is not capable of caring for him either. I'm going to order that the defendant be released on his own recognizance to the care of his mother. Should his mother's home not be deemed an appropriate place for the defendant, then I trust, Ms. Campbell, that you will find suitable arrangements for the defendant and keep the court notified."

"Yes, Your Honor," was all Elizabeth could muster. Not in the most optimistic scenarios that she had conjured in her head did she see that coming.

Judge Walters concluded the proceedings, and Elizabeth gathered her battle weapons and shoved them into her bag. As Elizabeth moved past, she was stopped by Assistant DA Burke.

"All prior deals are off, Ms. Campbell. The death penalty is back on the table. Be careful what you wish for."

Elizabeth didn't make eye contact but continued moving past, determined not to show any reaction to his threat.

❖

Raymond fussed in the front seat of Elizabeth's car, giving her the impression that he had little experience riding in a vehicle. Elizabeth jumped when he twisted the volume knob on the radio, sending music blasting through the speakers. Raymond quickly covered his ears and began rocking.

She twisted the knob back and offered soothing words to placate him, and he gave a sheepish smile in response. He turned to the window and looked out with interest.

"I know, I know." He clapped excitedly.

"You recognize the neighborhood, don't you?" she asked.

Elizabeth turned the corner to the street where the children had previously been playing soccer. She slowed down, remembering her last journey down this road. As she pulled in front of Raymond's home, he began fidgeting in his seat. She couldn't tell if it was excitement, nervousness, or both that kept him squirming.

"All right, Raymond, let's go see your mom."

Elizabeth hefted a small drawstring bag that contained Raymond's worldly possessions from prison. Raymond opened the car door after a few failed attempts at the door handle and followed her up the walkway. She knocked on the door, and it was yanked open.

"He's not staying here!" Delores Miller barked without waiting for Elizabeth to speak.

Elizabeth stared, her mouth slightly ajar.

"They called me. Told me he was coming," Delores said.

Elizabeth assumed "they" meant the prison. "But, Ms. Miller, Raymond needs a place to stay. You're his mother. This is the only home he knows."

"You got him out. He's your problem." Through the exchange, Delores never acknowledged Raymond's presence as he stood mutely at Elizabeth's side.

Delores closed the door, cutting off any rebuttal, and Elizabeth stood dumbfounded. She turned and headed back to her car with Raymond's bag dangling from her hand. It was only when she reached her car that she realized that Raymond remained standing on the porch staring at the closed door. She swallowed hard, her heart breaking for the childlike man standing at the door that his mother just closed on him. Elizabeth opened her car door and tossed Raymond's bag inside and headed back up the walkway.

"Come on, Raymond." She grasped Raymond's arm and led him back to her car.

❖

Elizabeth pulled her car into her parents' circular drive and cut the engine. She looked over to Raymond, who stared straight ahead. He hadn't moved or made a sound since leaving his mother's home.

"Okay, Raymond, we're here."

He offered no response and remained motionless in the front seat. She exited the car and circled to Raymond's door and opened it. She gingerly lifted his arm that rested in his lap, urging him to stand up, and kept a hold of his hand as she led him up to the large front door that stood guarded by two stone pillars.

As they crossed through the entryway, he stopped and took in the enormity of the room. She couldn't imagine how this compared in Raymond's mind to his shed. Elizabeth tugged on his sleeve to encourage him to continue following her as she led him into the kitchen.

"You must be hungry," Elizabeth said as she pulled open the industrial-sized refrigerator and surveyed the contents. While assembling the ingredients for two sandwiches, she asked, "Raymond, why did you tell them that you killed that priest?" She hoped a new setting would provide new answers.

Raymond stared down at the black and white floor, his lips slightly moving. He was counting the tile squares and simply shrugged in response to her question.

She wasn't sure if he was refusing to answer or really didn't remember. As she struggled with a jar of mayonnaise, Elizabeth watched him, still trying to figure out this boy trapped in a grown body.

"Here, Raymond, can you open this?" She held out the jar, and Raymond stretched his hand across the counter. She noticed a scar across his left palm that was once a deep cut, and she traced her finger across the raised edge that wrapped around to the side of his hand. "Raymond, where did you get this scar?"

He looked at his hand and tilted his head slightly as though noticing the scar for the first time, and as Elizabeth had come to expect, he again shrugged in a noncommittal answer. Before she could finish her questions or even embark on her sandwich preparation, Elizabeth's mother entered the kitchen.

"You're home early," her mother stated before she stopped in her tracks to stare at Raymond. "Who is this?"

"Hi, Mom, this is Raymond Miller. Raymond is going to be staying with us for a little while."

"Elizabeth, may I speak with you for a moment please?" she asked in an artificially nice tone.

Elizabeth drew in a breath for courage as she followed her mother into the sitting room.

"What are you thinking? I thought I raised you better than that. You don't just drag strangers into our home."

"Well, at least he doesn't shed."

As if on cue, Charlie jumped on the white sofa to allow Elizabeth to greet him.

"Ugh! That cat is a menace! He climbed the drapery. Did you know that?"

Elizabeth wisely chose not to answer the question because she knew there was no right answer. She also decided to withhold the information that Charlie had used her mother's prized potted plants in the sunroom as his personal kitty litter box.

"Mom, Raymond has no place else to go." Elizabeth told the story of Raymond Miller. The simple man whose mother rejected him and forced him to live in a shed, who was falsely accused of a crime that he didn't commit and duped into confessing, and who was viciously beaten in prison. Elizabeth could see her mother's rigid posture soften as the story unfolded. She knew by the end, she had reached her.

"All right, he can stay...for now," her mother said as she stood and headed back to the kitchen.

"Well, Raymond, if you're going to live in this house, I'm going to feed you right." She pushed aside Elizabeth's efforts at sandwich making and pulled out a skillet. "I bet you like pancakes."

Raymond's eyes widened and he clapped in approval.

Elizabeth had to give credit to her mother. She knew when to step up.

Chapter Twelve

Elizabeth opened a side door to St. Augustine, Father Rossi's former church, and strolled past a row of pews. She wondered when she had become so comfortable wandering into churches. At the forefront, a middle-aged man dressed similarly to Father Parker was lighting a candle on the right side of the chancel.

He turned to her as she approached. "You must be Elizabeth Campbell."

"Yes." She reached out and shook his proffered hand.

"I'm Father Estevan."

"Thank you for seeing me, Father Estevan."

"Anything I can do to help. Father Rossi's death was a shock to us all."

"I can only imagine. I'm sorry for your loss," she said.

"Thank you. How about we go into the office?" Father Estevan led her to a well-appointed office more lavish than Father Parker's.

Elizabeth learned that Father Samuel Rossi had retired from the day-to-day activities of the church about ten years prior, and Father Estevan stepped up to fill his role. After a pleasant conversation with the father, Elizabeth learned nothing more about Father Rossi than she had already gotten from the news coverage of his murder.

He discussed Father Rossi's background with confidence, as though he had become the recent authority on the man, at least with the media, since his death. Father Samuel Rossi was born in Italy in 1926 in a small town near the border of Austria, shortly after Benito Mussolini abandoned all pretenses of a democratically elected prime minister and set up his dictatorship. The events of the war shaped his childhood, and he pursued his calling to priesthood at the age of eighteen, in lieu of following the family business in medicine. His father was the town doctor where Father Rossi was born and raised, as was his father before him. Although Elizabeth found the father's early life interesting, it was unhelpful in her quest.

Defeated by the lack of new information, she rose and thanked the father for his time. She pulled on her coat and admired several photos hanging on the wall that chronicled Father Rossi's life. There was a photo of a younger Father Rossi in a crude rural setting with a group of smiling children surrounding a Spanish sign that announced San Salvador's Home for Children, a middle-aged Father Rossi posing with another man dressed in a purple cassock, and a more recent photo of Father Rossi at what Elizabeth presumed to be the Vatican.

Father Estevan came up beside her. "Father Rossi had a full life."

"He seemed like a wonderful man."

Elizabeth turned to exit the office but stopped in the doorway, causing Father Estevan to stop short before running into the back of her. She reached for the photo of Father Rossi standing with the other man dressed in purple, and drew it close to her face, scrutinizing the details.

"Where was this photo taken?"

"I don't know. It was many years ago. Why?"

"The gate behind them, it's familiar."

Behind a smiling Father Rossi was a black iron gate with the words "*Deo duce*" forming a circle around a cross in the center. The glossy, well-maintained gate indicated it was in much newer condition.

"Do you mind if I borrow this? I just want to make a copy. I'll bring it back tomorrow."

Without giving Father Estevan an opportunity to respond, she pushed the framed photo into her bag and headed for the door, not waiting to see if he was following.

❖

Elizabeth returned to the clinic but sat in her car in the parking lot with the photos of the first victim on her lap. After her encounter with Dan in her office, she felt the pirated file was safer in her presence and traveled with it. She held each photo from the file close to her face and compared them to the photo of Father Rossi. There was no doubt that the gate on which the killer displayed his first victim was the same as the one in the Father Rossi photo. What Elizabeth found curious was that the location where the first victim was found wasn't stated in the file. Was it an oversight?

She briefly considered paying Grace a visit but doubted she'd be forthcoming with the information. She hadn't seen or heard from her since the night her home was broken into, and she spent a great deal of time overanalyzing the detective's brief visit. Although she thought she saw true concern on Grace's face, in her frazzled state, she could have mistaken it for what was really professional sympathy. Showing empathy toward a victim was simply part of the job.

No, visiting Grace wouldn't be part of her plan, but neither would waiting and obtaining the information during the discovery phase of the trial. She didn't want to wait that long; she wanted to know now.

Elizabeth blew out a breath and walked to the clinic. The front desk stood empty, so she surreptitiously made her way to her office and closed her door. She half expected Dan to come barreling in accusing her of wasting time and resources chasing this case, but that didn't stop her from her research. However, a search of the Internet offered her no information on the gate.

"Somebody must know," she told herself and stared down at the photo. "You, you know." She pointed at the man dressed in purple in the photograph. "Who are you?"

CHAPTER THIRTEEN

Following a morning in court, Elizabeth made good on her promise and returned the framed photo to Father Estevan after making several copies. She made enlarged copies, as well as copies that zoomed in on the gate.

When she entered the church, she found Father Estevan kneeling at the front of the church, head bowed. She sat in a pew halfway down, patiently waiting, and was struck by the peace that seemed to come from the bent figure and envied the unquestioning faith that he seemed to possess. She leaned forward and rested her arms on the back of the pew in front of her. As she stared at the crucifix with Jesus taking center stage at the front of the altar, she pondered his blind faith and where it had led him.

Father Estevan stood and crossed himself. He turned toward her and offered a smile. "Ms. Campbell, back so soon?"

"I'm sorry to disturb you. I just wanted to return the photograph." She pulled the framed picture from her bag and handed it over.

"Ah yes, thank you."

"Thank you," she replied. "I don't want to keep you. I just had one question. Who is in the photo with Father Rossi?"

"That is Cardinal Ryan. He was a bishop then."

"Cardinal Ryan? Where is he?"

"He's the archbishop."

Elizabeth stared at him, hoping for more information. "Of our archdiocese," Father Estevan said with a slight inflection in his voice.

She made a mental note of his answer and figured she would look it up on the Internet later. "Great. Thank you again for everything."

"My pleasure. Take care."

Elizabeth made her exit with a plan of action and nearly walked into Grace, who entered through the vestibule.

Grace reached out to catch Elizabeth by her shoulders when she stumbled a little at their impact. "Ms. Campbell, I'd say I'm surprised to see you here, but that wouldn't be true." Grace allowed her grasp on Elizabeth to linger a little longer than necessary, and it didn't go unnoticed, but was also not unwelcomed.

"Just feeling the need for a little spiritual guidance, Detective."

"Maybe more than a little?" Grace snorted. "How about you stay out of trouble?"

Although they were being more cordial since Grace made an unexpected appearance at Elizabeth's home, they were not on the same side either.

❖

Elizabeth pulled her car into a parking garage of a high-rise building. The address she pulled up on her phone led her to this location for the archdiocese. After becoming well versed with the inside of churches, she expected to be led to a more spiritual location than an upscale office building. She guessed many of the building's occupants prayed to a different deity, one that controlled the stock exchange.

The lobby of the building oozed opulence with glossy marble tiles and columns. She approached the black security desk and faced a stern thirty-something officer dressed in a black uniform, with a large gold badge on his chest.

"How may I help you?" the officer asked in a professional tone.

"Good afternoon. I need to speak to someone in the archdiocese."

"Do you have an appointment?"

"Well, no, but I'm investigating a case that concerns the Church and needed to see someone—"

The security officer cut her off. "I'm sorry. If you don't have an appointment, then you can't pass through."

"Well, if you could just call and see if someone is willing to see me, now that I'm here." Elizabeth started to remove her identification from her bag.

"Please put that away, ma'am. You'll need to contact the archdiocese and schedule an appointment. Have a good day."

She got the none too subtle hint and turned away without another word. She returned to her car, discouraged but not defeated. Her prior research on the archdiocese listed a cathedral where the archbishop performed mass. She pulled up that address and continued on her quest.

Elizabeth could see the cathedral before she reached the parking structure down the block. She walked toward the church and was in awe of the size. The cathedral was substantially larger than the other Catholic churches she visited. The architecture reminded her of European churches she had seen on her trips abroad. Two large gothic spires extended above the church, one on each side of an elaborate entrance with stone pillars. Large gold-plated doors with oversized handles stood in the center.

Elizabeth walked along a stone pathway that cut through a lush green lawn and climbed a set of stone steps. She stood at the front doors, intimidated. After a deep breath, she pulled on the door, but it didn't budge. She figured it would be a bit much to expect to find the front doors open and be able to stroll in. She rounded the building and found a modern structure that boasted a gift shop and what she hoped to be offices. She walked in the gift shop, thankful that it was open, and perused the selections. The store offered T-shirts with embroidered photos of the cathedral, postcards, and other religious-themed trinkets. A woman who was restocking a glass case emerged from beneath the counter.

"May I help you?"

Unsure where to start because of her last encounter at the office building, she hesitated. "Hi, um, I'm Elizabeth Campbell. I was wondering if there is anyone here I can talk to about a photograph."

The woman stared at her completely confused. "A photograph?"

"Yes, sorry. I'm not being very clear. I'm investigating a case that involves the death of Father Samuel Rossi." Elizabeth heard the woman let out a small gasp. "I have a photograph of Father Rossi and Cardinal Ryan taken many years ago. I'm trying to identify the location of the photo. This may prove to be very helpful in my case."

The woman stared at her. "Let me see who can help you. One moment, please."

"Thank you," Elizabeth called after her as the woman disappeared through a side door. She resumed inspecting the store and picked up a small glass bottle with a cork. The label told her that it was "Holy Water Blessed by Cardinal Ryan." While she was closely inspecting the divine water, the clerk reentered the store followed by another woman. Elizabeth gently set the bottle back down, afraid of breaking it, and moved to the new woman.

"I'm Jenny Tulls. I'm the manager here. I understand that you have a photograph that you were looking for help with?"

Elizabeth repeated the woman's name in her head and took a breath to stifle her laugh. The woman cocked her head at Elizabeth, oblivious to the humor she found in her name.

"Sorry, yes, I have it here." She pulled out a copy of the photo and handed it over.

"Yes, that's Cardinal Ryan and Father Rossi."

Elizabeth nodded at the information she already knew. "I was hoping that someone could identify where the photo was taken."

"Hmm, well, I'm not really sure." The woman gripped her chin with her thumb and forefinger as she spoke.

"Do you know if there is anyone else here that might be able to identify it?" *Like maybe Cardinal Ryan*, Elizabeth finished in her head.

"I don't know, but we of course always want to help the police when we can. I'll go check. Why don't you go out to the garden and have a seat on the bench?" The woman pointed to a stone patio ringed by marble benches and returned the picture.

It wasn't lost on Elizabeth that the woman believed she was with the police investigating the case. She felt no need to correct her. She figured this was the reason why she was getting some cooperation, as opposed to her encounter in the other building. She took a seat on the bench as instructed and waited. She turned to admire the vast green lawn and garden of well-manicured roses boasting a diversity of colors. The minutes stretched on, and she started to fidget on the hard bench, the roses long since losing her interest. She started to wonder if they figured out she was an imposter and were keeping her there until the "real" police arrived. She reasoned with herself; it wasn't a lie, but an omission.

Elizabeth's internal discourse was cut short when a man dressed in a black cassock with a purple sash crossed the patio. She stood as he approached. Unsure of the protocol, she held back her urge to extend her hand and remained still.

"I'm Bishop Pallone," the man said. He extended his hand that was adorned with an engraved golden ring.

Elizabeth forewent the urge to bow or kiss the ring and grasped his hand and shook it. "Thank you for seeing me, Bishop Pallone." She hoped that was the right title to address him. He didn't react to her greeting, so she figured she did the right thing.

"Certainly. I understand that you're looking for assistance in Father Samuel Rossi's murder."

"Yes." She was really hoping she wasn't going to hell for her lie of omission. Elizabeth pulled out the photograph and handed it to the bishop. He studied it for a moment while she remained silent. He lifted his head and made eye contact with her. "Yes, this is Father Rossi with Cardinal Ryan. Cardinal Ryan was a bishop at the time this photograph was taken."

"Bishop Pallone, I was hoping you could tell me where the photo was taken." She moved to him and pointed at the gate in the picture. "I'm trying to locate this gate."

The bishop stood still for a moment, looking her directly in the eye, as though sizing her up. "May I ask why you want to know this?"

"Is it a secret?"

The bishop blew out a soft breath. "No. I just don't see the relevance to Father Rossi's death."

"You might be right, and it might not be relevant, but until I know the location, I won't know for sure."

"What is your name again?" the bishop asked.

Uh-oh. "Elizabeth Campbell," she answered.

"Ms. Campbell, where do you work?"

She momentarily froze. *Busted.* However, before she could respond, she was saved by another member of the church approaching from behind the bishop. She watched the man dressed in a red cassock move toward them. The bishop turned to follow Elizabeth's gaze and expelled a breath.

"Cardinal Ryan." The bishop bowed slightly, and the cardinal extended his hand. The bishop grasped it and kissed a ring on his finger. He then extended his hand toward Elizabeth, and she followed the bishop's actions and bowed and kissed his ring.

The cardinal addressed her. "I understand you're looking for assistance in Father Rossi's death. I was told you have a photograph."

She tried not to stutter. "Yes, Your Honor."

The cardinal smiled at the title. "I think *Your Honor* may be appropriate in the court. The official title is 'Your Eminence,' but you can simply call me Cardinal Ryan," he corrected her good-naturedly.

"Thank you, Cardinal Ryan." Despite his higher ranking, she was more comfortable in his presence than with Bishop Pallone.

"Now, where is this photograph?" he asked.

Elizabeth pointed to the photo still clenched in the bishop's hand. He reached for it, and Bishop Pallone released his hold. Cardinal Ryan looked down at the photo, adjusting its distance from his eyes, until he could see it clearly. A small smile crept across his face.

"I do remember this day. I went to visit the school."

"The school?" Elizabeth asked.

"Yes." The cardinal pointed to the gate. "This is, or was, Saint John's Boys School."

"I've never heard of it."

He looked off, momentarily lost in thought. "It closed down many years ago. Father Rossi ran the school."

"Where was the school?"

"It was near the old textile mill on the county line. That area is deserted now."

Cardinal Ryan handed Elizabeth back the photo. "Is there anything else?" he asked.

"No, thank you. You've been extremely helpful."

The cardinal smiled. "Well, I'm glad to have helped. Have a nice day."

Elizabeth offered a slight bow as he turned and walked toward the garden with the bishop in tow. She hurriedly exited the church property and walked back to her car, afraid someone would realize who she was before she made her escape. Her heart was thumping in part from excitement from her meeting with the cardinal, but also from the revelation of the photo location.

Cardinal Ryan walked at a measured pace, hands clasped behind his back, a deep crease etched into his brow. His red cassock flowed slightly with each step as a slight breeze played with the fringes. A bed of roses struggled to show the last of their color. Autumn was becoming crisper with each passing day.

Bishop Pallone kept pace, waiting for him to wake from his reverie. The cardinal was methodical and spoke precise, measured words, and as Bishop Pallone knew, would speak only when ready. For this reason, he remained silent on their traverse through the cathedral garden.

When they came to a gray marble bench, Cardinal Ryan sat as though a heavy weight pulled him down, and Bishop Pallone joined him. The silence was starting to eat away at his patience. Unlike the cardinal, Bishop Pallone was a man of many words.

"You realize that we cannot continue with this. I've been negligent in my duties to have allowed this to happen." The cardinal finally spoke.

"With all due respect, Your Eminence, we don't know if the killings are related."

The cardinal balked. "This we know. The branding and manner of killing is the same. We were wrong to believe that the simple man was responsible for the first death. We created this monster, and he's back. We must act this time and not hide like cowards."

"Your Eminence, we cannot act rashly. Think of the archdiocese."

"I am, and I know what we must do."

"Your Eminence, just a bit more time."

"We have run out of time, I'm afraid."

Cardinal Ryan rose and made his way back down the path. Bishop Pallone remained in his seat, lost in thought.

CHAPTER FOURTEEN

While reading a message on her phone as she walked, Elizabeth nearly ran into Father Parker as she exited the church. "Oh, I'm sorry, Father. I was texting and walking."

"Yes, I've heard that's not a good combination. Is everything all right with Rosa? I wasn't expecting you today."

"Oh yes, everything's fine. I just made some last-minute changes to the affidavit and needed to get Rosa to sign it again."

"You are doing good work. You make a difference in the lives of those you touch."

Elizabeth had heard this before, but coming from Father Parker, it held a special meaning. "Thank you, Father."

"And how are things with Raymond Miller?"

"Well, I'm heading out to Saint John's Boys School now," she responded as though that sufficiently answered the question.

"Saint John's? That school has been closed for what, thirty years?"

"So I've been told. You know the school?"

"I've heard of it."

It wasn't lost on Elizabeth that she might have been able to avoid her adventure at the cathedral if she'd only thought of going to the library with the photo to research it or had shown it to Father Parker.

"If I may ask, why are you going there?"

"Well..." She paused, unsure of how much to reveal.

"You needn't tell me. I'm only concerned for you. That area has been abandoned for a very long time, and it doesn't seem wise to go there alone."

Touched by his honest concern, she went on to explain the iron gate and how she tracked it to the school.

"I'd like to come with you, then."

"Father, that isn't necessary. I'll be fine. I'm just going to take a quick look around."

"Then you won't mind some company. It would give me an opportunity to avoid the administrative work waiting for me, the part of the job that I could live without," he replied with a smile. "I'm not comfortable with you going out there alone. It really is an isolated place. There's a homeless camp not far from there," Father Parker said in a more serious tone.

Elizabeth considered this information. She couldn't see how much protection an ordained priest could offer in hand-to-hand combat, should she find herself in such a situation, but she did appreciate his support. Since the day she started looking into the Raymond Miller case, she'd been met with resistance, and in some instances, downright hostility. Father Parker's concern was a nice change. "All right, if you're sure I'm not taking you away from anything important."

"Would I lie?" the father quipped back. They walked side by side to Elizabeth's car. "Wow, she is a beaut."

"Thank you, I'm rather fond of her."

Father Parker settled himself into the passenger seat and stroked the soft leather. "I can't say I've experienced this luxury before. I could get spoiled."

"You haven't seen nothing yet. Hang on." She shifted the car into reverse and punched her foot down on the pedal. The tires screeched, leaving tread marks in her wake.

"Oh, dear Lord," the father cried out as he reached for the ceiling handle and pushed his body back into the seat.

After a quick journey, Elizabeth stopped the Roadster at the entrance of the school property. Two large black wrought iron gates that had once stood proudly protecting the school, now lay open, sagging on their hinges. She observed the elaborately designed cross engraved into each gate. Surrounding each cross, in the shape of a circle, were the words "*Deo duce*."

"Do you know what that means?" asked Elizabeth.

"It's Latin. It means 'God as my leader,'" he responded.

She passed the gates and pulled into a mostly dirt parking lot dispersed with chunks of gray asphalt that had been chipped away with time. Large weeds threatened to overtake the lot. She killed the engine, and the father finished a silent prayer and made the sign of the cross.

"It wasn't that bad," she said.

"No, but it was a close second to being run through the spin cycle in a washing machine."

Chuckling, she exited the car and approached the cement foundation of what looked to have once been a large building, the structure itself long since demolished. She circled the foundation and stood at its back side. Overgrown trees ringed the school property, and high grass blanketed the terrain. Smaller buildings were spread throughout the grounds, but most were torn down with only a cement foundation, like the main structure. Those that were still intact exhibited signs of rot. Parts of their roof tiles were missing, and colorful graffiti decorated their side paneling.

Elizabeth approached the largest of the buildings that were still standing. It was a three-story structure with the windows boarded. The bottom portion of the outside walls was covered in a green mold. Two doors stood on each end of the building and a set of double doors in the center. As she completed a circle around the building, she found each door was locked. Metal latches were drilled into each door and frame and were secured together by heavy padlocks to keep out trespassers. She pulled on each door for good measure only to find them securely fastened.

She turned to keep track of Father Parker and found him roaming the grounds admiring the wildflowers that had taken root. Elizabeth moved on to one of the smaller, partially intact structures that appeared to have been a storage facility and peered inside a window whose board had been pulled away. Bricks, ceiling tile, and debris littered the inside. "Well, this is a whole bunch of nothing," she said to herself.

At the back of the property stood a chapel. Elizabeth identified the building by the steeple still standing erect on the top. She walked the circumference of the church and found it locked and boarded like the rest of the structures.

She remembered that she didn't come alone and turned to see where the father had wandered, but lost sight of him. After retracing her steps back toward the car with no sign of Father Parker, she walked to the edge of the school property where the boundary of a dense forest began. She softly called out for the father and received no response. She moved farther into the trees and called again, her concern building for the welfare of the priest.

"I shouldn't have brought him," she scolded herself.

As she was prepared to call out his name again, she noticed

another small structure mostly obscured by trees and brush, about fifty yards in. She made her way through the underbrush that threatened to tangle her feet to a dilapidated outbuilding. The building abutted a stone mountain behind it.

The structure offered no window to look through, so she pushed down on a long handle on the door. The handle easily moved, but the door wouldn't open. She banged her shoulder against the door, hoping to jar it free. After several attempts, she slumped against the door, closed her eyes, and tried to slow her breathing from the exertion.

"What did you find?"

Elizabeth jumped. "Ah, you scared me!" She had momentarily forgotten about Father Parker.

"I'm sorry. I should have announced myself."

"I don't know what it is. The door is jammed." She demonstrated by pulling down the handle and pushing and pulling on the door to no avail.

"Well, have you tried turning the handle up?" he asked.

Elizabeth realized the absurdity of that, but decided to humor him. As she pulled up on the handle, the door easily opened.

"One should always strive for up, rather than down," Father Parker sagely advised.

She rolled her eyes, then turned to face the inside of the structure. "This looks like an entrance to a tunnel, perhaps a mine."

She crossed the threshold into the darkness and walked about ten feet, until she came to a metal grate pulled shut across the passageway, blocking any further excursion. A rusted lock held the gate in place. She yanked down on the lock hoping time had compromised its strength, but the lock held. She then yanked up, and the father chuckled behind her.

"I think we've reached a dead end, Ms. Campbell."

"You give up too easily, Father, and please call me Elizabeth."

"All right, Elizabeth, what do you propose?"

She pulled the grate away from the wall. "I think I can fit through here."

"Oh no, Ms. Campbell—Elizabeth, I don't think that is such a good idea. That gate is meant to keep people out."

"Where's your sense of adventure, Father? Didn't you ever see Indiana Jones?" Without waiting for a reply, she turned and trotted back to her car. Moments later, she trotted back with a large flashlight in her hand.

"I'm always prepared," Elizabeth said as she turned the flashlight on and off.

She walked past Father Parker toward the structure. "When I was little, I wanted to be a Boy Scout. But my father told me that Boy Scouts were for boys, and Girl Scouts were for girls. I argued that Boy Scouts were so much cooler than Girl Scouts. The Girl Scouts did sissy stuff. I wanted my father to file a class action lawsuit based on gender discrimination on behalf of all the girls being denied entrance into the Boy Scouts. I think that's when I knew that I wanted to be an attorney to defend the rights of others who couldn't defend themselves."

He listened with interest to her story and momentarily forgot about the adventure on which she was about to embark. When they reached the metal grate, Father Parker again pleaded with her not to enter the tunnel; however, Elizabeth's mind was set. She pulled the grate to one side and squeezed herself through the gap. He stood at the grate, watching the light of her flashlight move farther away. "This is absurd," he called after her.

Father Parker sat in a dilemma. He knew entering the tunnel was not only dangerous, but illegal. However, allowing Elizabeth to walk in there alone and come across who only knew what kind of danger was morally wrong. His moral stance won out, and he pulled the grate to the side and squeezed himself through. "It looked much easier when she did it," he muttered.

He walked quickly, following the beam of light in the distance. "Elizabeth," he called out. The light stood still, and Father Parker caught up.

"Glad you could make it."

"Against my better judgment," he countered.

The tunnel was dank and musty. Small streams of water ran down the coarse rock walls. He stayed close behind her, explaining to himself that it was because she had the light.

"Aaahh, what was that!" Father Parker screamed and jumped forward, knocking into her. Elizabeth dropped the flashlight and quickly bent to pick it up before it rolled away.

"What's wrong?" she asked in a slight panic.

"Something ran across my foot."

She shined the light on the ground around him. A small pack of rats squealed and scurried away from the light, one making its way across his foot in its escape. Father Parker screamed again and jumped from foot to foot.

"They're just rats."

"*Just* rats?"

"I never would have taken you for being so squeamish," Elizabeth stated as she turned and continued walking. He jogged to catch up to her.

"I'm not squeamish. I just don't like rats."

"Don't worry, Father. It's our secret," she teased him.

"It's not a secret. Most people, excluding you, don't like rats."

They bantered back and forth for a few minutes, walking single file with Elizabeth in the lead, as the tunnel gradually descended deeper into the earth. She came to a sudden stop, and Father Parker ran into the back of her, causing her to lurch forward.

"You know we could make this easier, and I could give you a piggyback ride," Elizabeth quipped, as she regained her balance.

"Why did you stop?"

She shined the light on the wall, which revealed a concrete door.

"Where do you suppose that goes?" she asked, pushing on the immobile handle, but the door didn't budge. "It must be locked from the other side." Elizabeth continued down the tunnel.

"Maybe we should turn back now. I think we've gone far enough," Father Parker offered in response.

"Turn back? This is just getting good."

"Elizabeth, we don't know how safe it is in here. This tunnel could give way and trap us in here." Father Parker's breathing was coming harder with a small rise of panic at the thought of a cave-in.

"Relax, Father. This tunnel has probably been here for a hundred years."

"That's not reassuring," he said.

"Just a little bit farther. This has to lead somewhere. Otherwise, why would it be here?"

He conceded not because he agreed with her logic, but because Elizabeth had the light. After a few minutes, they came to a mouth of a small cavern. She entered the space with Father Parker right behind her.

"You think a bear lives here?" he asked.

"A bear! Yes, that's it, Father. This is a bear's house. A bear who secures his home with a metal gate and lock."

Elizabeth moved her light around the cavern, which revealed a decrepit couch with no legs sitting against one wall, along with articles of trash and ancient tin beer cans littering the ground around it. Several round white candles with the wicks burned halfway sat on the ground and ringed the walls. Against the back wall sat a long wooden table with a faded red cloth covering the top. Several more candles sat in the center of the table.

Elizabeth broke the silence. "What is this place? It looks like a cross between a frat house and an altar."

Father Parker offered no response as he took in the makeshift room.

She approached the table and lifted one of the candles that was turned on its side. A deep layer of dust covered it, along with everything else on the table. Beneath the candle, a darker red ring formed where the table had been protected from dust and aging. As she redeposited the candle on the table right side up, she noticed a small pendant the size of a dime partially embedded in the wax. Elizabeth used her fingernails to scrape around the wick and free the disc.

She continued to shine the light around the walls and took in the display of spider webs crisscrossing the walls and ceiling. She stopped on a crude wooden cross made of two sticks tied together hanging upside down on the wall above the table.

Now officially spooked, Elizabeth shoved the pendant into her pant pocket and turned to find the father who had been unusually quiet. Not finding him, she walked back toward the entrance of the room and softly called out, "Father, where are you?" She received no answer. "Father?" she called a bit louder.

"Yes?" His voice caused her to catapult and send the flashlight across the room. Father Parker chased after the light.

"Jesus Christ!" She remembered who her companion was and quickly recovered. "Sorry, I didn't mean that, I meant damn, darn it."

"It's all right, Elizabeth. In times like these, a curse word or two is appropriate. Besides, who's squeamish now?"

"That's not fair. I didn't go creeping up behind you after coming across some religious altar thingy."

Elizabeth turned to continue down the tunnel, and Father Parker stayed close beside her. Less than fifty feet beyond the cavern, the tunnel came to an abrupt end. The passageway was fully obstructed by rock debris. Apparently, the tunnel was not as sturdy as Elizabeth had claimed.

"Are you ready to go back now?" he asked.

"Yes."

Father Parker didn't hesitate to lead the way back with the light in hand, leaving her to keep up.

They reached the parking lot in a fraction of the time compared to their inbound trek. Elizabeth stopped at the school entrance as they were leaving and took several photos of the gates, including close-ups of the engraved cross encircled by the Latin words. As she and Father Parker drove back to the church, she asked, "What does that old school have to do with the murders? The school was closed down long before Raymond was born." She gestured with her right hand to emphasis the point.

"Can you put both hands on the wheel, please?"

At the end of their drive, Elizabeth pulled into the church lot, and he breathed a sigh. "Thank you for coming with me, Father."

"I'd say it was my pleasure, but I wouldn't want to lie. Let's say it was an adventure, as you called it."

Satisfied with that, she gave him a smile.

He exited the car and bent his head into the door. "Please keep me posted on what you're doing. It seems very dangerous, and I'd like to help if I can."

"As long as there are no rats?" Elizabeth asked.

Father Parker chuckled and closed the door with no response.

❖

Elizabeth returned to the office late for a scheduled client. She rushed through the front door and issued several apologies to an elderly African American woman sitting by the window.

Amy pulled her to the side. "What's up with you?"

"What?"

"What were you doing, crawling in an attic?"

"No, crawling in a tunnel." Elizabeth looked down at her pantsuit that was covered in a fine layer of dust, with a few cobwebs mixed in. Black streaks were smeared across her chest from squeezing herself through the grate.

"Fine, don't tell me, but you have to get yourself cleaned up," Amy said.

Elizabeth turned to the elderly woman. "Mrs. Francis, I'm so sorry. I'll be right back."

After making herself as presentable as possible, but with a black streak still across her chest, she set out drafting a healthcare proxy for Mrs. Francis. She had drafted many over the years, so she was able to accommodate the woman's needs quickly to make up for the time she left her sitting in the lobby. As Mrs. Francis signed the documents, relief washed over her face. "Now I can die in peace."

Elizabeth wanted to chuckle at the remark but realized that it wasn't meant to be a joke. She escorted the frail woman back to the reception area.

"Mrs. Francis, how did you get here?"

"I took the bus."

"Oh, I can't let you take the bus back."

"It's no problem, child. I was taking the bus before you were born."

"Please let me call you a cab."

"Oh no, child, cabs are too costly."

"Not this cab. It's free. It's a special service. Please," Elizabeth begged.

"Are you sure it's free?"

"Absolutely. Have a seat, and I'll get that cab for you."

Elizabeth walked back to her office and called the local cab company. She gave them her credit card number for the fare and a hefty tip if the driver got there in five minutes. Three minutes later, Mrs. Francis was safely tucked inside the back of a cab. Elizabeth ducked into the cabby's window. "Take good care of her. She's a special one," and stuck a twenty-dollar bill in his front shirt pocket to add to the generous credit card tip.

The cab driver beamed. "Thank you, ma'am."

Elizabeth stood watching the cab until it turned the corner and then made her way back into the clinic. She shoved her hands in her pockets as she walked past the bank of cubicles and felt cold metal in her right pocket. She pulled out the small coin-shaped pendant and studied it. It appeared to have been blackened by the candle, which made it difficult for her to make sense of the image. She rubbed at the pendant with the bottom of her shirt.

A picture of a man clothed in robes carrying a child on his back emerged. As the writing became visible, she read, "Saint Christopher, protect us," around the circumference of the image. She figured finding a religious medal in a hangout behind a Catholic school wasn't so unusual and dismissed it.

Determined to find the link between the school and the murders, Elizabeth ran a search on her computer for the history of Saint John's, but the information was sparse. A single news article revealed that it was an all-boys Catholic school founded in 1943. Years of financial difficulties resulted in the school's closure in 1982. Beyond that, the school seemed to drop off the grid.

Further research on the tunnels yielded even less information. Mining tunnels, some legal and others not, were dug throughout the state over a hundred-year period starting in the mid 1800s. She could find no specific details on mines in the area of Saint John's, which led her to believe that the tunnel was an excavation of the illegal kind.

Elizabeth pulled up an aerial map of the area and saw the skeletal remains of both the school and the mill. She recalled the concrete door that she and Father Parker discovered in the tunnel and wondered if similar tunnels ran toward the mill. *If they did, why? Perhaps another adventure is in order.*

Chapter Fifteen

After a cursory grand jury hearing the week prior, Raymond Miller was again held to answer for the charge of a single count of first-degree murder, not to Elizabeth's surprise. It was the trial that would test the government's case against him.

Elizabeth sat at the counsel table as the court clerk read off the instructions for jury selection. Raymond was conspicuously absent from the proceedings, with the judge's approval. Elizabeth feared that Raymond would be a distraction to her and the potential jurors if he had to sit through the arduous process of jury selection. As the morning wore on with mundane procedural issues, Judge Rose Walters called an early recess, ordering all parties and potential jurors back at one thirty to start the selection process. Elizabeth waited until the jury pool was released before she packed her belongings to head for an early lunch.

Mayor Reynosa leaned back in his leather chair, tipping it perilously toward the window behind him without care. He clutched a small stack of papers in his hands as he pored over the list of the potential jurors.

"When does jury selection begin?"

"This afternoon."

The mayor ran his finger down the paper and stopped on a name. "Bruce Jessup, on disability. Filed for bankruptcy. He's our man. Get him on the jury."

ADA Burke agreed and rose from his chair opposite the mayor. As he pulled on his coat, he asked, "How is this going to work?"

"Let me worry about that. You do your job and leave it to me."

Burke shook his head and turned to depart. He pulled open the door and found Simon at the ready. He offered a nod to acknowledge him as he passed.

❖

Elizabeth resumed her seat at the counsel table and propped her hand under her chin, a little sleepy from lunch. The names of the first twelve potential jurors were read, and she watched as each rose and took their seat in the jury box.

She observed what potential jurors brought with them to keep themselves occupied. She favored those that brought books over those that brought cell phones or other electronic devices, believing that jurors that read as a pastime would be more methodical and patient. Those that preferred mysteries would be more engaged in the minute details and fitting the pieces together and lead the group in discussions. Those that read romance novels would be more emotional and could be easily drawn in by the puzzle solver. Those that needed electronic devices to fill their time wanted quick answers and would rush to judgment. She needed the passionate thinkers on this jury.

As the afternoon continued, one juror was dismissed because of her difficulty with the English language, a second because he expressed an opinion that organized religion was nothing more than voodoo. Elizabeth pondered that statement for a while as ADA Burke jumped up requesting that the juror be excused with cause. Elizabeth kind of liked the juror. *Too bad.* Two more jurors were excused due to their religious beliefs and another very pregnant juror because of an impending due date. By the end of the afternoon, Burke used all of his peremptory challenges to dismiss jurors without cause, which she found unusual, but assumed that he had a method similar to Elizabeth's preference for readers.

After a day of voir dire, a jury of eight women and four men with two alternates was impaneled. Elizabeth blew a sigh of relief. Although she disliked this part of the process, she felt good about the selection. The jury was full of bookworms.

❖

"We have a problem," ADA Burke said as soon as Mayor Reynosa picked up the line.

"Now what?" Reynosa asked impatiently.

"Jessup is the first alternate on the jury."

"What the hell are you doing over there?"

Burke released an irritated breath. "I don't have control over this. You're lucky he made it there. Campbell didn't use all her peremptory challenges."

"Remember who you're talking to. I can pull up my shirttails that you so comfortably ride on."

Burke had his eye on the district attorney's seat, but he didn't have the political capital to make it happen, at least not without the discreet help from the mayor. Mayor Reynosa wouldn't balk at discarding his long-term relationship with the current district attorney if it suited him. As far as the mayor was concerned, the current district attorney was too squeamish and continually required cajoling to do the work that the city needed done.

A stubborn silence filled the line, a battle of wills. The mayor broke first. "Christ, I'll take care of this. Just do your job."

Burke disconnected the line without a further word.

❖

Bruce Jessup exited his rusted two-door coupe and slammed the door shut. The door bounced back open in an act of rebellion. He slammed it again, jamming his hip against it to keep it closed. He crossed the cracked asphalt that was dimly lit by a single streetlight and entered the liquor store, setting off a beep as he entered and alerting the clerk at the front to his presence. Jessup pulled open a glass door that stood in the back. The refrigerated air hit his face, causing him to blink. He grabbed his usual six-pack of beer and retreated to the counter, pointing to a case of cigarettes above the clerk's head. "One pack of the red ones."

After he completed his purchase, Jessup yanked a can free from its plastic holder and popped it open. He threw back his head, drinking the contents as he walked to his car. Only when he reached his car did he notice the man sitting on the trunk. "Get the fuck off my car, asshole."

The man slid off the car and leaned against it. "No disrespect intended, man. Just wanted to talk."

"What do you want?" Jessup demanded.

"Just looking to help you out a bit. Make some cash."

Jessup took another large gulp from the can. "I don't sell drugs. Now go."

"Oh no, this is much simpler and safer and much more lucrative. You interested?"

"I'm listening."

They stood close together as Jessup listened with rapt attention.

CHAPTER SIXTEEN

On the first day of trial, Elizabeth's mother sat in the front row behind Raymond, who was dressed in blue slacks, a white dress shirt with sleeves too long, and a silk striped tie, loaners from Elizabeth's father, and it showed. Judge Rose Walters arrived in the court more than half an hour late and took the bench. Everyone sat again as the judge called the court to order. She called Elizabeth and ADA Burke to the bench. The judge advised them that juror number three would be replaced by the first alternate. She explained that the court received notification from juror three's daughter that the elderly woman was hospitalized the night before from a fall, resulting in a broken hip.

After a series of procedural discussions and detailed instructions to the jury, Judge Walters ordered ADA Burke to call his first witness.

"The People call Detective Grace Donovan to the stand."

Although she knew Grace was on the witness list, Elizabeth still felt her heart quicken at the sound of the name. Trying to feign disinterest, Elizabeth busied herself with her trial notes as Grace passed and settled herself on the stand. She was dressed in a black suit with a white collared shirt, and Elizabeth chastised herself for not looking sooner because now she didn't know if Grace was wearing pants or a skirt, as her bottom half was hidden below the witness stand.

Elizabeth smiled to herself at the absurd thought and leaned back in her chair and quietly observed as the ADA and Grace went through a well-orchestrated question and answer session in which Grace detailed the arrest and search of Raymond Miller, after responding to a call for trespassing. Grace's stop and search was textbook, leaving no room for Elizabeth to challenge it, which was crucial to the DA's case. The search warrant and subsequent confession were all based on Grace's arrest and search of Raymond. Pleased with himself, the ADA sat back in his chair and turned to Elizabeth with a smug look. "Nothing further of this witness, Your Honor."

"Ms. Campbell, do you wish to question the witness?" asked the judge.

"Yes, Your Honor, thank you."

Raymond started fidgeting, bored of the proceedings. She knew that he didn't understand most of what was happening.

"I just need a moment, Your Honor." Elizabeth laid a soothing hand on his arm and calmly asked him to relax. She tore a few pieces of blank paper from her legal pad and asked him to draw some pictures.

As she returned her attention to the court, Elizabeth was taken aback by Grace's direct stare. It was the first eye contact they made all morning. Uncertain if Grace was trying to unsettle her, she took in a fortifying breath before proceeding. "Detective Donovan, the call complaining about Mr. Miller trespassing, that call was anonymous, correct?"

"Yes, I believe it was."

"Isn't it true that Mr. Miller had been going through trash cans and Dumpsters collecting recyclables for years prior to that arrest?"

"That is what I understand," came the curt reply.

"And at no prior time was there a complaint about Mr. Miller, correct?"

"I suppose."

"So why that day?"

"I'm sorry. I don't understand the question."

"Why on that day, the day that Raymond Miller was carrying the cross in his pocket, was an anonymous call placed about Raymond Miller?"

"I don't have any knowledge of that," Grace responded coolly.

"Objection, speculation," the ADA interjected.

"Sustained," said the judge.

Elizabeth was unperturbed; she didn't really expect the answer. She was simply trying to plant the seed in jurors' minds. "Detective, you are currently investigating a new murder, a Catholic priest. Correct?"

"Yes, but I'm not at liberty to discuss that case. We're currently investigating it."

"Isn't it true that this latest victim had a carving on his stomach that looked like this?" She raised a copy of the sketch of the circle with the three triangles.

The ADA jumped up. "Objection! That case has no relevance here.

It's an ongoing investigation, and as the detective stated, she cannot compromise her investigation by discussing it in open court."

Elizabeth calmly responded, "Your Honor, this case has been all over the news. This carving," she pointed to the sketch, "has been spelled out in detail in at least four papers. I'm not asking the detective to discuss anything that hasn't already been released to the public."

"I agree," responded the judge. "Detective Donovan, please answer the question."

"Yes, the victim in my investigation did have a carving on his stomach that looked something like that."

Without missing a beat, Elizabeth asked, "Isn't it true that in the killing for which Mr. Miller is accused, the victim had the same marking, the circle with three triangles inside, carved into his stomach?"

"Yes." Elizabeth couldn't help but note that Grace's eyes never wavered and continued in their challenging stare.

"Isn't it true that during the investigation of the first murder, the police withheld from the public the fact about the triangle carvings?"

"I wasn't the detective on that case, so I cannot answer that."

"I have nothing further, Your Honor." Elizabeth turned her back, abruptly ending the verbal sparring, and took her seat, once again busying herself with her notes.

After ADA Burke waived redirect examination, the judge said, "We got a late start this morning, so I think we're going to call it a day."

Grace stepped down and moved past, but Elizabeth refused to look up and acknowledge the blue eyes once again; however, she did watch the long legs stride past her table. *Pants.*

Chapter Seventeen

On the second day of the trial, Elizabeth brought a small box of crayons and a book of coloring paper to keep Raymond busy. Again, Elizabeth's mother sat behind him.

The ADA first called a forensic expert to testify, who confirmed that the blood on the rosary beads matched that of Father Francis Portillo. He also described the injuries the victim sustained, the circle with the trio of triangles carved into his abdomen, likely with a hunting knife, and his cause of death. There were no surprises for Elizabeth. A second expert went on to establish that the fingerprints of Father Francis Portillo were found on the Bible in Raymond's shed. Elizabeth attempted to shake the forensic experts' findings, especially with the passage of time, but with no success.

"The People call Patrick Sullivan to the stand."

The former detective was what Elizabeth thought to be the epitome of a seasoned detective. He had mostly gray, thinning hair. He carried a slight bulge in the middle. Deep creases were etched in his forehead.

Patrick Sullivan detailed his history with the police force and his date of retirement, which came weeks after the conviction of Raymond Miller. A series of questions allowed him to explain the search of Raymond's shed, the discovery of the victim's articles, and finally, the confession of Raymond Miller. Multiple photographs depicting the victim and the shed were introduced and displayed on several easels within the jury's easy view.

In closing his examination, the ADA inquired about the anonymous phone call that lead to the arrest of Raymond Miller, an obvious attempt to alleviate any doubt Elizabeth might have raised during her cross-examination of Grace.

"The police receive anonymous phone calls all the time. Some people are reluctant to give their names for fear of retaliation. Just because this was the first time someone called to report Mr. Miller doesn't mean it hasn't been on their minds for a long time. Sometimes God acts as our leader. Who knows how many more he would have killed."

"Objection!" Elizabeth dropped her pen as she quickly rose, nearly knocking over her chair.

The judge didn't wait for Elizabeth's explanation. "Sustained. The jury will disregard the witness's last two statements. Mr. Burke, please proceed."

Self-satisfied, he said, "I have nothing further, Your Honor." He knew that even with the judge's admonishment, the jury would never disregard the former detective's statements.

"Your witness, Ms. Campbell."

"Thank you, Your Honor. Detective Sullivan—"

"I'm retired. I'm no longer a detective," he interrupted.

"Yes, of course. Mr. Sullivan, did you personally search the shed?"

"Yes."

"Did anyone open the shed before you got there?"

"No. I arrived with the first unit."

"Was the shed locked when you got there?"

Sullivan paused for a moment as though searching his mind. *Aha, a question you hadn't rehearsed.*

"Yes, I believe it was."

"You believe it was?"

"It was locked," he said more firmly.

"How was it locked?"

"I don't understand," he puffed out in irritation.

"You said it was locked. What kind of lock was on the shed?"

"I don't know. One of those kind you need a key."

"So how did you get in the shed?"

"His mother must have opened it." He gestured toward Raymond as he spoke. "She let us in."

"I'm looking at the inventory report from the items removed off of Raymond Miller when he was arrested. Raymond didn't have a key. So how did Raymond get in his shed?"

"His mother, I suppose."

"Did you talk to Raymond Miller's mother?"

"Yes, when we conducted the search. As I said, she let us in. She spoke to us freely."

"Did she tell you that Raymond Miller couldn't tie his shoes?"

"So what?"

"The government's forensic expert testified that the victim's wrists and ankles were securely bound by a rope. How is it that Raymond Miller, a person who cannot even tie his own shoes, was able to securely tie him up?"

"I've seen much stranger things in my years as a detective."

"Isn't it possible that Raymond Miller didn't tie up the victim and someone else did?"

"No!"

"Why not?"

"He confessed to killing the priest."

"Ah yes, the confession. How long after his arrest did Raymond Miller give his confession?"

"A day, I believe. We first got the search warrant based on the rosary beads we found on him and searched his mother's home and the shed."

"Did anyone talk to Raymond from the time he was arrested to the time you questioned him?"

"No. He stayed in an isolation cell in the jail."

"Wasn't Raymond confused when you questioned him?"

"No. He knew why he was there."

"Did you offer him an attorney?"

"I read him his Miranda rights."

"You read off a legal statement to a person with an IQ of a young child and believed that was enough?"

"I did what the law required."

"How long did you interview Raymond before he confessed?"

"Not long, five, ten minutes. He was happy to talk."

"Mr. Sullivan, isn't it possible that Raymond Miller found the cross and Bible in a trash can? After all, that's what he was doing when he was arrested."

"Not likely."

"Why is it not likely?"

"He confessed to killing them," he said, drawing every word out slowly, as though Elizabeth was dense.

"Did Raymond have a car?"

Sullivan hesitated. "A car, uh, no."

"Did Raymond even have a driver's license?"

"No, I don't believe so."

Elizabeth turned and pointed to Raymond who was selecting a crayon from the box. "So it's safe to say that Raymond doesn't know how to drive a car, correct?"

Sullivan crossed his arms. "Yeah."

"So, then how did he transport the victim?" She gestured to the picture of Father Francis Portillo. "Did he carry him through the streets without anyone noticing?"

"I don't know."

Shifting gears, she asked, "Are you aware that there was another murder much like this murder?"

"I read something about it."

"Did you also read that the newest victim had the circle with triangles carved into his stomach?"

"I didn't pay that much attention."

"Well, let me help you out. Detective Donovan testified earlier that this newest victim had the triangles carved into his stomach, just like that." She pointed to the close-up picture of Father Portillo's abdomen.

"Then I guess it is so," he said.

"Isn't it true that in this case the police didn't release to the public the fact that the victim had the triangles carved into his stomach?"

"I can't remember that detail. It's been several years."

"Here, let me help you refresh your memory." She pulled out the former detective's investigative notes that she had copied from the Raymond Miller file and handed it to him. "These are your notes from the investigation, correct?"

He reviewed the notes as Elizabeth stood in front of him.

"Yes, these are my notes."

"Will you read the bottom of page two?"

He complied, moving his lips as he read. When he lifted his head, she asked, "Do you recall now?"

"Yes."

"Let me ask again, isn't it true that in the case of this murder, the murder of Father Francis Portillo, the police did not release to the public the fact that he had the circle with three triangles carved into his stomach?"

"Yes."

"Well, Raymond Miller has a pretty solid alibi for the latest murder, considering he was in prison at the time. Isn't it possible that someone else killed Father Portillo and made this carving?"

"No."

"Why?"

"Because he confessed."

"The confession was from a child who doesn't even understand what was going on. The confession doesn't explain how a fact that had never been disclosed, this carving, could end up on a new victim, unless Raymond Miller was not the killer."

"No, that's not true. Mr. Miller could have relayed that information to someone else. He could have set this whole thing up. Have someone kill another victim the same way he did, so he could get his conviction overturned."

"I see." She turned and looked at Raymond who was hunched over his paper, busily coloring a picture, oblivious to the world around him. She pointed to him. "You think he's a criminal mastermind?"

The ADA stood, "Objection, argumentative."

"Sustained."

Elizabeth rounded the defense table and sat in her chair. She looked down at her notes from the direct examination of Patrick Sullivan. Most were scribbles, as his testimony followed the script.

"Ms. Campbell, do you have any more questions?" the judge asked.

"No, Your Honor." As she said the words, she focused on a single phrase, *God is our leader.* She underlined the words and popped up out of her chair.

"I'm sorry, Your Honor. I actually do have a few more questions."

"Proceed then."

"Mr. Sullivan, where did you go to high school?"

On cue, the ADA jumped from his chair. "Objection! How is that relevant?"

"Ms. Campbell?" the judge looked at her questioningly.

"Your Honor, if you just allow me this line of questioning, its relevance will become apparent."

"Ms. Campbell, I will allow you to proceed, but be advised that I expect this to be going somewhere."

"Thank you, Your Honor."

Turning her attention back to the former detective, she said, "Mr. Sullivan, you attended Saint John's Boys School, correct?"

"Yes," Sullivan replied dubiously.

Elizabeth flipped through her file and pulled out two enlarged photographs that she took of the school gate. She placed one copy on the prosecutor's table, then crossed to the witness. "This is a photograph of the front gates of Saint John's Boys School. Do you recognize it?"

He squirmed in his seat. "Yes."

She then walked to the enlarged photo of Father Francis Portillo and tapped it. "What is the victim here hanging on?"

"A gate."

"Yes, thank you, we all see it's a gate, but what gate?"

"The front gate of St. John's Boys School," Sullivan said without looking at her.

Elizabeth held her photo of the school gate next to the photo of Father Francis Portillo, so the jurors could compare.

"Father Samuel Rossi, the current murder victim that Detective Donovan is investigating, who also had this carving," she pointed to the Father Portillo's abdomen in the photo, "did you know him?"

"What?" Sullivan asked, a little surprised.

She expelled a breath. "Did you know Father Samuel Rossi?"

"Objection, relevance!" the ADA barked.

"If Mr. Sullivan would answer the question, the relevance would be apparent."

"Objection overruled. Answer the question," Judge Walters instructed.

"Yes, he was in charge of the school."

"By 'school,' you mean St. John's Boys School, the school that you attended and where Father Portillo was left hanging on the front gate."

"Yes," he said, exasperated with her.

"Interesting. It all seems to be coming back to this school."

"Ms. Campbell, is there a question there?" the judge asked, preempting ADA Burke's objection.

"No, Your Honor. I'm finished with this witness." Elizabeth returned to her table and didn't need to make eye contact with Sullivan to feel the daggers that were directed at her.

After the prosecution rested, Judge Rose Walters turned to Elizabeth. "Is the defense ready to present its case?"

"Your Honor, I respectfully request a brief recess to be able to present my witness. She's not in the courtroom."

"It's just as well," responded the judge. "It's Friday. We can pick this up on Monday." She then turned to the jury and issued a series of instructions before rising from the bench and making her exit.

Elizabeth breathed a sigh and turned to Raymond. "Okay, Raymond, let's go home."

Elizabeth walked Raymond and her mother to her mother's black Mercedes and stood watching until they drove safely out of the parking lot, and then she turned toward the direction of her car, hitting her car remote to follow the beep. After settling behind the wheel, she noticed a white slip of paper sticking out from her windshield wiper. Frustrated that vendors would have the audacity to distribute flyers in the court parking lot, she lifted herself out of the seat, leaned over the car door, and snatched the paper. She crumpled the offensive advertisement and threw it on the passenger seat.

Using her Bluetooth, Elizabeth dialed Father Parker, and Mary answered on the third ring, breathing heavily.

"Hi, Mary, this is Elizabeth Campbell. Is Father Parker available?"

"I'm afraid not. He's counseling a parishioner. May I take a message?"

"Yes, thank you." Elizabeth recited her phone number and disconnected.

Uninspired to return to the clinic, Elizabeth decided to visit a friend at the county recorder's office.

❖

"Hey, Rich, how's it going?" Elizabeth offered as a greeting, as she strolled up to the counter of the county recorder's office.

Rich Porter was a lifer in government service. He had been with the county recorder's office since before there were computers. He was tall and extremely slim, and a worn black belt circled his waist, not for fashion, but for necessity. A few gray wisps of hair were combed over the top of his shiny head in hopes of disguising his impending baldness.

Elizabeth met Rich shortly after joining SILC when she was on a mission to dig up an old property deed of a slumlord's apartment building. Over the years, Rich proved to be invaluable. He knew where every record was kept, even documents not housed at the county recorder's office. He had a network of connections. Elizabeth was able to repay the favors with a dismissal of an overdue parking ticket that would have cost him half a month's salary. For that, he felt indebted;

however, to make sure he never lost that feeling, she plied him with jelly beans, Rich's vice, every time she came.

"Well, hello, stranger," Rich called back to her.

As he approached the counter, Elizabeth dropped the colorful bag of beans in front of him. "A bribe."

"Not necessary, but much appreciated. What can I do for you?"

"I was hoping you could dig up any information you can find on a school that was closed down about thirty years ago."

"Which one?"

She provided the minimal details that she had. Rich scratched his head, causing a rogue hair to stand on end, and she tried not to stare at it.

"That's a tough one. It may take some time," he replied.

"I appreciate anything that you can find."

"This may be a two-bagger job," he joked as he juggled the bag of jelly beans in his hands.

"I'll get you the whole candy store, if needed. Thanks, Rich."

After an endless Friday, Elizabeth pulled up to her parents' home and dragged herself up the steps. When she opened the door, swing music filled the entryway. She crossed the foyer to the sitting room to investigate and stared in incomprehension at the sight in front of her. Her mother and Raymond were clasping hands and moving their feet. *I think they're dancing.*

Her father sat on the couch clapping along to the beat and offering words of encouragement to Raymond. Raymond's face was red with exertion, but he beamed with excitement. Elizabeth stepped into the room, letting her presence be known. "Who are you and what did you do with my parents?"

Her parents both laughed, but her mother and Raymond continued their dance.

"Your mother is teaching Raymond how to dance," her father explained.

Elizabeth observed Raymond stepping on her mother's feet several times in his desperate attempt to keep up, but it only caused her mother to laugh harder. Bewildered, but enjoying the show, she joined her father and clapped along. However, her joy was short-lived, as she realized that if she failed, she would not only be letting down Raymond, but her parents.

❖

Patrick Sullivan paced the dimly lit room wringing his hands. "She's putting it together. Something must be done."

Mayor Reynosa raised a tumbler of aged scotch to his lips and took a slow sip. He savored the taste in his mouth before swallowing. "Relax, will you. Sit down. You're making me seasick watching you."

Sullivan sat at the edge of a textured print chair with dark wooden trim and rapidly bounced his knee. The delicate chair seemed an odd match for him. "I'm not going down alone."

"Don't forget who you're talking to." After another languorous sip, Reynosa continued. "The jury is ours."

"What do you mean?"

"You don't think we'd leave this to chance, now do you? Let's say we have an insurance policy."

Sullivan shook his head. "How does that help? You buy off a juror, Miller's found guilty, then what? That doesn't tell us who killed Rossi." He got himself worked up, and his tone increased as he spoke.

Mayor Reynosa stared at Sullivan, his drink perched halfway to his lips. "The confession of the retard was real, yes?"

"Yes. Miller's confession was clean."

Mayor Reynosa raised his hand in surrender, attempting to placate him. "I don't doubt you. Think about it; if he confessed, it means either he's behind this or he knows who is, and we need that name. Unless Mr. Miller is securely locked up again in our fine institution, we'll never get the name out of him."

Sullivan worked his mouth from side to side, and then finally nodded.

"Now leave before anyone sees you and don't come here again," Reynosa commanded.

Sullivan rose and walked toward the door.

"The back way," said Reynosa.

Sullivan changed his direction and exited.

"Moron." Reynosa removed a phone from the drawer of a dark mahogany table. He pushed a series of buttons, and a male voice answered, "May I help you?"

"This is Mayor Reynosa. May I please speak with Bishop Pallone?"

"It is rather a late hour. May I ask what this is regarding?"

"A confession."

While placed on hold, Reynosa resumed his affair with his scotch.

CHAPTER EIGHTEEN

Elizabeth was startled awake by a metallic-sounding version of "Happy." Disoriented, she slapped at her alarm clock, but the offending noise continued. She pulled herself up on her elbows, opened her eyes half-mast, and snatched up her cell phone.

"Hello?" she croaked.

"Elizabeth?"

"Yes, who is this?"

"This is Father Parker. I'm sorry. Is it too early?"

"What time is it?"

"About nine a.m."

Elizabeth's eyes flew wide open. "Holy shit."

The father softly chuckled.

"Sorry, Father." She banged the palm of her hand on her forehead. "Should I call back later?"

"No, I'm good. I didn't mean to sleep this late. Thanks for calling me back."

"I didn't see your message until this morning. What can I do for you?"

"I was wondering if you have some time to meet and go over the Raymond Miller case. It seems you're the only person I can talk to about it."

Father Parker agreed, and as Elizabeth hung up, she sat staring at the phone in her hand, thinking of the strange turn of events. A Catholic priest had become her closest confidant.

When she walked into the kitchen, she found Raymond, with the upper half of his body covered in a fine white powder, eagerly stirring a sticky mixture in a bowl with a wooden spoon. His tongue jutted out of the side of his mouth as he worked, and Elizabeth's mother stood over him offering words of encouragement.

"What ya making?" Elizabeth asked him.

"Pancakes!" Raymond said with more volume than necessary.

"Wow, that sounds great. I'm hungry."

"He did it all by himself," Elizabeth's mother said with pride.

"I can tell," Elizabeth responded, looking at the various spills on the counter and floor.

After a satisfying breakfast with an overabundance of syrup, compliments of Raymond, who insisted on serving, Elizabeth set out to meet Father Parker.

As she pulled up into the church parking lot, she found him standing by the church entrance. He approached her car, and she rolled down her window. "Hi, Father."

"Good afternoon, Elizabeth. Beautiful day. I thought I'd get a bit of sun while I waited for you." He leaned into the open passenger window. "If you don't mind, I thought we could get a cup of coffee. Mary is a wonderful and very efficient woman, but her coffee leaves something to be desired."

"Coffee it is," Elizabeth responded. He opened the door and reached down and picked up a crumpled paper resting on the passenger seat before sitting. She took the crumpled paper from his hand and shoved it into her sweatshirt pocket as Father Parker pulled the seat belt tight. She chuckled. "I'll take it easy on you."

After a relatively subdued ride to a coffee shop, by Elizabeth's standards anyway, they settled into a shiny red booth opposite each other and perused the menu. They placed orders for coffee and slices of pecan pie, and she went into story mode, giving him a rundown of the trial.

"But here's the kicker. When asked about the anonymous phone call, Sullivan said something about God leading him. That made me think of the school motto on the gate, 'Does do.'"

"*Deo duce*," the father corrected her.

"Right. You said it means 'God leads us.'"

"'God as our leader,'" he corrected her again.

"So, I'll bet you the check where he went to school."

"Saint John's," he responded.

"Bingo."

"Well, what do you think that means?"

"I'm not sure. Maybe it's all a coincidence, but somehow I don't think so. I was hoping you might have some thoughts."

"I do think that it's curious, but maybe he didn't see the relevance of the school, other than it being a remote location that served as a safe final resting place for the victim."

Elizabeth sat twisting her napkin as she contemplated his statement. It sounded reasonable, but she was up to playing devil's advocate with a priest.

"What if there's a connection between the first priest that was murdered and the school, like Father Samuel Rossi. What if he worked there too? And based on Sullivan's age, he would have been attending the school around the time it closed."

"Assuming this were true, what does it mean?" the father asked.

"I don't know yet, but I intend to find out."

"Why does that frighten me?" he asked.

She ignored him and continued in her thought process. "Sullivan found a convenient scapegoat in Raymond Miller, who, for reasons we don't know yet, confessed to the killing. Perhaps Sullivan forced Raymond to confess. A confession means the case doesn't go to trial, and it's all closed out neat and simple."

"Perhaps."

"That's it. Perhaps?"

The waitress returned with their order, and Elizabeth and the father sat quietly until she left. "I don't know what disturbs me more, the murder of innocent people, or the thought of an officer covering a murder and framing an innocent boy," Father Parker said as he wrapped his hands around a cup of coffee.

Elizabeth watched the father's internal turmoil as a grim expression crossed his face, and they finished their coffee in silence. The waitress's offer of a refill woke them, and they both declined. Elizabeth reached for the bill and jammed her hand into her sweatshirt pocket for money. She pulled out the crumpled paper that obstructed her access and threw it on her plate, then picked it up again for a better look.

"What the…?"

"What's wrong?"

She remained silent as she read what was on the paper. "This was left on my car yesterday when I got out of court. I thought it was just an advertisement, but there's a note or…something on the back." Elizabeth handed the paper to him.

Buried beneath the lovers' tree
Lies the secret of Infinity
Thirty B, upon level three
Continued the devil's iniquity
Sins of our fathers will always be
For children to bear indemnity

Elizabeth looked at Father Parker as he read the lines several times over, trying to make sense of it. She was grateful that she uncovered the note in the father's presence because for reasons she couldn't explain, it spooked her. When he didn't speak, she tried to lighten the moment, more for herself than the father. "You think it could be more obscure?"

Father Parker returned the paper. "I'm sorry. I don't know what it means."

"I guess it would be too easy if you did."

❖

Elizabeth returned Father Parker to the church and went to the clinic to research the cryptic note, believing it would be quieter than her parents' home. Based on the last several days with her mother and Raymond, who knew what activity they would be engaged in.

As Elizabeth pulled on the clinic door, she found it locked. Not overly surprising for a Saturday, but she half expected to find Dan there, as he often worked on weekends, citing it to be the best time to get anything done. However, today it looked like she'd be doing it alone. She pulled her keys from her bag and fumbled through them trying to locate the correct one, contemplating when she last had to open the front door. Once inside, she secured the lock again and headed to her office.

As she walked through, the clinic seemed different. It was devoid of the usual ordered chaos of bustling people trying to manage an impossible load, all the while quelling the rising rebellion of the office machines. Instead, Elizabeth was standing in quiet, but for the soft humming of a computer as it slept.

She moved past to the sanctuary of her office and flipped on only her office light. She looked at BD. "Looks like it's just you and me." She stroked its top and took a seat and booted up her computer. She turned to her CD player to fill the silence and wiped a thin layer of dust on the cover. Despite her love for music, she never got the opportunity to use the player because Dan deemed it a distraction. But when Dan's away, Elizabeth shall play. She popped in a *Heart's Greatest Hits* disc and cranked it up, taking advantage of the empty office.

She laid the paper flat on her desk and smoothed it over several times with her hands. She stared at it, waiting and hoping that something would stand out, then she read it aloud slowly. "Buried beneath the lovers' tree / Lies the secret of Infinity / Thirty B, upon level three / Continued the devil's iniquity / Sins of our fathers will always be / For children to bear indemnity."

She blew a raspberry with her lips and cradled her chin in her hands over the paper. "Seems clear enough," she snorted.

She turned the paper over and studied the flyer on the backside, which commemorated the city's year-long anniversary celebration. The multiple graphics made it difficult to take in all the information the celebration had to offer. She might have overlooked a small photo of Mayor Reynosa in a ribbon cutting ceremony mixed in the collage, but a goatee and set of horns colored on the mayor's image caught her eye. Elizabeth turned to her computer and searched for the event, which honored the opening of the city's first civic arts center. The performance selection got her attention, a modern rendition of the 1960s play *The Devils* by John Whiting.

She turned the paper back over to review the line, *Thirty B, upon level three, Continued the devil's iniquity.* She drummed her fingers next to the keyboard and then pulled up the theater's website. Although she realized it might be a stretch, it was the most sense she could make of the piece of paper that was left on her car, and she reserved two seats for the show.

Elizabeth closed down her computer, followed by her CD player, and glanced at her watch. It was later than she expected. She turned to look through her bar-covered windows and saw that the alley was covered in shadows. It was suddenly deathly quiet in the room with the absence of the music, and a chill ran down her spine.

She rose, gathered her things, and turned off her office light as she exited. Now plunged into darkness, she carefully made her way forward, a little uneasy in being cast alone in the nearly black office. She allowed her head to wander, envisioning herself in a parody of a slasher movie. A few steps into her journey, she was stopped by the light touch of something striking her in the face. "What the—"

She quickly stepped back into her office, banging her shoulder into the door frame on her way in, and switched on her light. As she re-emerged, she sucked in a sharp breath and pushed her body back against the doorway, dropping her bag to the floor. Dangling from a light fixture, a hangman's noose swayed side to side, as though mocking her. Elizabeth quickly stooped, grabbed her bag, and ran for the exit. She yanked on the front door to find it already open. She didn't stop to lock it, and she ran, not looking back. Her heart pounded in her ears, and spots began to swim in her eyes. Her knees threatened to betray her, as they shook violently with every step. Sheer fear forced her on, and she didn't stop until she reached her car.

Nearly hyperventilating, she practically dove into her car and hit the locks. She dialed Dan's home number, but it went to voice mail. She disconnected and dialed his cell, and he picked up on the third ring. Without waiting for a greeting, she jumped into her story at a rambling pace, not leaving out the detail that she was sure she had locked herself in the office.

"Dan, I just ran. I didn't even lock the door."

"All right, just breathe. Get home. I'll go to the office and look around."

"We need to call the police."

"I'll take care of it. Just go home."

Elizabeth did as she was told for a change and pointed her car in the direction of her parents' home. As she pulled her car into her parents' drive, she debated what to tell them. She feared if she revealed her story, her parents would have more ammunition in their fight against her work with the clinic. Deciding silence would be her best course of action, she took several deep, stabilizing breaths before entering the house. However, she found the usual suspects absent, and the house quiet, for which she was grateful, and she settled into the safety of her childhood bed.

She called Michael and unburdened on him, but instead of offering the support she had hoped for, he jumped on her parents' bandwagon. "Girl, it's not worth it. Get out of there and away from this case and don't look back."

"I can't. Raymond is here. This case is a part of all of us now. I can't just walk away."

Michael offered a sigh in response. "I'll protect you, then."

"I don't think they'll be afraid of your skillet."

"You mock my skillet?"

Elizabeth enjoyed the senseless banter and took a cleansing breath. "Come with me to the civic center tomorrow night."

"What's playing?"

"*The Devils*."

"Sounds like that will cheer you right up," he said.

Elizabeth gave a quick rundown of the surreptitious note on her car. "I got tickets on level three, and there's a row thirty. I figured it's a start."

"Oh, yippee."

A loud grumble could be heard across the phone line.

"What was that?" Michael asked.

"My stomach. I've only eaten pancakes and pie today."

"What are you, three? You have a stash of Halloween candy under your bed?"

"No," she answered. "In my closet. My mom will find it under the bed."

Michael laughed, but little did he know, she wasn't kidding.

"Shut up and good night. I'll pick you up tomorrow." Elizabeth ended the call and debated raiding the refrigerator downstairs. She set her feet on the floor, then she pulled them back up and sank under the covers. *Maybe I'll wait until my parents get home.*

❖

Elizabeth and Michael arrived at the theater early, and Elizabeth approached her seat on level three and moved up and down the row. The chairs were red cloth seats that reclined slightly, offering greater comfort to their occupants. She ran her hands along the cloth of the seats feeling for any anomalies. Finding nothing irregular, she got on her knees and searched underneath. She continued down the row of seats, groping at the cloth as she went.

"Get up. What are you doing? The floor's disgusting, and I can see more than I care to," Michael protested as he stood behind Elizabeth.

She ignored him and ran her hand along the underside, finding a wad of gum stuck at the bottom of an armrest. "Gross. What's wrong with people?"

"Coming from a woman in a dress crawling under the seat."

"Shut up. You're not helping."

"I'm sorry. Should I go around the back and stick my head under the seat from the other side?"

She ignored him and resumed scanning the bottom of the seat, its sides, and the floor for any markings.

"Excuse me, may I help you with something?"

Michael turned to find a young man dressed in a gray suit with the theater's logo emblazoned on the pocket. "Oh no, we're fine. She's just really into the theater experience, and it isn't the same if she can't roll herself on the ground under her seat to feel the aura of those who sat there before her, as well as find any loose change that might be hiding."

The attendant backed away. "Okay, sir."

Elizabeth rose and plopped herself into the seat. "Nothing," she sighed. "Here." She deposited a pink lump into Michael's hand.

"What's this?" He stared at his hand and then shrieked. "That is disgusting." He chucked the gum to the front of the theater. "I can't take you anywhere. Where were you raised, in a barn?"

"You were just complaining about being hungry."

As the theater started to fill up, they settled into their seats. Halfway through the performance, Michael slumped into his chair with his elbow on the armrest propping up his chin. He leaned into Elizabeth and asked in a stage whisper that would make even the best thespians proud, "Can't blame the nuns for being so angry, look what they had to wear, and there's no sex. Maybe that's why they're called nuns. Because they get nun, nada, zilch."

Elizabeth swatted his arm, causing his elbow to slip off the armrest and his hand to lose its position under his chin, resulting in Michael's head flopping forward. She giggled and was shushed by several annoyed patrons. Resigned that the theater was a bust, she pulled on his arm. "These people don't know real slapstick comedy when they see it. Let's go." They rose and unsuccessfully tried to withhold their laughter until they exited the main theater.

CHAPTER NINETEEN

On Monday morning, Elizabeth sat herself behind the defense counsel table. She pulled out Raymond's crayons and a new coloring book that Raymond picked out while shopping with her mother. In addition to the new coloring book, their shopping excursion scored Raymond several new clothes, including the navy blue suit that he was currently yanking on. It was clear that the suit was a new experience. Her mother was in her customary seat behind Raymond.

The judge entered the courtroom, and Elizabeth stood, pulling Raymond up with her. He clutched at the crayon in his hand, slightly annoyed at the interruption in his coloring.

The judge looked to Elizabeth. "Is the defense ready?"

"Yes, Your Honor, the defense calls Delores Miller."

Delores Miller stood up in the gallery, and Elizabeth held the swinging wooden gate open for her as she passed. She moved to the witness box with exaggerated effort, clearly hoping to garner some sympathy from the jury and spectators. After taking the oath, Ms. Miller stared straight ahead at Elizabeth with her hands resting on her lap. She wore a dark green dress that was pulled tight around the waist by a thin white belt. She appeared much better groomed than the last two times Elizabeth saw her.

"Ms. Miller, what is your relationship to the defendant?"

"I'm his mother," she said.

"Before Raymond was arrested, where did he live?"

"With me."

"When you say with me, do you mean he lived and slept in the main house where you sleep?"

"No, not exactly."

"Then where exactly?"

"In a separate room behind the house, in the backyard."

"That separate room, is that the shed?"

Ms. Miller muttered something inaudibly.

"I'm sorry. I couldn't hear that. Will you repeat that please?" Elizabeth asked.

"Yes, it was like a shed."

"Thank you. This shed, did it have an air-conditioning or heating system?"

"No."

"How about water?"

"No."

"Wasn't the shed meant to be a storage shed?"

"Raymond liked it in there," she responded defensively.

"When Raymond lived in the shed, was the shed kept locked?"

"No."

"Why not?"

"Because then Raymond couldn't get in. If I put a lock on it, he wouldn't remember the combination. He's not right in the head."

"Did you ever have a lock that needed a key on the shed?"

"No, Raymond would only lose the key. And what's the use? Who would want to go in there anyway, besides Raymond?"

"Good question, Ms. Miller. Because there was no lock on the shed, couldn't anyone go in the shed when Raymond wasn't there?"

"I suppose, but who would want to go in there? It's just a bunch of crap, I mean junk, in there."

"Perhaps someone who wants to plant items in the shed to make your son look guilty would go in there."

"Objection!" the ADA shouted.

"The jury will disregard the last statement. Ms. Campbell, please move on."

"Yes, Your Honor." Elizabeth turned to Ms. Miller. "Do you remember about two months ago, I came to your home?"

"Yes."

"During my visit, you told me about what it was like caring for Raymond. He has difficulty doing some simple tasks."

"Yes," Ms. Miller responded with an exasperated breath. "He always needs help with something. He's like a child, but worse."

Elizabeth cut her off because she knew that Ms. Miller was only getting started on her rant. "You mentioned something about Raymond having difficulty tying his shoes. Do you remember that?"

"Yes, Raymond never learned to tie his shoes. It was difficult to find the Velcro strap shoes for his size, so I was always having to tie his shoes."

Elizabeth crossed the courtroom to the board where the photos were displayed and pointed to a photo of the victim tied to the gate. "Can you see these ropes?" She tapped the photo in each place where the victim was tied.

"Yes."

"Could Raymond have tied these?" Ms. Miller's face changed, as though a light had gone on in her head.

"No, he couldn't. Absolutely not," she stated firmly, as her son's innocence washed over her.

"Thank you, Ms. Miller."

Elizabeth returned to her table and sat. The judge turned to the ADA, and he passed on questioning Ms. Miller.

With the lunch hour approaching, the judge found it a good stopping point and called a recess.

Elizabeth found Ms. Miller standing outside the courtroom, and she took Raymond's hand and approached her. Ms. Miller looked at him. "Hi, Raymond."

Raymond offered a shy greeting in return.

"Ms. Miller, we're going to get some lunch across the street. Would you like to join us?" Elizabeth asked.

"Well, I, uh, don't think so. I need to get back."

"Okay then. Well, thank you for being here."

Ms. Miller offered a tight smile. "I'll see you later." She turned and walked away, but Raymond didn't seem to notice.

As they returned from lunch, Raymond sat contentedly. Elizabeth's last witness, Dr. Janice Delaney, remained outside the courtroom. Dr. Delaney would echo her report that was filed in support of the motion to vacate hearing, challenging Raymond's competency and thus his ability to carry out the murder. She hoped it would be enough to cast doubt in the minds of some of the jurors.

More than thirty minutes had passed since the court should have been called to session, but there was no sign of the judge or jury. Elizabeth twirled her pen in her hands, anxiously waiting. Elizabeth's mother leaned over the railing to her and whispered, "What's taking so long?"

"Not sure."

As if on cue, the judge entered the courtroom and stood behind her bench. "I need to see counsel in my chamber." Elizabeth quickly rose and crossed the well of the courtroom, following the judge to her inner sanctum. She waited for the judge to take a seat behind her desk, then seated herself in a large high-back leather chair facing her, as ADA Burke settled in the chair next to Elizabeth.

"Juror number three has been recused," the judge said.

ADA Burke spoke first. "Why?"

"We received information that the juror had been communicating with outside sources regarding the case. The juror was questioned and admitted to being offered money for his vote in this case."

Elizabeth sat with her mouth open.

"Where did this information come from?" Burke asked.

"The court received an anonymous letter." The judge handed over a copy of the letter to both of them. A typed letter detailed the name of the juror, the amount he was paid, and the task the juror was paid to complete, which was not only to vote to convict Raymond Miller, but to sway the other jurors to do the same, by bribe if necessary.

"We've begun interviewing the remaining jurors to determine if anyone else is involved with or was even aware of juror three's plan. I intend to continue this case to next Monday for a status conference, after a full investigation has been conducted."

"Yes, Your Honor," Elizabeth and Burke responded in unison.

Elizabeth pulled into the parking lot down the street from the clinic, but she couldn't remember how she even got there. The revelation of jury tampering left her dazed. She gathered her things and walked to the clinic, staring at the ground as she went. She resisted the urge to think aloud and talk to herself.

Amy had the phone to her ear and gave Elizabeth a quick wave as she passed. Instead of settling into her office, she walked to Dan's and knocked on the door, waiting until he acknowledged her. She realized that things had changed. Before, she wouldn't have thought twice about walking into his office without an invitation, but things were different between them after the Miller case.

Dan watched Elizabeth sit. "I didn't expect to see you here. I thought you were in trial."

"I was, but it's been continued until next week."

"Next week? Why?" Dan looked concerned.

"Well, it seems that there's been a little jury tampering, and the court needs to figure out how deep this goes."

Dan sat quietly staring at Elizabeth. She could see the movement of his knee as his leg bounced up and down below the desk.

"How does the court know?" he asked.

"There was an anonymous letter sent in. It spelled it out and named the juror."

"Did it say who was working with the juror?"

She released an exhausted breath. "Nope. It just said that he was being paid to deliver a guilty verdict. It didn't give names."

"Wow. That's pretty incredible."

"Definitely a first for me. Everything about this case is unusual. So what did the police say on Saturday?"

"What?" Dan looked confused.

"The noose. I went screaming like a banshee out of here. I called you, hysterical." She gestured with her hands as she spoke for emphasis.

"Right. I came and removed the rope. It was just a Halloween prank."

"That's what the police said?"

"Well, no. I didn't call them. I didn't see the need. It was just a silly prank."

"Are you serious? Dan, I locked myself alone in this office, at least I thought I was alone. Someone left a noose outside my office door. With everything going on in the Miller case, you think that was a prank?" Elizabeth's voice rose as she spoke.

"Lower your voice, please. Look, no harm done. The clinic doesn't need any negative publicity. That's exactly what we'd get. Just be more careful."

"I don't believe this." She snatched up her things and stormed to her office, slamming the door behind her.

CHAPTER TWENTY

On Tuesday, Elizabeth headed to the clinic early in hopes of catching up on cases that she neglected because of the Miller trial. She was buried in an unlawful eviction case when she was startled by her telephone.

"This is Elizabeth Campbell."

"Hey, Elizabeth, it's Rich."

"Hi, Rich. How's it going?"

After a minute of friendly banter, Rich gave her the information she had been waiting to hear—the school and the surrounding property were owned by the archdiocese. Although initially a Catholic prep school, the school shifted to boarding boys with troubled pasts. Many of the students that were sent there were school delinquents and one step away from the justice system. Other boys were referred over from the juvenile courts in an attempt to straighten them out before they spiraled down the felonious path.

The school closed in 1982, but unlike the reports Elizabeth read about the closure, the school was operating at a profit up until the end. At the city's request, the archdiocese demolished most of the neglected and decaying buildings in an attempt to thwart a vagrancy problem. The few remaining buildings were boarded and secured, to which she could attest.

After promising a refill on his candy stash, she hung up and leaned back in BD. She remembered herself and sat forward and propped her hand under her chin on the desk. Although she didn't find a smoking gun, she found the information curious. *If the school was operating at a profit, why did it shut down and allege financial problems?* She decided to answer her question with a return visit to the school.

She kept herself in her office for the rest of the day, only emerging for bathroom and coffee breaks, and sustained herself on energy bars that she had stashed in her drawer. As the sun began to set, she packed up, not wanting to be in the clinic after dark. She successfully avoided Dan as she exited.

❖

ADA Burke and Mayor Reynosa sat opposite each other across a fireplace in the mayor's sitting room.

"Who the hell sent the letter?"

"I don't know," said Burke, as he clutched the armrests. "What I do know is that I'm out."

"The hell you are. You walk away and I'll make sure you're doing traffic court for the rest of your life."

"Fuck you," Burke said. He stood and grabbed his coat. "I'd rather be in traffic court than prison, which is where you'll be if the court traces this back to you."

"If I go down, I'm taking you with me," the mayor spit out.

Burke left without comment and passed Simon sitting outside the door without acknowledging his presence.

❖

Elizabeth walked into the church and found it empty, not a surprise for a Tuesday evening. She continued to the side door that led to the office and rapped on the open door. Father Parker sat behind the desk immersed in his reading and jumped at her knock.

"Sorry, didn't mean to startle you. I should have called first."

He stood and motioned to the chair across his desk. "Not at all. Please come in and have a seat." He waited until she seated. "Is everything all right?"

"Yes and no. First, how are Rosa and Hector? I'm still waiting for a response from the court."

"They're doing very well. Rosa has started venturing outside, and she and Hector accompanied Mary to the grocery store."

"That's great. Thank you for taking such good care of them."

"It's nothing. I enjoy having them around, and I know Mary does as well." Father Parker paused and looked at her, as though sizing her up. "I don't think you came here to check on Rosa and Hector."

"No, I came to talk to you about the Miller case. It seems you're the only one I can really trust."

He settled back into his chair. "I see. I'm always here for you."

"Thank you. I really do appreciate that, more than you may know."

He smiled and gestured for her to continue, and she filled him in on everything that transpired since their last meeting in the diner, including the noose, the anonymous letter to the court, and the new information she learned from Rich.

He blew out a breath. "Wow, that's a lot. I'm not even sure what to say."

"Don't worry. I wasn't looking for answers. I wanted to see if you would go with me back to the school."

"When?"

"Now."

"Now! It's dark out. It's dangerous."

"That's okay. I understand. Don't worry," she said as she stood.

"Wait. What are you doing?"

"I'm going to the school," she casually replied.

"Now? Alone?"

"Looks that way."

"Ugggghhh," he said in an elevated tone, surprising her at his outburst. "You can't go alone. That's not right. Hold on, let me get my coat."

She smiled when his back was to her.

After he scribbled a quick note for Mary, they approached Elizabeth's car, and he said, "I just ate. You might want to take it slow," and crossed himself before getting in.

"Don't I always?"

When they passed through the iron gates of the school, Elizabeth turned to him. "You can open your eyes now." She exited and moved to her trunk and pulled out a large black backpack and two heavy-duty flashlights.

Father Parker watched on. "What is all of this?"

"I did a little shopping after work."

"I see. Is this that Boy Scout thing?"

"Yep, always be prepared."

She hefted the pack on her back and handed one of the flashlights to him and started toward the buildings. He called out after her, "Is there a reason that this has to be done at night?"

"Because that's when the rats come out." She threw back her head and laughed.

"I'm not going to like this," he said.

Elizabeth strolled to the three-story building that sat at the center of the grounds and stood at the door on the side of the structure, sizing up the padlock. She dropped the pack and pulled out a pair of bolt cutters.

"Oh no," cried Father Parker, as she snapped the lock with one try. "This is breaking and entering," he reprimanded her.

"Well, technically, it's cutting and entering. Did you see that lock pop off?" She pulled open the door and crossed the threshold.

"Is temporary insanity a defense?" he asked.

"Don't worry. I know a good lawyer."

"Is this the same lawyer that is well versed at committing felonies?"

"Maybe."

She moved her light up and down the hallway and noted the series of doors that lined each wall. Gray carpeting covered the length of the corridor. "This looks like it was a dormitory."

She walked down the hall shining her light on the first door and pushed it open, finding the room nearly vacant but for two twin beds that stood opposite each other on both sides of the door. The mattresses were gone and only the wooden frames of the beds remained. The beds appeared to be bolted to the floor. It was probably the only reason why they still remained. She observed the rest of the room and took in the dusty hardwood floor and light blue painted walls with a few nails protruding. The father peeked his head into the room and took it in. She was alerted to his presence by the second beam of light in the room and instructed him to search the rooms on the right side of the hallway as she searched the left.

Each room was the same as the first, no furnishings but for the two twin beds. The floor held two bathrooms, one on each end, with multiple sinks, toilets, and showers efficiently lined up. As they made their way to the end of the hallway, she turned back to a wooden stairway that stood in the middle, opposite the main exit at the front of the building. They resumed their plan of each taking a side and searched the rooms, finding the second and third floors duplicates of the first.

The building was now barren, devoid of any indication that life once existed. It almost reminded her of a sunken ship that had been scavenged. There was no treasure here.

"Well, this is a whole lotta nothing," she stated as she headed back to the stairway and walked down two steps before stopping. Father Parker remained at the top of the stairs and watched her walk back up. She moved down the hallway and stopped in front of a door with her arms crossed.

"It's a door," he said, stating the obvious.

"I see that." She shook her head, "Look." She shined the light on a brown plastic marker next to the door that displayed a white number with two empty slots below.

"Yes, the rooms all have that. It's the room number, and the empty slots next to A and B probably listed the occupants' names."

She gave him a look and then realized she would need to explain. "This is Thirty B, upon level three."

He stared at her.

"The poem," she blurted out. "Thirty B, upon level three / continued the devil's iniquity."

"You think the devil lived here?" he asked with a straight face.

"Or someone close to it."

Father Parker stayed silent with a serious look.

"We need to know what happened here."

He inspected the sign as she turned and walked back down the steps.

"What, that's it?" he called down to her. "You're not going to break down the wall?"

"Not today. Didn't bring the right tools."

When they exited the building, Elizabeth closed the side door behind them to make their intrusion less obvious to anyone who might pass by. She moved on to the church that stood at the far end of the property and circled the structure, stopping at the front entrance. Before Father Parker could offer a protest, she snipped the lock off with her cutters, and he let out a groan but otherwise remained silent. She figured the father had given up protesting by now.

After shouldering her pack, she walked to the front of the church with her flashlight trained straight ahead. A thick layer of dirt blanketed the inside, and with the windows boarded, the room was engulfed in darkness. She banged her knee into the side of a pew and bent to rub it, which caused her light to bounce around the enclosed space as she tended to her leg. When she stood again, she turned to face the pews and shined her light around the church. The walls were a simple white, with a slight texture, and wooden beams ran across the roof and down the side walls in between the windows.

She shuddered as an uneasy feeling crept through her. "How would you like to do Mass in here, Father?"

"Probably better than in a prison," he replied from right behind her, causing her to jump.

She ignored him and stepped up to the altar as she moved her light across the surface. It was clear that the church had been vacant for a substantial period of time and nothing had been disturbed in the interim. The only thing that remained was the furniture that was attached to the ground, and she wasn't sure if that was because the archdiocese removed the belongings or the trespassers did it for them.

The architecture of the chapel was simple. It was a solitary building roughly shaped like a square, unlike most modern Catholic churches that were laid out as a cross. There were no passageways leading off to other rooms outside of the main church. The room seemed large enough to only accommodate Mass for the students at the school. Four sets of doors led out of the church, including a double set of doors at the back of the church from which they entered, two single doors at each side of the church, and a single door at the front near the altar.

She moved to the door near the altar. "There were only three doors to the outside when we walked around it. Where do you think this door goes?"

When he didn't answer, she asked, "Father, are you there?" She turned and shined her light right in his eyes.

He shielded his face from the glare and responded. "Yep, I'm here."

She twisted the handle on the door but found it locked and fumbled with her bag and pulled out what she was looking for.

"A crowbar? You can't be serious. What law school did you go to?"

She only chuckled and wedged the bar between the door where the lock met the frame and heaved, using her body weight. There was a cracking sound, but the door didn't give way. She continued with no success as Father Parker watched on.

"A little help here?" she asked.

"Oh no, not me."

"Let's see, you've broken into two buildings, but you draw the line now?" She used all her weight, pushing on the crowbar, making grunting noises with each thrust.

"Fine," he said. He took Elizabeth's position, and with one push, the door frame cracked, and he pulled open the door.

"Thank you," she said, removing the crowbar from his hands and redepositing it in her backpack.

He shined his light inside the open door and down a set of stairs. "It looks like a basement."

She joined him, shining her light down, and then descended the stairs as he stood at the top.

"I don't suppose there's any way of talking you out of this?" he called down.

"You can try."

"That's what I thought." He released a breath and took careful steps down the wooden stairs.

Elizabeth stood at the base of the stairs and methodically trailed her light from corner to corner. The room stood vacant but for a harvesting of spider webs and dust. She took a few steps in the room as Father Parker remained on the bottom step. She abruptly stopped and took a few steps back, until she banged into him.

"What is it?" he asked, alarm in his voice.

She shined her light on the floor. "Footprints."

"How? The doors were chained shut."

She moved the light around the room until it landed on a set of cement steps leading to a cellar door. She crossed to it and pushed up on the rusted metal doors, and they gave way, exposing her to the night air. The cellar doors on the outside were camouflaged by brush strategically placed around the entrance.

"They got in through here. It looks like it had been pried open."

"Probably someone looking for a warm place to sleep," the father reasoned.

Elizabeth circled the room until she came to a concrete door. "What do you suppose is in here?"

Father Parker remained perched on the last step as she turned the handle and pushed. She struggled with the door and pushed with her shoulder, putting her body weight into it. "It's heavy," she grunted.

He came to help just as she got the door open, and she shined her light in first and inspected the room, finding wall-to-wall concrete. Confident that the room was empty, she stepped down a small flight of cement steps and stood in the center. The father joined her and added his light for a better view. Thick metal clasps drilled into the wall and floor were evenly spaced on one side of the room. She would have questioned the purpose, but the same clasps were affixed to the ceiling near the center of the room and floor below with heavy chains attached.

"What the hell is this place? Looks like the Spanish Inquisition."

The father didn't respond but instead sat in a solitary chair that stood next to a small wooden table. Elizabeth crossed to a metal shelving unit that was bolted to the wall and pulled down a cardboard box containing cleaning solvents and supplies. She pulled down the second box with the same contents.

"I just don't get it." She cocked her head as she spoke, noticing a second concrete door near the table where the father sat. It nearly blended in with the cement wall. He followed her gaze. "This just keeps going on," she stated as she moved to it.

She pulled hard on the door until it gave and released a squeak as the hinges moved. The noise caused Father Parker to jump, and he muttered just loud enough for her hear, "Why did I agree to this?" He rose and dutifully followed her, but stopped in the doorway. "Ugghh, not the rat tunnel," he groaned.

"This is the door we saw the first time, see?" She pointed, trying to contain her excitement. She pulled the door halfway closed, forcing the father to hop into the tunnel and out of the way, and shined the light on the backside of the door. "Why do they need a secret passageway? This just gets curiouser and curiouser."

She started down the tunnel toward the chamber they previously discovered. "Elizabeth, I don't think this is a good idea," the father said. She didn't answer, and he moved to the middle of the tunnel, away from the sides. From the corner of her eye, she saw his light move around his feet looking for rats. A large bang echoed through the passageway, causing small rocks to fall from the ceiling.

She ran back to him, breathing heavy. "What was that?"

"The door. It closed," he responded.

She went to the door, and it was sealed shut. "What did you do?"

"Do? I didn't do anything. I was standing right here." Father Parker took a deep breath and collected himself, and she waited patiently, realizing he was truly spooked. He looked directly at her. "It could have closed by itself."

"We should go back."

The father turned toward the entrance of the tunnel, and she followed directly behind him. He breathed an audible sigh when they came to the metal grate, and he pulled it away from the wall, holding it open for her. She tossed her backpack through first and followed it, then held the grate so Father Parker could pass. She opened the wooden door that shielded the tunnel from the outside world, and a burst of cold air hit her face. She relished it, breathing it in deep. She could hear the father do the same as he closed the door behind them.

"Never thought I would be so happy to be in the middle of the woods," he said.

Elizabeth stepped through the dead foliage, making her way back to the school. After a few moments, Father Parker put his hand on her shoulder, causing her to flinch.

"I think we need to go that way." He pointed to the right.

"No, I'm pretty sure it's this way." She shined her light straight in front of her.

"For once, how about you follow me?"

She conceded and stepped behind the father, letting him lead the way. After several minutes of wandering, she finally spoke up, "I think we need to go back that way." She pointed to the direction she was originally heading. "We should have come up to the school by now."

He turned to face her and caught his foot in the underbrush, causing him to drop his light. He reached out to Elizabeth for balance, and she grabbed a hold of his arm and helped steady him.

"You all right?" she asked.

"I'm fine. I just got caught up." He kicked at some low brush as he spoke.

She bent and picked up his light and handed it to him, but pulled it back just as he reached for it. She shined both lights on a tree behind him and moved to it, keeping the lights trained on the tree.

"Uh, a little light here, please."

"Oh, sorry." She turned and handed him back his flashlight.

"Buried beneath the lovers' tree / lies the secret of Infinity," she recited.

He scrunched up his nose. "What?"

"The poem, remember? It said, 'Buried beneath the lovers' tree / lies the secret of Infinity.'"

"Okay," he drew out.

She realized that he didn't see it and shined her light close to the tree trunk. Two sets of initials surrounded by a heart were carved into the tree. "It's a lovers' tree."

The father stepped close and shined his light. "But it could be any tree."

"Perhaps," she responded. "Or perhaps it's this tree, behind the school, outside the secret tunnel." She gestured with her hands to emphasize her point, and he shrugged, unconvinced.

Elizabeth turned back to the tree and dropped the pack off her back. He pointed to the backpack and replied, "Oh no, don't tell me you have a shovel in that thing too?"

"Nope, no shovel. Didn't think of it. Next time." She circled the tree slowly, shining her light around the trunk and the ground. She widened her circle, scouring the ground and kicking at the leaves that cracked as they moved.

"Shhh," the father said. "You're too loud."

"Afraid I'll wake the bear?"

He shook his head. "No, I'm afraid you'll wake whoever it was that closed the door."

"Good point." She assumed that the door closure was simply a result of a draft or gravity pulling on the door, but she knew they couldn't be too cautious in case the father's paranoia turned out to be right. She slowed her movements and then crouched to the ground for a closer inspection, and after several minutes of searching, gave up. "We need to come back in the light." She moved her light up the tree as she stood and arched her back for a stretch, causing the light to bounce randomly. She then stood still, grasping the light in both hands, and moved it slowly over a low-hanging branch. The light glinted off an object dangling, nearly concealed by leaves, and she moved to it and stretched up, but couldn't reach.

"What is it?" asked Father Parker.

"I don't know. Can you reach it?"

He reached up and pulled the object down, bringing a small part of the branch with it. He gave it to Elizabeth, and she turned it over hands.

"It looks like a name tag. The kind you see in the military. I can't tell what it says. It's too dirty."

"Let's find our way back, and we can look at it when we get out of here."

"Okay, hold on a sec." She reached for her backpack and dropped the necklace in a side pouch and then pulled out the crowbar.

"What are you going to do with that?"

"Mark the trees so we can find our way back here. Follow me."

She held the light in one hand and the crowbar in the other and etched a mark into each tree as she passed. She moved in the direction that they were originally heading before Father Parker had changed their course. After a brief walk, the clearing came into view, and Elizabeth held back an "I told you so."

Without a word, they walked to the parking lot, scanning the property as they moved, and she clutched the crowbar in her hands in a defensive manner. When they reached the Roadster, he let out a breath. "Made it. Never thought I'd be so happy to get in your car."

She gave him a weary smile as she opened her trunk and dropped the backpack inside. After closing the trunk, she spat out, "God damn it."

The father turned in alarm, not even fazed by her language at this point. "What?"

She kicked the tire that was flat and circled the car, kicking each tire as she went. "They're all flat. Someone slashed my tires."

Father Parker leaned against the car and put his head in hands. "This night will never end."

Elizabeth pulled her cell phone from her pocket and called roadside assistance.

CHAPTER TWENTY-ONE

Bishop Pallone knocked on the ornately carved door, and a thin, frail man with white hair who had Pallone beat by at least twenty years in age pulled it open. Pallone entered and crossed the room. "Your Eminence."

"We can dispense with the formalities. Please have a seat and join me," said Cardinal Ryan. The cardinal sat savoring his tea from a delicate floral-patterned cup, his beloved morning routine, as he basked in the warmth radiating from a fireplace at his side. Pallone took a seat in an antique floral-patterned chair opposite the cardinal. He pondered whether the teacups and the chairs were meant to match. A silver tea set sat on the table between them, and the white-haired man stood beside Pallone and wordlessly bent to pour him some tea.

"Thank you." Pallone accepted the cup, trying to keep a neutral expression. He detested tea but couldn't refuse the cardinal's invitation to partake in his favorite ritual.

"Thank you, Edmund. That will be all," Cardinal Ryan said to the man.

With a slight bow, the man slowly but steadily moved to the door and securely closed it behind him. The cardinal waited until he left before he spoke. "So tell me, have you spoken to the police?"

"Yes, I have a meeting arranged for Friday and have put the necessary documents in order."

"Excellent. I know you don't agree, but it's the best thing. We should have done this thirty years ago. We must accept our responsibly in all of this."

Pallone offered an insincere smile and then released a violent cough, spilling some tea on his lap. He leaned forward and set the cup on the table.

"Are you all right?" the cardinal asked with concern.

Pallone waived his hand in embarrassment. "Yes, I'm fine," he choked out and felt his face flush. "I seem to have swallowed wrong." He relaxed back into his chair and calmed his breathing.

"Let me get something to help clean you up," the cardinal offered.

Cardinal Ryan rose and crossed the room to a side door and disappeared. Pallone took advantage of the cardinal's departure and removed a small glass vial from the folds of his robe. He poured a generous amount of its contents into the cardinal's cup and a fraction of the amount into his own. He threw the empty container into the fireplace, shattering the glass against the back wall. He watched as the flames momentarily flared, licking at the shards of glass, devouring the chemical traces.

"Here you go," Cardinal Ryan said as he reentered the room with a small white towel dangling from his hand. Pallone graciously accepted it and wiped at his lap. After he reseated himself, the cardinal picked up his cup and resumed their conversation. Pallone followed and lifted his cup, taking small sips.

Cardinal Ryan spoke of the integrity of the Church at a time when there had been much scrutiny and scandal. "I alone shall bear this cross."

Pallone found the cardinal's words poetic and ironic.

Having said his peace, the cardinal moved the conversation on to more mundane Church matters, and Pallone welcomed the change. As Cardinal Ryan poured the last of the tea into his cup, he attempted to stifle a yawn. "I'm sorry. It seems that our meeting has been a bit taxing." The cardinal smiled as he spoke.

Pallone offered a smile in return and set his cup on the table. "Well, I should let you get to your other matters. I enjoyed our visit. Thank you."

Cardinal Ryan did not protest at Pallone's departure.

❖

Elizabeth lifted the metal tags dangling from a silver chain from the jar of cleaning solution and wiped. Layers of dirt and rust had enveloped the necklace from years of exposure to the elements, and she scraped at the lingering crust with her nail, removing the last of the crud. The front side of both tags bore a picture of a red cross. The backside of the first tag listed a name, David Collins, with an address and phone number, and the second tag advised that David was allergic to bee stings.

She turned the necklace over in her hands. *Who are you, David Collins?* It would have to wait because she was running late. She tucked the piece of jewelry into her bag and headed down the stairs. She heard the sounds of a television and found Raymond sitting on the couch watching cartoons with a bowl of cereal in his lap. She shook her head. She would have never gotten away with eating anywhere but at the table. She waved good-bye to Raymond, who nearly spilled his milk as he eagerly waved back. She walked to the place where her car should have been parked, but then she remembered the prior evening's events. She blew out a breath and jogged back to the house for the keys to her parents' "spare" car.

She spent a tedious morning drafting motions on Dan's orders that were not due for several weeks, assuming this was her penance for disobeying him. Fortunately for her, she had templates that sped up the process, leaving her time to research the origins of the mysterious tags from the tree. Several hits came up on the computer for the name, none of which appeared relevant, at least she didn't think so, unless the David Collins she was looking for was a Facebook devotee or an aspiring bodybuilder, both of whom were born after the school closed. She Googled the address on the tag to gauge its location, figuring another road trip was in order. She escaped the clinic after lunch to file one of her motions, and with the task complete, punched the address into her GPS. She was led to a quiet middle-class suburban area a few towns away and parked in front of a single-story stucco home. As she walked to the porch, she could hear barking from inside the house and decided there was no going back. She knocked on the door, and a small girl answered.

"Hi, is your mom home?"

The girl stood staring up at her and nodded, her pigtails bouncing in rhythm with her head.

"May I speak with her?"

The girl turned her head and yelled, "Mom! Someone's at the door!"

Elizabeth flinched at the girl's volume.

A woman she guessed to be only a few years younger than her came to the door. "Can I help you?"

Elizabeth lied and stated that she was preparing a genealogy report and was looking for the Collins family, who she believed might have lived in the home. The woman was interested, but was unable to help. As she turned to leave, the woman stopped her. "Wait. Mrs. Becker might be able to help you." The woman pointed to the house next door. "She's lived here forever."

Elizabeth thanked her and trekked next door. An elderly woman she calculated to be in her seventies pulled open the door. She quickly explained her mission regarding the genealogy report and the missing information of the Collins family. She was surprised at how easily it had become for her to fabricate stories, whether it was outright lies or lies of omission.

The woman seemed grateful for the company and invited Elizabeth inside. She sat at a white laminate table with gray specks throughout, with matching faux white leather chairs completing the set. The woman offered coffee and started pouring her a cup before she could answer.

Elizabeth spent the better part of an hour with Mrs. Becker, who talked about her deceased husband, her children who visited infrequently, and the old neighborhood. She learned that the Collins family purchased the home in the early seventies. Mrs. Becker characterized them as a lovely family with one child, a son named David.

Elizabeth perked up at the name. "Where is David now?"

The woman shook her head, and a grim expression overtook her. Mrs. Becker explained that the parents were killed in a car accident in 1981, and with no other family, David ended up in foster care.

"I never knew what became of that boy. I prayed for him. I wanted to take him in, but we had three children of our own," she said.

Elizabeth expressed her understanding, and with a bit of effort, finally made her exit with a promise that she would come back and visit. It was a pledge she fully intended to keep.

Elizabeth reasoned that David would have been placed into foster care by the local children's social services office, so she looked up the information on her phone and weighed her options, go there now and try it alone or wait until tomorrow and go with a particular priest. She figured she would have better luck getting information with Father Parker accompanying her. She might find someone willing to talk to the man of the cloth.

❖

Patrick Sullivan stumbled out of the pub, and good-natured shouts from his fellow drinkers could be heard through the doors. A green neon light depicting a four-leaf clover illuminated the sidewalk that seemed to sway slightly as Sullivan studied it. He moved his feet forward, trying to negotiate the course to his car. He reached his silver compact across the parking lot and fumbled in his pocket for his keys. He attempted to fit the key into the lock but lacked the dexterity for this maneuver, and the keys clanked to the ground.

"Goddamn it," Sullivan slurred out. He bent to retrieve the keys and banged his head into the car door as the ground began to sway again.

"Here, let me help you," a man said, standing over him.

Sullivan stood erect and rocked on his feet as he let the stranger pick up his keys.

"I'm not so sure you're up to this," the stranger said. "How about a lift?"

Sullivan rebuffed the offer. "Give me the damn keys." He attempted to snatch the keys from his hand but missed and fell against the car. The stranger grabbed at him before he fell and propped him up.

"You're coming with me." The stranger wrapped his arms around Sullivan's waist and half dragged him to his car.

CHAPTER TWENTY-TWO

Elizabeth entered her office earlier than usual to make up for her early departure the day before, and only one of the clerks had beat her in. With David Collins on her mind, she picked up her phone. "Morning, Mary, this is Elizabeth Campbell. Is Father Parker available?"

"Hi, Elizabeth, I'll go check. He was in the rectory last I knew."

She looked over her schedule as she waited and reviewed her possibilities of schedule changes should the father agree to go with her.

"Good morning, Elizabeth. What can I do for you this fine morning? Perhaps we can plan a bank heist or maybe smuggle some aliens across the border?" The father greeted her in an upbeat tone.

Elizabeth laughed. "Now that was actually funny. I was planning on something more subdued."

"Such as?" he responded suspiciously.

She updated Father Parker on what she had learned about David Collins the previous day.

"How may I help you with social services?"

"Well," she drew out, "I think that if a Catholic priest is with me, someone might be more apt to give me some information."

When Father Parker didn't respond, she asked, "Father, are you there?"

"Yes, I'm here. I'm just shaking my head, which I seem to be doing a lot lately."

"So are you in?"

"In?"

"Yeah, come on, take a ride with me. No tunnels, I promise."

He blew out a breath. "Why do I feel like you're using me for my collar?"

"Because I am. It looks better on you than me."

"Fine," he said. "But I have a matter to take care of this morning. How about after lunch?"

"I'll see you then." She disconnected and started clicking on her calendar, freeing up her afternoon. Moving an interview with a homebound client up to the late morning gave her an alibi with Dan when she left.

She closed out her calendar and opened her browser and stiffened when she read the news headline, *Cardinal Ryan in Critical Condition.* She clicked on the story and learned that the cardinal had suffered ricin poisoning, along with Bishop Pallone, the day before. An elderly staff member who had worked with the cardinal for many years was suspected of lacing the cardinal's tea. A picture of a white-haired, innocuous-looking man was prominently posted next to a photo of the cardinal.

A chill ran down Elizabeth's spine as she remembered the congenial man. She couldn't help but wonder if his poisoning wasn't a coincidence to her earlier visit, but shook it off. "Now I'm paranoid," she scolded herself, but it didn't give her relief from the pit that formed in her stomach.

Sullivan awoke with an intense throbbing in his skull. "Cheap beer," he muttered without opening his eyes, fearing what the light would do to the pain. He attempted to lift his head, but the pain only increased with the movement. His stomached grumbled in protest, and sour acid pushed up his esophagus. He moved his hand to cover his mouth but found it held tight out to his side. He yanked on his other arm and found it the same. A panic rose in him that trumped the pain, and he lifted his head to look at his arms. He was secured at his wrists and ankles, with his arms and legs spread apart.

"Holy shit! What the fuck is this?" He surveyed the rest of his body and found himself naked with dried vomit on his chest and stomach. The rank of the puke hit his nostrils, causing his stomach to roll and lurch, and the acid that had been contained in his throat erupted and flew out of his mouth.

"I should make you clean this up," said a man dressed in a dark cloak, who calmly sat in a chair a safe distance in front of him.

After regaining his voice, Sullivan scratched out, "Who the fuck are you? Release me, you asshole."

"What language from a good Catholic boy. I'll tell you how this works." The cloaked man crossed to a hook hanging on the wall and pulled down a coiled rawhide whip.

Sullivan urinated on himself as he watched the man thoughtfully unfurl the leather and run his hand along the length of it.

"No, no, please," Sullivan begged. Without knowing a name, he understood who the man was and what he was capable of doing. "I'll give you whatever you want, just please don't hurt me," he sobbed.

"You can never give me back what you took. You laughed at the suffering. You are the monster." Without warning, the cloaked man violently jerked and turned to the corner, which caused Sullivan to whimper. "I wish you would stop sneaking up on me," he said to the empty corner with a tremor in his voice.

Sullivan stared at the man with the whip, confused, searching for an answer to give him. The cloaked man nodded vigorously before he turned back around and lifted the whip over his head. He brought it down, and Sullivan screamed out before it touched his skin.

❖

Elizabeth greeted Father Parker with a wave as she drove up. The father settled himself in the car and fastened his seat belt as she watched him.

"What, you're not going to cross yourself or say a prayer?"

He chuckled. "No, considering the other adventures we've had recently, driving with you pales in comparison. I'll save my prayers for the big stuff, like a cave-in or getting arrested."

She pulled out of the parking lot and momentarily debated whether to mention the story she read about the cardinal. "Father Parker, did you hear about Cardinal Ryan?"

"Yes, it's rather shocking."

"I met him and the bishop." She explained her trip to the cathedral and chance meeting with the cardinal. "He was very nice. The bishop, I'm not so sure about."

The father offered a small smile but didn't reply. She assumed he needed space in his own head to process the tragic event, and they fell into a comfortable silence as Elizabeth let the GPS guide her to the social services office.

After pulling into a concrete parking structure across from the building, she turned to him, "Okay, let me lead in there."

"No problem there."

Father Parker pulled open the glass door for Elizabeth and then followed behind her. A gray counter ran the length of the room with several people at computer terminals behind it. A line neatly curved through metal chains connected to posts that marked the path. They took their place at the end, and Elizabeth reminisced about her visit to the police station where she first met Grace. That felt like a lifetime ago, before she became so entangled in the Raymond Miller case.

Elizabeth and Father Parker made their way to the top of the line, but she held the father's arm when they were summoned to the counter by a woman with an extreme fondness for eye makeup. Elizabeth turned to the man behind her. "You go ahead. I'm not quite ready. I have to find something."

The man didn't need to be told twice as he moved past her to the counter.

"Why did you do that?" asked the father.

"Because we want him." She subtly pointed to a Hispanic man behind the counter at the end.

"Why?"

"See the cross he's wearing?"

"You're exploiting his religious beliefs?"

"You say exploiting, I say being observant."

The clerk that Elizabeth was waiting for became free and beckoned them. The clerk straightened at the sight of Father Parker, who stayed silent as Elizabeth spoke. She explained the information she needed, but the clerk shook his head.

"I can't give out that kind of information," he said apologetically, looking at the father.

"But David Collins isn't a minor anymore," she said. "We need to know what happened to him. It seems he disappeared after he was placed by your agency. We only need to know where he was placed."

The clerk sat quietly and absently played with the cross around his neck.

She watched the clerk debate with himself. "We're investigating a murder where an innocent man is being accused. We believe that whatever happened to David Collins is a key. We need to know where he was placed after his parents died."

The clerk started typing. "When did you say he was placed?"

"In nineteen eighty-one."

"I'm not sure I'll have those records on the computer. The county didn't go fully digital until two thousand and five." The clerk typed furiously, and Elizabeth held her breath during the silent waiting.

"I'm sorry. There's nothing here. My system just doesn't go back that far."

Elizabeth sighed. "Well, thank you for looking."

The clerk looked at Father Parker, who gave him a grateful nod, and began once again playing with his cross. "I'll tell you what, my boss can access that information. He's linked to the archives. I can ask him for you. Do you want to hold on?"

Elizabeth grasped the man's hand with both of hers. "Yes, thank you." She released her hold, and the clerk gave an awkward smile and stumbled as he walked away.

Father Parker finally spoke. "I think that young man was smitten."

"By whom, you or me?" she answered back with a little smile.

Father Parker's sole response was the usual shake of his head.

Elizabeth began idly spinning a pen that rested on the counter until it pointed toward the father. "Truth or dare?"

"I live my life by truth and have had as much dare as I care to since I met you, so I'm good, thanks."

For once, Father Parker stumped her, and she stared at him with no comeback.

"My boss will see you. I explained how important this is," the clerk proudly announced as he returned.

"Thank you so much." Elizabeth again grabbed his hand and shook it, causing a prominent blush to form on the clerk's face.

After being buzzed through a nondescript beige door, Elizabeth and Father Parker were escorted past several rows of cubicles, until they stopped in front of a small office. A man with a crooked toupee sat behind the desk with a telephone to his ear. With some time to contemplate the hairpiece, Elizabeth decided it looked more like a dead animal sprawled across his head, and it deserved a name. *Mr. Sparkles*. Named in honor of the hamster that she had in third grade. While they continued to stand in the doorway, she observed the utilitarian office, which contained a gray metal government-issue desk with a matching gray metal bookshelf off to the side. Several bound manuals were neatly aligned on the shelves. Behind the desk stood a bank of windows that looked out to the neighboring building. Elizabeth acknowledged that, despite the bleakness of the office, it was a step up from her own.

The man finally disconnected his call and gestured for them to enter. "Have a seat. I'm Frank Barns. What can I do for you?"

She reiterated her story as Frank sat listening, bobbing his head from time to time, and Mr. Sparkles held on for dear life.

"Well, I'm not sure I can help you. Let me see." He began pecking at his computer with two fingers in a slow rhythm, inputting the limited information that Elizabeth gave him.

She stared intently at Frank's fingers as he typed, wondering how he could be in the computer age and type like that. After a very long silence, he completed his pecking and sat back to await the results, before finally making a sound. "Hmm."

She sat up in her chair. "Did you find something?"

"Yes, I see his file here. It's very limited. It only contains the information about his placement and the preliminary home visit. Then it just stops."

"Can we have the location where he was placed?"

He took a deep breath and expelled it, causing Elizabeth to sit back when she got a whiff of garlic. "He was a minor. We can't just release this information without a court order."

"But that was more than thirty years ago," she said, trying to reason with him.

Frank thought about it for a moment. "Hold on. I need to check with our counsel. I'll be right back." He exited out of the computer and walked to the door, giving Elizabeth an opportunity to view Frank in his entirety, including one black and one brown shoe to complete his outfit.

As soon as he left the room, she stood. "Guard the door."

"What are you doing?" Father Parker asked with a bit of alarm in his voice.

"Just watch the door. Let me know when he comes back. I'm going to look it up myself." She was already in Frank's seat and typing as she spoke.

"How do you know how to work that thing?" the father asked as he stood near the doorway.

"I watched him type. He was typing so slow I could read everything he input." She typed in the password, which engaged the system. She had a decent view of the screen when Frank worked the computer, so she could mimic his moves. A small icon circled in the center of the screen as the computer processed the information.

"Come on, come on," Elizabeth demanded of the computer, nervously tapping her fingers on the desk.

Father Parker shifted from one foot to the other as he tried to inconspicuously stand guard. "I can't believe I'm a part of this. Since I've known you, I have trespassed, burglarized a school, and now I'm complicit in breaking into a government system and stealing confidential information. Did I leave anything out?"

Elizabeth didn't have time to respond as the requested information popped up on the computer screen. She snatched a pen from a cup on the top of the desk and searched for a piece of paper to write on. She started pulling open the side drawers, only finding files stuffed with forms. She yanked open the top drawer and hastily moved things around, pushing aside a container of Tic Tacs. *I think Frank could have used some of these.*

"Hurry up. He's coming!" Father Parker said in a loud whisper.

"Damn it!" She took the pen and started writing on her arm.

"Three seconds!" he said in a panic, wringing his hands.

Out of time to exit the computer, Elizabeth pushed the button on the computer, shutting it off. She leaped from the chair, and without enough time to return to her seat without Frank seeing her dive for it, she moved to the window and stared out.

"Sorry to keep you waiting so long," Frank said to Father Parker as he approached him.

"Oh, no need to apologize," the father replied. Frank passed him in the doorway, and Father Parker followed and took his seat as Elizabeth turned from the window and casually retook her seat.

"Well, I'm sorry to say that I've been advised that I cannot release that information without a court order."

Elizabeth wasn't surprised, as she already knew this would be the answer if Frank consulted with department counsel. She rose and put out her hand, and Frank firmly gripped it. "Thank you anyway, Frank. I appreciate that you took the time to check for us."

"I wish I could have been more help."

She gave him a small smile, and Father Parker stood without making eye contact and made a quick escape without saying a word.

Father Parker finally spoke as they reached Elizabeth's car. "I think I need to go to confession. Care to join me?"

She smiled. "It's all for the greater good, Father."

The father simply shook his head once again and opened the car door.

Seated in the car, Elizabeth pulled out a small pad of paper from her glove compartment and copied down the information from her arm. Father Parker remained silent, and she felt slightly guilty for putting him through that. She knew that he had a different set of rules that he played by, and she had caused him to run afoul of them several times. She would think twice before she called on him again to go out on one of her missions.

After Elizabeth dropped off Father Parker, she headed to her parents' home, her head filled with thoughts of a hot bath and reading a book curled under the covers; however, her dreams were shattered when she opened the front door and heard her mother call out to her, "Hurry up, Elizabeth. We're going to be late."

She scrunched up her nose at her mother who was standing at the top of the stairs. "Late for what?"

"Honestly, Elizabeth. How do you keep your life straight? I told you last week about the cocktail party that the mayor is hosting."

"Uh, no you didn't," she responded with her eyes wide.

"Elizabeth, I don't have time for this. Come upstairs and get ready. Wear that little black dress you had on last New Year's Eve. I think Thomas will like it."

"Thomas?"

Her mother blew out an exasperated breath. "Thomas Whittaker. I told you about him. He's made partner at his brokerage firm." She gestured with her hand in the air for emphasis. "He's meeting us here in less than an hour." She turned to walk away.

"But I'm not going," Elizabeth stuttered out.

Her mother stopped, turned, and leveled a glare down at her. "Oh yes, you are. Stop this foolishness and get upstairs."

"What about Raymond?"

"Roberta is going to stay the night and watch over him," she responded with the superiority of motherhood.

"How come he doesn't have to go?" Elizabeth whined out. She couldn't believe that came out of her mouth. She cringed. This was what her mother reduced her to, a whining, selfish two-year-old.

Her mother simply shook her head in disapproval and walked away. "You have forty-five minutes."

Elizabeth threw up her arms. "Welcome to hell."

A short hour later, she strolled down the stairs in her tight-fitting black cocktail dress, just as her mother ordered. She considered wearing something dowdy or even a pair of jeans but realized how juvenile that would be, and she had to redeem herself from the Raymond comment earlier. Her act of rebellion came in being fifteen minutes late coming downstairs. Thomas stood watching her descend, wiping his nose with a handkerchief.

"I swear this must be one of Dante's circles of hell," Elizabeth whispered to herself.

Thomas held out his hand to assist her down the last step, and she reluctantly accepted it. *Shoot me now, please.*

She rode with her parents in the back of the limousine, with her date seated at her side, and sat staring out the window the entire ride, ignoring the conversation around her. When the car pulled up to the entrance of the posh restaurant, she resisted the urge to open the door and start running.

Inside the restaurant, Grace stood with a passive smile, nodding on occasion at the dribbling of conversation that was surrounding her, hoping that she at least gave the appearance of paying attention. She hated events like these, but attendance by all the detectives and upper ranks in the department was deemed mandatory by the captain to show support of the city. Grace arrived early in hopes of making a quick showing and then an even quicker exit, with still enough of the evening left to salvage the night.

She knew of a women's bar less than ten minutes away, and although she would be overdressed, she would garner the attention of the women, just as she had of the men thus far, who made no effort to hide their gawking at her form-fitting navy dress. Thoroughly bored and wondering if she had stayed an appropriate period of time, she looked to the entrance to gauge how many were still streaming in, when a familiar face caught her attention. Her eyes greedily trailed the form that occupied the sleek black dress. She realized her unabashed stare and visceral reaction and repositioned herself, which allowed her to inconspicuously watch Elizabeth as she stood impatiently at the entrance, waiting for the security to discreetly search her small purse that was dangling from her wrist.

As she observed Elizabeth look on with disinterest at the restaurant that was bustling with the political and social elite, a man at Elizabeth's side leaned into her ear for a whisper before grabbing her hand and leading her through the crowd. Not wanting to witness any more of the intimate display, Grace turned away and lost herself in the crowd, narrowly missing Elizabeth as she passed. She did not turn back as she headed toward the exit, dispensing with the thought of continuing her evening at a bar with anonymous company.

❖

Elizabeth freed her hand from Thomas and paused as a familiar scent washed over her. She quickly scanned the perimeter, hoping to find its source, but realized she was being ridiculous and once again allowed Thomas to recapture her and guide her without protest to his clients, who he had spotted across the room. The two men who had been engrossed in conversion stopped and looked up to acknowledge them.

"Thomas, good to see you," offered one, and he extended his hand in greeting.

"It's good to see you." Thomas turned to her. "This is Elizabeth Campbell. Elizabeth, this is Seth Lowry, the CEO of IPR."

"IPR?" she asked, although not particularly interested.

"We're a pharmaceutical research company," Lowry said.

Elizabeth recalled reading a newspaper article about the start-up pharmaceutical company, with its success and rapid growth. "Yes, of course. I read about your company."

He was clearly pleased.

"So what's your secret?" she asked.

"Excuse me?" Lowry asked.

"From what I read, IPR has seen quite a bit of success for a start-up," she explained.

"Ah well, it's a combination. We hired some very smart people, invested our capital into the proper research, and well then, there's also just plain luck."

"IPR's innovative and thorough research has streamlined their clinical trials, and they're now in the final stage with a patent pending. It's all hush, hush, but it's going to be big. This is a company to watch," Thomas said, clearly trying to earn some kudos from his client.

"We've been lucky," Lowry said.

The second man, who had been silent through the exchange, finally spoke up and began the topic of the morning's stock market report, and Elizabeth tuned out. The men quickly forgot about her presence, and she felt like an interloper and excused herself, claiming that she recognized someone and wanted to say hello.

As she wandered through a sea of people, a clear swan carved from ice stood above a table of appetizers in the corner and beckoned her over. The swan sat elegantly atop a block of ice in a small glass pool, with small fish swimming around the base. Elizabeth looked closely at the pool and noticed a fish floating at the top. *Poor guy. I know how you feel.* She turned her thoughts to the swan and couldn't resist the urge to reach out and touch the sculpture to verify its authenticity. She ran her hand over its smooth, cold back and ran it up to the head. She traced the beak with her fingers, grasping the end when she got to it. To Elizabeth's horror, the beak snapped off in her hands.

"Oh shit!" *Maybe my parents should have brought Raymond and left me home with the sitter.* She furtively looked around to see if anyone had noticed her faux pas. Convinced she went unnoticed, she tried to reattach the beak, hoping if she held it firmly enough, the ice would melt together. No such luck. A waiter approached with a tray of champagne flutes, and she held the beak behind her back out of the waiter's view and politely declined the drink. She looked around trying to find a place to inconspicuously stash the chunk of ice. Her hand was freezing. The ice was dripping through her fingers, and she could feel it trickling down the back of her legs.

She moved away from the wounded swan and headed toward the bathroom with the intent of flushing the evidence but was abruptly stopped by Mayor Reynosa, who stepped out in front of her path.

"Ms. Campbell, I thought that was you," the mayor said. Several other guests turned to see who garnered the mayor's attention.

"You know who I am?"

"Well, of course. I make it my business to know the infamous people in this town."

"Infamous? How so?"

"The Raymond Miller case, of course. That was a bit of a surprise."

"I'm sure it was," she said without care as to how it sounded.

"It's a shame that the city must waste its resources to retry a man who admits his own guilt."

She bit the inside of her cheek. "I certainly didn't ask for this. It was your idea for a full review of all major crimes convictions. I did my job. I reviewed the case. It didn't add up."

The mayor shook his head with a small laugh, like he was

addressing a child who misunderstood the point of her parent's lecture. "My dear, I believe you are confused. I certainly did not request a review of this case. The man confessed. End of story. There was no review needed." He droned on about her fruitless expedition squandering the city's money, but she paid little attention. She was lost in the mayor's statement that he didn't request for Raymond's case to be reviewed. *If he didn't, then who sent it to SILC for review?*

She tuned back in to hear the mayor's condescending tone as he continued to lecture her. "I suppose jury tampering is a way to ensure that the city's integrity remains intact. I'm not so sure about its budget. What's it cost to buy a juror?"

"Excuse me?" asked Mayor Reynosa, indignation evident in his voice.

"You heard me."

"You should be careful, young lady. Slander can be costly."

The mayor turned and walked away, flagging down another guest.

Another waiter passed by, and Elizabeth raised her hand in the air to stop him. The ice was still clutched in her raised hand, and she placed the beak on the tray and grabbed a glass. The waiter furrowed his brows at the beak and then looked up at her.

She took a large sip of alcohol before responding to the waiter's unasked question. "The swan had a bit of a mishap." She pointed to the beakless ice sculpture. "It was a drunken fish. He got too frisky. The swan fought nobly but lost his beak in the end." The waiter remained motionless as he stared at her.

She knew that it would be a good time to make her exit and placed her now-empty glass on the tray next to the beak and bid the waiter a good evening and headed for the door. She passed Thomas on her way and informed him that she was leaving, claiming a headache, and told—no, more like ordered—him to stay. "I've called a friend who's picking me up. You stay and enjoy the evening. Will you tell my parents that I left when you see them?" She didn't wait for a response and turned and walked out.

She pulled her phone from the black purse and dialed Michael's number, but it went to voice mail, and she puffed out a brisk message explaining her surprise date with the runny nose man, as she came to dub him, and found herself in need of a ride. She hugged her torso and vigorously rubbed her arms in an attempt to generate some body heat as she impatiently waited his return call.

"It's warmer inside."

She turned to find a man on the shorter side with a crooked bow tie, standing a few feet away. "No doubt, with all that hot air."

"I'd have to agree. I came out for a bit of fresh air. It's a bit stuffy in there, and I don't mean the temperature."

She instantly liked the man. "I'm Elizabeth Campbell." She unwrapped one arm from her body and offered a handshake.

"Nice to meet you, Ms. Campbell. I'm Simon Fisher. I work for the mayor and am forced to be here."

"I'm sorry," she said.

"Me too," Simon responded.

Before Elizabeth could continue their conversation any further, an SUV pulled up to the curb, and the passenger window rolled down. "Need a ride?"

Elizabeth peered inside to see Grace behind the wheel and debated her options: sit outside and wait and hope Michael returned her call, return to the party and her date, or get into the car with Grace. Elizabeth turned to Simon and bid him good-bye and quickly stepped into the SUV. She turned the car vent, allowing the heated air to blow on her.

"This dress was a stupid idea. I'm freezing."

"You should have waited inside," Grace said.

"Hell no," she replied through chattering teeth.

"Am I missing the opportunity for a hell freezes over joke here?"

Elizabeth turned and looked at her as if recognizing her for the first time, and she admired her navy dress from the top of the cleavage to the bottom of the hem that came mid-thigh. "What are you doing here?"

"I was just about to escape when I saw a stupid woman with no jacket, standing out front, and being that it's my duty to protect and serve, I rescued her."

"I don't need rescuing."

Grace put the car into reverse and started to back up to the restaurant entrance. "All righty then, I'll just put you back where I found you."

"Wait. Fine. I need a ride."

"Please," Grace corrected her like she was a small child.

"Please and thank you," Elizabeth said through a false smile.

"Won't your boyfriend be missing you?" Grace asked.

"My boyfriend? Oh God no, the runny nose man was my mother's doing, a surprise date."

"The 'runny nose' man?" Grace laughed.

Elizabeth's phone rang and she snatched it up. "Michael, where have you been?"

"Where are you? I'll come and get you."

"Never mind, Detective Donovan is giving me a ride."

"Ooohh, this sounds interesting. Two lesbian lovers sitting in a tree, k-i-s-s-i-n-g, first comes love, then comes vows, and somewhere in there, a rented U-Haul's involved."

Elizabeth hung up the phone and jammed it into her purse.

"Everything all right?" Grace asked.

"Yes, just my soon to be ex-best friend Michael."

"I met him at your house. He seems like a nice guy," Grace said.

"Figures. You two would get along just great."

Realizing that Grace was heading the wrong way, she started pointing out directions to her parents' home, and then they finally sat lost in their own thoughts, until Grace broke the silence when she pulled up to a fortified gate. "Wow, did you grow up here?"

Elizabeth felt slightly embarrassed for her privileged upbringing. "It all started with my great-grandfather's bootlegging."

Grace looked at her sideways.

"Oh, never mind. Just pull up there."

Elizabeth waited until Grace made it safely back outside the gate before she dashed in the house. *Bootlegging? That was smooth.*

With Grace no longer clouding her mind, she returned her thoughts to earlier in the evening. *If the mayor didn't want this case reviewed, then how did it end up at SILC with the other cases? Someone knew. I think it's the same person who left me the note on my car.*

CHAPTER TWENTY-THREE

Grateful for a quiet Friday morning, Bishop Pallone sat in the floral-patterned chair that Cardinal Ryan occupied the last time they had met. He'd been released from the hospital that morning and still felt weak from his ordeal, and he rested his head against the chair. The base of his cognac glass balanced on the arm of the chair as he loosely held the stem between his fingers. With his other hand, he absently rubbed a Saint Christopher medallion hanging around his neck that was usually concealed beneath his clothing. He looked about the airy room, redesigning the space in his head to meet his liking. The cardinal's tastes were much simpler than his own.

With Cardinal Ryan's passing, a vacancy was left at the top of the archdiocese pyramid, and it was only a matter of time before a papal appointment would place him in the seat. He had been revered as a hero by many after surviving the ricin poisoning that claimed the cardinal's life. The cardinal was loved by all in the archdiocese, and he was able to point the authorities to the person responsible. The cardinal's trusted servant and companion of many years proclaimed his innocence in the murder of Cardinal Ryan and attempted murder of Bishop Pallone, but the old man was another expendable person.

A knock sounded at the door, waking him from his reverie. He remembered that he was alone with no one to open the door and called out, "Come in." The knock sounded again and he realized that his voice would not carry through the heavy wooden door. He begrudgingly set down his glass and rose from the chair, yanking open the door. "Yes?"

A man dressed in a black suit, who equaled Pallone in age, stood with a silver tray in his hand, and he sized him up. This was the old man's replacement.

"Your Excellency, a message was left for you, and I believe it is urgent."

He snatched up the envelope resting on the tray. "Who sent it?"

"I don't know, Your Excellency. It was left for you on the bench in the garden with a note attached." He pulled out a folded note from his pocket.

Pallone took the note in his other hand and unfolded it. The note advised the reader that the enclosed envelope was an urgent message for him addressing a confidential Church matter. He turned the envelope over in his hands, and the back side revealed a waxed seal that secured the flap. He looked at the embossed seal closely. "*Deo duce*" was written in a circle with a cross in the middle.

"Shall I send it to security?" the servant asked.

"No, I shall take care of it. Thank you." Pallone turned and closed the door behind him and retook his seat, laying the envelope in his lap. He stroked the perfect block lettering that spelled out his name on the front of the envelope and then flipped it over. He studied the red waxed seal; it wasn't a church seal, but he recognized it. He passed through those gates often enough in his youth.

He broke the seal and pulled out a white card with the same block lettering as the envelope.

> *Tuesday at dusk, the white chapel on the hill next to the iron cross is where you will find the information you need to end the bloodshed. For a small fee, of course. Bring $50,000 cash. If you are not interested, then I am sure the Church will find it useful.*

After reading the note over again, he dropped it to his lap and covered his face with his hands. He was so close. Why now? He knew it could be a trap. He knew he should notify the police, but he also knew the risk if he did. He had worked hard for his stature within the Church. He was on the cusp of being archbishop, and this information in the wrong hands could destroy him. He had worked hard to keep his misdeeds of the past buried. He would go alone.

The fee would be a minor issue. Pallone had become adept at manipulating church funds. He had covertly maneuvered the sizable church accounts many times, including a fairly recent withdrawal of $100,000 for a donation to a certain legal clinic. Some would call it embezzlement, but Pallone saw it as his due for his years of service.

CHAPTER TWENTY-FOUR

As Monday morning finally arrived, Elizabeth sat behind the counsel's table nervously awaiting the judge's arrival. She had never been in this situation before. Jury tampering was outside her well of experience as a lawyer. Raymond sat beside her busily coloring, wearing the same navy suit that he had on the last time they were in court. However, this time, he seemed more comfortable in it, but that didn't surprise her. He'd become comfortable in his new life living with Elizabeth and her parents. She was amazed at his ability to adapt to the changes life threw at him.

ADA Burke sat hunched over his phone, furiously typing. He didn't acknowledge her, but she casually watched him from the corner of her eye. His leg anxiously bounced up and down under the table, and it reminded her of Dan the day she told him about the jury tampering. She filed that thought away for later processing.

The oak door behind the judge's bench opened, and Judge Walters entered. The bailiff called the court to order, and Elizabeth rose. Burke fumbled with his phone, hastily trying to shut it off, and nearly knocked it toward the center of the court when he bobbled it. The judge raised her eyebrow at him but didn't say a word, and he sheepishly slipped the phone into his briefcase. "Sorry, Your Honor."

Judge Walters leaned forward on the bench with her hands clasped in front of her. "As the parties are aware, the court received disturbing information about one of the jurors that caused this case to be placed in recess since last week. The court has conducted a thorough investigation, including interviewing the juror in question as well as the remaining jurors. The court has not yet learned the identity of the person or persons responsible for contacting juror number three. As such, the court cannot say with certainty that no other juror has been compromised. For this reason, the court will declare a mistrial."

Elizabeth inhaled a deep breath through her nose at the judge's words. Although she knew this could be a possibility, she was still shocked to hear it. Burke kept his head bowed, staring down at his file.

"All jurors will be recused. We will continue this case to next Monday afternoon for the district attorney to decide how they wish to proceed. The defendant will remain free on his own recognizance."

The judge rose and exited the courtroom as the court remained absolutely still. It seemed as though everyone present waited until the judge left to exhale. As soon as the door closed, a cacophony of voices erupted.

Elizabeth turned to Raymond, who was still working on his artwork, oblivious to the chaos around him. She laid her hand on his back. "We're all done. Let's go home."

Without waiting for them to leave the table, Elizabeth's mother rushed around and grabbed her in a hug, and then grabbed Raymond and squeezed him tight. He squealed in delight.

The three of them exited the courthouse with Raymond walking in the middle of them and Elizabeth's and her mother's arms protectively wrapped around his shoulders. Elizabeth slowed her gait when she noticed a figure leaning against her car and stopped to turn to her mother. "You two go ahead and enjoy your day. I have some things to take care of." She gave her mother and Raymond quick hugs and sent them on their way toward her mother's car and stood watching until her mother exited the parking lot before she approached her car.

"Something I can do for you, Detective Donovan?"

"A word with you…please."

"How did you know it was my car?"

Grace broke into a crooked grin and looked around at the selection of sedans in the parking lot. "Oh, I don't know. It kinda stands out. I remembered it from the last time we met in a parking lot. I believe that was when you told me I had my head up my ass."

Elizabeth smirked, remembering that early confrontation. *Okay, maybe it was a bit harsh. She did save me from the mayor's party. Perhaps an apology is in order…Naaahhh.*

"Something funny?"

"Just replaying it in my head and enjoying it for a second time." Elizabeth smiled.

Grace offered a smile in return, but quickly resumed her stoic demeanor. "Truce, we need to talk."

Elizabeth raised her eyebrows but remained silent, and Grace continued. "Sullivan's dead."

She pushed the lock release for her car and opened her door. "Get in."

After circling the car, Grace opened the passenger door, and Elizabeth waited until she settled. "What happened?"

"His body was found in a private garden behind the archdiocese cathedral. He was hung on a wooden cross like Father Samuel Rossi. A gardener found him. The archdiocese has agreed to keep it quiet for now, given the state they're in with the death of their cardinal. They didn't want any more negative publicity."

She waited for more information to come, but Grace sat silently staring off. Unwilling to wait any longer, she asked, "How was he? I mean, what was the condition of his body?"

"His body was like the others." Grace's voice trailed off, and Elizabeth sensed that this death was more difficult for her because it was closer to home. "Did he have the circle with the triangles?" Elizabeth asked, while gesturing to her abdomen.

"Yes," came the whispered response. "His car was found at O'Shays Pub. I think that's where he grabbed him."

"So now what?"

"I know you're investigating these murders. It makes sense that we work together," Grace replied.

She gave Grace an innocent look.

"Don't think I don't know that you've been sneaking around, poking your nose into things."

"I can neither confirm nor deny that accusation. So does this mean you don't think Raymond Miller is guilty?"

Grace let out a humorless laugh. "I used to think Miller was guilty. He confessed, the crucifix in his pocket, the Bible in his shed. I was so sure. Sullivan…" She took a breath. "He told me so." Her words sounded weak. "God damn it!" She threw her head against the headrest before turning to Elizabeth. "Why did he confess? Why did he have the cross in his pocket and the Bible?"

"I don't know. I'm not sure he knows," she replied.

Grace ran her hands through her hair and stared off. "I don't know who to trust," she whispered.

Elizabeth truly understood the loneliness of that statement. "It's the school," she finally responded. She weighed the situation, unsure how much to reveal, but she felt at a stalemate. Breaking and entering could only get her so far. "It's all tied to Saint John's Boys School," she explained.

"I've never heard of it."

"It was a Catholic school on the east side on the town's border next to a mill. The school and the mill closed down in 1982."

"Yeah, I remember it. The school's torn down. The kids liked to vandalize it. What does this have to do with anything?" Grace asked impatiently.

"Well..." she drew out, irked by Grace's tone. "The first victim, Father Portillo, his body was left hanging on the front gate of the school; Father Rossi worked at the school before it closed down; and Sullivan testified that he attended the school."

"This is all very interesting, but it could be nothing more than a big coincidence." Elizabeth suspected that Grace was intentionally being difficult and chose to ignore her. She produced the David Collins necklace from her bag. "I found this hanging on a tree behind the school."

Grace took it from her and held it close to her face, reading the inscription. "Yeah, so?"

"Well, David Collins's parents died in 1981, and he was placed into foster care. David was in a home at least a thirty-minute drive away, so what was he doing up at the school? And according to my, um, research, the social services records for David cease to exist shortly after he was placed."

"You know this how exactly?"

"Very diligent research." She smiled.

"Right."

Elizabeth sat with her hands folded in her lap waiting for her to speak.

Grace finally looked at her. "Show it to me." Elizabeth stared back at her.

"The school," she clarified. "Show it to me."

"Now?" Elizabeth realized she sounded like Father Parker. "Fine," she said resolutely. She started her engine and drove the now familiar route as Grace gripped the door handle during the ride, her knuckles turning white. Seeing that gave Elizabeth a perverse sense of pleasure, and she put a little more pressure on the gas pedal.

Elizabeth pulled into the school lot and parked in what she now considered her spot. Grace exited the car and started walking toward what was left of the foundation of the main building, without waiting to see if Elizabeth followed.

Elizabeth caught up with her as she was approaching the dormitory building and steered her toward the side door. Grace grabbed the padlock hanging from the chain, and it came off in her hand. "Hmmm, can't imagine how this happened."

Elizabeth handed her one of the flashlights she was holding. "Here, you might need this."

Grace accepted the light. "Experienced at this?"

Elizabeth didn't answer but stepped past her through the open door. The inside of the building seemed less ominous in the daylight. "All the rooms are the same. If you've seen one, you've seen them all," she said as she moved directly to the third floor. She didn't need to turn to see if Grace was following because she could hear her footsteps on the staircase behind her. This was another difference from Father Parker, who was stealth-like and could sneak up on her. She stopped in front of room thirty.

"Yeah, so?" Grace asked unimpressed.

"Thirty B / upon level three / continued the devil's iniquity," she replied like it was normal conversation.

"What have you been smoking?"

"Oh, that's right." Elizabeth remembered that she had left out the detail of the surreptitious note on her car. She recited the poem from memory and explained its mysterious arrival as they made their way back out of the building.

"So what's it supposed to mean?" Grace asked.

"Beats the hell out of me."

"Hmmm, there's an option," Grace said loud enough for her to hear.

After replacing the chain on the door, Elizabeth walked to the front doors of the church, and Grace kicked at the chain and broken lock still lying on the ground from Elizabeth's last visit and shook her head. "Coincidence? Two broken locks. I think not."

Offering a noncommittal shrug, Elizabeth pulled on the door, and not finding anything of interest in the church the first time through, walked directly to the basement, and descended the stairs. Grace remained silent about the broken doorjamb, where Elizabeth and Father Parker pried the door open. Elizabeth figured she had given up by now.

"It's a basement," Grace said, stating the obvious.

Elizabeth didn't respond, choosing to ignore her, and shined her light on the metal cellar doors. "These doors were pried open, and it looks like some from the homeless camp might have come in here."

Grace shook her head at this information as though to say "How do you know?"

"There were footprints on the floor." Elizabeth realized that she just confessed her past indiscretion of breaking and entering, and Grace snickered.

Elizabeth walked to the concrete door and heard something skitter across the floor when she kicked it, and she bent over to pick up a discarded book of matches. Grace moved past her and pushed open the door. Elizabeth shoved the matches in her jacket pocket and followed her through the open concrete door.

"What the hell is this?" Grace asked. "Looks like some kind of bomb shelter. When was this place built?"

"The school was built in the 1940s, but I think this was added after, probably in the fifties, Cold War era," Elizabeth replied. "Here's the interesting thing." She shined her light on the metal hooks protruding from the ceiling and walls, and the chains hung motionless. "Want to venture a guess what was going on in here?"

Grace shook her head and walked the circumference of the room, meticulously scanning the floor and walls with her light. Satisfied that the room was empty, she sat on the chair next to the small table and leaned her head against the wall. "Not sure what to think."

Elizabeth stood in the center of the room looking up at the dangling chains and shuddered. Mistaking the cool atmosphere of the room as the cause of her shivering, Grace stood. "Let's get out of here." She started back to the basement.

"Hold up," Elizabeth called out. "This way."

Grace turned and watched her pull on a matching concrete door directly across from the first concrete door. "You've got to be kidding me."

Elizabeth walked into the tunnel and waited for her as Grace moved to Elizabeth and stood close, nearly touching her. Although Elizabeth noticed, she chose to stay quiet and enjoy the close proximity for the moment and shined her light down the tunnel. "If you keep going down this way, the tunnel is blocked by debris. It looks like part of the tunnel gave way."

Elizabeth could feel her shudder at that bit of information, and Grace quickly turned the opposite way. "Where does this way lead?" she asked, shining her light down the tunnel.

"Out."

"Out it is," Grace said as she started walking toward the tunnel entrance. Elizabeth had to skip a few steps to keep up with her quick pace, and when they reached the metal grate, Grace turned to her. "Now what?"

Elizabeth pulled the grate away from the tunnel wall and squeezed through.

"Oh great, I thought we were going to have to scale a cliff or something."

"No, not yet. That's next," Elizabeth responded without turning.

"Seriously?" she asked, and Elizabeth released a laugh, fully enjoying watching Grace's tough demeanor erode away.

She opened the wooden door to the outside. "No."

Grace didn't waste any time squeezing herself through and followed Elizabeth out the door. "Where are we?" she asked as she turned around in a circle.

"The woods."

"Oh, thanks, I was confused for a moment and thought we were in a shopping mall."

Elizabeth pointed. "The school's that way, but I want to show you something." She walked in the general direction of the lovers' tree, scanning each tree trunk, looking for her markings. When she finally found her trail, she turned to Grace. "It's over here." She led her to the tree. "This is where I found the metal tags for David Collins."

"How did you find them out here? That's like a needle in a haystack."

"Well, it was close. We were wandering around trying to find our way back to the school—"

She interrupted her. "We?"

"Never mind, just stay with me," Elizabeth responded without missing a beat. "And I saw this carving." She pointed to the heart etched into the tree.

Grace stared at her, and Elizabeth realized she would need to explain further. "This is the lovers' tree, you know, from the note."

Grace crossed her arms and moved closer to the carving. "Did our poet sign this note?"

Elizabeth gave her a look. "No, if I knew who wrote the note, I probably wouldn't be traipsing through the woods, or tunnel for that matter."

"I'm not so sure about that," Grace said under her breath, but loud enough for her to hear, and Elizabeth opened her mouth to defend herself but realized it was pointless because it was true. Traipsing through the woods and secret tunnels wasn't so bad.

Grace circled the tree and sized it up. "So wait, does this mean that there's something…" she paused for a moment, "or *someone* buried beneath this tree?"

"I don't know. I didn't have my shovel."

"Is there anything else you want to show me?"

"Nope, that pretty much concludes our tour."

"Thank God. Let's go."

Elizabeth navigated her way back to the school and checked the church and dormitory doors to make sure that they were secure, while Grace stood facing toward the tunnel entrance. Elizabeth stood next to her, and Grace pointed. "The tunnel entrance is there. From what I can tell, the tunnel ran this way and would have continued going down there." She pointed out the path as she spoke, and she was now pointing in the direction that led farther down the road past the school.

"What's down there?" Elizabeth asked, following her finger.

"Let's find out."

When they returned to the car, Elizabeth inspected her tires, which were intact.

"What are you doing?"

She relayed the story of the mysterious closing of the tunnel door and slashing of her tires on her last visit, conspicuously leaving out Father Parker's name in the retelling to protect him from any possible repercussions.

"Oh, now you tell me," Grace said.

Elizabeth shrugged and pulled her keys from her pocket, pulling the matchbook out with them. She opened her car door and tossed the matches into the center compartment and started the engine, then casually watched and waited as Grace settled in. Even though they were being friendly, she knew their alliance was fragile.

She turned the car down the road past the school. On her prior visits to the school, Elizabeth had never ventured past the school, and she was now curious. In less than a half mile, a building emerged, and the road abruptly ended. "This must be the mill."

Although the building still stood, time had not been kind. What was once a proud building now sat sagging and weathered. The paint was faded and peeling, with the wood supports showing signs of rot. The windows were boarded, likely to keep out vagrants and troublemakers. With no one to defend the building's integrity, the overgrowth of the brush from the woods was encroaching upon the grounds surrounding the building. Weeds were erupting between the cracks of the blacktop and overtaking the parking lot. Elizabeth felt a sense of sympathy for the structure.

Grace clearly didn't share the same sentiment. "This place is a piece of shit." She opened the car door and began circling the structure while scanning the grounds as she walked. Elizabeth walked around the other way. A moment alone from Grace was needed to settle the mixed feelings Grace aroused in her, a combination of agitation and exhilaration.

As Elizabeth scanned the property, she noted that there was nothing remarkable about the location, other than the fact that it was isolated, but for its only neighbor, the school. The woods surrounded the three sides, and she guessed that Grace was right. The tunnel did appear to head in this direction. As she stood at the side of the building staring out toward the direction of the school, Grace stole behind her. "Boo!"

Elizabeth jumped and impulsively turned and slapped Grace in the arm. "Damn it! You scared me," she said.

"Ouch, you hit me," Grace whined while rubbing her arm.

Elizabeth turned away from her and gave a small smile. "Did you see anything?" she asked.

"Nothing but a dilapidated building."

"Well, if the tunnel does come this way, it could have an entrance in the basement, like the church," Elizabeth reasoned.

"I think the bigger question is why?"

Elizabeth shook her head in response.

"Well, let's get out of here."

Normally, Elizabeth would have protested and argued to explore the woods for another entrance or use her handy bolt cutters to get into the building, but she suspected Grace was less inclined to recklessly follow her on one of her adventures. In that regard, Father Parker was more fun. *Who would have thought I would have found a priest more fun?* They spoke very little on the return drive to the courthouse, and the bit of conversation they had related to the case. It was as though by silent agreement they had resumed their professional status once again.

"So, you said that you learned the identity of the foster parents of David Collins?" Grace asked.

Elizabeth nodded.

"Have you talked to them?"

She shook her head.

"Do you speak?"

Elizabeth nodded, her professional demeanor waning. Why did she enjoy irritating Grace so?

"Give me their information, and I'll check them out," Grace said.

Usually, Elizabeth would have been taken aback by being ordered around, but she saw the advantage of allowing Grace to do this assignment. A detective would likely have greater access to any additional information out there about David's placement and subsequent disappearance from the system, and Elizabeth would be free to search the origins of the mill.

When she pulled up to the court parking lot, Elizabeth pulled out the slip of paper with the requested information and read it off, and Grace exited the car with a promise of letting her know what she found out. Elizabeth took a brief moment to rest her eyes and reflect on the changing relationship with Grace from one of hostility, to an indifference, to...what? *A cordial working relationship? No, it seems more than that, perhaps a working friendship. That's it, a working friendship.*

Elizabeth returned to the clinic, but only after stopping off to see Rich at the county recorder's office. She wanted to know who owned the mill and hoped this would help piece together what she was missing.

As she strolled through the reception area of the clinic, Amy sat in her usual spot with a phone to her ear. She lifted her index finger in the air, beckoning Elizabeth to stop, and she waited patiently as Amy finished her call.

"Dan wants to see you," Amy said with a blank expression.

"Thanks." Elizabeth gave her a tight smile. Somehow, she knew this wouldn't be good.

She approached Dan's office and rapped on the door frame as he sat with his back to her, staring out the window. His view was no better than hers, so she knew he wasn't taking in the scenery, but lost in thought. He swiveled his chair to face her.

"Come in," he replied without making eye contact.

She took the seat across from him, dropping her bag at her feet, and clasped her hands in her lap, waiting.

"I heard about the court ruling this morning."

She remained silent, curious as to how he had come to learn this information, or more appropriately, from whom?

"Elizabeth, I think it's time that we part ways."

Although she expected a reprimand that wasn't deserved, she didn't see this coming. "You're firing me?"

"I'd like to say that we have grown apart, and we no longer see eye to eye on what's in the best interest of this clinic."

"You can't be serious. This is all about the Raymond Miller case. I may actually prove that an innocent man went to prison, and you think this isn't in the best interest of the clinic. What you really mean is, it's not in the best interest of your donors, like the mayor and his cronies." She didn't care how much she angered Dan because she had nothing to lose. She was being fired.

Dan flinched at the remark, but didn't respond to it. "Please close out what cases you can by the end of the week. What you can't complete, leave a detailed memo of what must be done and leave it with me."

She figured that he must still have some trust in her as he was giving her until Friday to finish up, instead of booting her out on the spot. For that, she was grateful because she hated the thought of leaving her clients and their cases hanging. At least she had time to put closure on some of the pending matters.

Elizabeth rose and grabbed her bag without saying a word and exited, crossing the office past Jeff who was standing at a large copy machine, whistling a nameless tune. This wasn't the defective machine with an attitude that threatened Jeff within an inch of his life the last time she saw him standing at a copy machine. This was a technologically advanced machine that hummed in appreciation at being given the opportunity to serve its master. She shook her head at the machine. *The donors must have paid their dues.*

Chapter Twenty-five

Elizabeth was awakened by her cell phone and momentarily stared at it, trying to remember how to answer it. With success, she put it to her ear, but before she could speak, she heard, "Pieter Spiedel."

"Uh, who is this?" Her voice cracked as she spoke.

"It's Rich, and it's Pieter Spiedel of the Spiedel Trust," Rich answered with excitement.

Elizabeth looked at her bedside clock that read 6:45 a.m. Confused, she asked, "Do you know what time it is? Where are you?"

"Not where, who."

"What?"

"No, who," he corrected her.

She scratched her head, "Am I Abbott or Costello?"

"Don't you get it? The Spiedel Trust owned the mill."

"Oh, okay," she said, closing her eyes and sinking back into her pillow.

"The mill was owned by a series of holding companies, so I had to dig through and really trace them, but eventually it led to the Spiedel Trust, which is, or was, controlled by Pieter Spiedel. The trust is responsible for funding some of the country's most cutting-edge and sometimes controversial medical research."

Elizabeth sat back up, resigned that she wasn't going to get the extra fifteen minutes of sleep. "So, the mill wasn't a mill?"

"No, it was. It operated as a textile mill, but from everything I see, at a loss for many years before it closed down. I'll send you the information."

They exchanged good-byes, with Elizabeth expressing her gratitude for Rich's diligent work, and he was pleased to have earned her praise.

❖

Elizabeth spent the morning locked in her office sorting through files and preparing to-do memos for the unfinished cases. Satisfied that she at least had it organized, she turned her attention to the information Rich had emailed her.

Pieter Spiedel was a man of substantial wealth as an innovator in the stock and bond market. As Rich had briefly explained on the phone, the sole purpose of his namesake trust was to fund novel medical and scientific research. She learned from Rich's extensive background information that Spiedel suffered from multiple sclerosis and was looking for the Holy Grail in medical research, which he apparently did not find, as he died in 1985. However, the trust and Spiedel's quest continued to live on with Spiedel's nephew, Bradley Iverson, as successor trustee.

Rich understood Elizabeth well and had the forethought of providing Bradley Iverson's information, but in reviewing Iverson's bio, she knew that they didn't run in the same circles and wouldn't likely have a chance encounter at the corner deli. Fortunately for her, Charles Campbell did run in Iverson's circle. Campbell, Roberts, Addelstein, and Krass were the counsel of record for Spiedel Trust, and she was going to need her father's name to get her on the inside. Two months ago, she would have balked at this idea, but not now, not since Raymond entered their lives. Little did she realize how much Raymond had changed them. Elizabeth saw her parents very differently now.

She lifted her receiver and dialed a familiar number. "Hi, is Charles Campbell available? This is his daughter."

❖

Bishop Pallone knew the iron cross to which the covert note referred. It was in the memorial cemetery located at the base of the hill, upon which the white chapel sat. As the evenings were arriving sooner now, he decided to leave early. It would do him no good to be late and possibly miss his informant.

Despite his position within the church, he had little freedom or power in his own life to come and go as he pleased. He couldn't simply request a car; he had drivers. He couldn't simply walk the streets without a care; he would be noticed, but he had time to think it through.

A quick visit to a church donation center supplied him with street clothes, clothes he hadn't worn in thirty years. He neatly folded the clothes into a canvas bag, placing them on top of a neatly wrapped white package, containing bundles of hundred-dollar bills. He concealed the bag below his tunic, which rubbed uncomfortably against his leg. After starting out on his routine walk through the garden, he turned off and entered a public bathroom where he changed, stuffing his tunic into the back of a cupboard below the sink.

When he exited the bathroom, he assumed his new identity of a common man. He quickly moved to the street, enjoying the freedom of movement that his new clothes offered, a freedom he had long forgotten. He walked to the main boulevard and raised his arm at an oncoming taxi, but the taxi passed him by, and he muttered under his breath. He continued his quest, at first raising his arm at the oncoming cabs, but later he resorted to flapping and waving his arms in the air after he was passed over several times. He realized that his church clothes offered him privileges that he was now sorely missing. At long last, a cab driver took mercy on him and pulled to the curb.

Pallone looked down at the dingy faux leather seat that sported gray tape to seal the cracks. The driver didn't turn but watched him through his rearview mirror. "Where to?"

He provided his desired location, and the driver raised his eyebrows but didn't say a word and pulled into traffic, earning a few honks by other drivers that caused Pallone to cringe and grasp his chest. The driver easily navigated the city and quickly pulled up to the gates of the cemetery.

"You sure this is where you want to go?" asked the taxi driver.

"Yes. How much?" He pulled out a wad of cash stuffed in his front pocket that he had "borrowed" from the petty cash fund. After paying the driver, he was left alone at the entrance, and he cautiously entered, thankful that the gates were still open. The sun was quickly setting.

The iron cross could be easily spotted in the center of the cemetery. He approached it and stood at its base, staring up at the enormity of it. To its left, a cement pathway wound up the hill to a church, and he moved to it and ascended the hill. He approached the front door and pulled, surprised to actually find it open.

"What idiot actually leaves a church wide open just waiting for hooligans?" he said.

He slowly stuck his head in the door and peered around the room. It was small, with less than a dozen rows of pews, clearly meant for small funeral services only. Assured that he was alone, he entered the church and sat in a middle pew, without offering the sign of the cross. He pondered his lack of church etiquette and decided it was the clothing. It made him a different person, a person who wasn't expected to worship any particular god or religion. He found that liberating in a way that surprised him.

He closed his eyes, taking advantage of the solitude, and waited. His stomach fluttered in anticipation of what was to happen next, and he took slow breaths to calm his nerves, until his breath became shallow. His head fell forward and startled him. He looked out the stained glass windows to his side and realized darkness had fallen. He wasn't sure how long he'd been asleep and urgently looked around the room and found that he was still alone.

Unsure if he was relieved or disappointed, he pulled himself up, leaning on the back of the pew for support as he rose. Lamps from the outside offered a little illumination into the church, and Pallone slowly navigated his way up the aisle toward the back of the church through the near darkness. As he reached for the door, he heard a small noise from the front of the church and jumped at the sound.

A man rose from the front pew and started toward him. Pallone's breath quickened, and he considered running out the door and down the path but knew that based on the quick stride of his unknown companion, he wouldn't be able to outrun him.

"Who's there?" he said.

The man didn't answer but continued to move forward.

"I said who's there?"

The man stopped short with his hands clasped behind his back.

Pallone breathed a sigh of relief. "Oh dear Lord, you startled me. I didn't mean to intrude. I was waiting for someone, and I must have fallen asleep."

The man offered a smile but stayed quiet.

"Well, good night then," Pallone said, and as he turned, he felt a heavy blow to the back of his head, which sent a sharp pain through his skull before everything turned black.

❖

Elizabeth stood at the front of the glass turnstile door trying to time the right moment to hop in. Most people were exiting the building for the evening, making it more of a challenge to enter. She made her leap forward but missed her stop when a crowd of employees escaping for the day blocked her in and she had to circle around again before she made it into the building. She approached the imposing gray marble security desk that reminded her of her visit to the corporate offices of the archdiocese; however, this time, she had an appointment.

"May I help you?" asked a stern-faced woman.

"I'm Elizabeth Campbell. I have an appointment to see Bradley Iverson," she said, putting a little emphasis on the word "appointment."

"One moment please," the guard replied and began furiously typing before she asked, "Identification, please."

After Elizabeth completed the security formalities, she was presented a plastic visitor's badge and escorted to a bank of elevators. The elevator came to rest on the twenty-fourth floor, and the doors effortlessly glided open. As soon as she stepped forward, she was greeted by a jovial woman behind a large glass desk. "Good evening, Ms. Campbell, please have a seat. Mr. Iverson will be with you shortly. May I get you something?"

Elizabeth declined the offer but was impressed with the efficiency of the office; even the variety of magazines displayed on the table were up-to-date. Before she could get settled in and catch up on the latest gossip, the phone buzzed and the receptionist rose. "Ms. Campbell, if you will follow me."

The receptionist ushered her into a well-adorned corner office with floor to ceiling windows. Night had fully fallen, and she could see the lights of the city come to life. A well-manicured man stood from behind the desk and came forward to greet her. "Ms. Campbell, it's a pleasure to meet you. Your father speaks of you often. He tells me what great work you do."

Elizabeth opened her eyes wide at the comment.

"You seem surprised?"

"Let's just say that my father and I don't see eye to eye on my career choices."

"Ah yes, he would prefer you to work in the family firm, but let me tell you, he's proud of your accomplishments, nonetheless."

She was awestruck and momentarily rendered speechless. After recovering, she moved along. "Thank you for agreeing to see me on short notice and at the end of the day."

He gestured to a chair. "Please have a seat." He retook his seat and leaned back. "So what's the interest with the old mill?"

"The mill is next to a school that was abandoned around the same time as the mill. I'm actually interested in the school for a case that I'm researching."

"Yes, your father told me."

She gave a small smile and began to wonder what her father hadn't told him. "I was hoping to find out what the mill was doing before it closed down."

"Well, it was a textile mill," he replied.

"But what interest does Spiedel Trust have in a textile mill?"

Iverson crossed his arms over his chest and smiled. "A good question, and one that I was curious about as well when I got your call this morning. So I did a bit of digging." He took a long pause, but she remained still, never breaking eye contact. "You have to understand, my uncle was a very smart man, but also very desperate. Desperate men can do desperate things."

She calmly nodded, effectively disguising the impatience growing inside her.

"Would you like a drink?" he asked.

She clasped her hands together in her lap, and her fingers started to turn white. "No, I'm fine. Thank you."

He rose and moved to a well-stocked bar in the corner and began speaking again as he prepared himself a drink. "My uncle had enough money to buy anything he wanted, anything but his health. As I'm sure you know from your research, he suffered from MS. He was convinced that with enough money, a cure could be found."

"So he established the trust to fund medical research," Elizabeth said to show that she was keeping up with the conversation.

"But my uncle knew little about medical research, so any snake oil peddler that came to the door with his hand out received a grant."

"And the mill?"

"Well," he took a long sip and savored it, "that is interesting." He took a seat and withdrew a manila folder from a drawer and tossed it on the desk in front of her. "There isn't much information on the mill. The money was given to a man named Henry Gesler. He was a doctor or researcher who claimed to be working on a breakthrough. It was Gesler that chose the location. That was where he wanted to work."

She lifted the folder and scanned the information as Iverson continued. "That's all the information I have. The mill closed down. It was bleeding money, and best I know, Gesler disappeared. You can keep that," he said, pointing to the folder.

"Thank you, and I really appreciate your time on this."

He raised his glass in salute and took a sip before he stood. "I'll show you out." He walked beside her and waited for her to gather her things, and they walked side by side to the lobby with his hand on the small of her back, which didn't go unnoticed.

Iverson offered his hand. "It was a pleasure meeting you. Please give your father my regards."

She returned his firm grip. "I will. Thank you again." She retreated into the open elevator and escaped.

Once she reached her car, Elizabeth locked herself in and reviewed the folder. It contained very few documents, including a research paper in medical terminology that she couldn't decipher, but she assumed was the basis of Gesler's work, and a curriculum vitae for Henry Gesler. First thing in the morning, she planned to comb through the CV and check its veracity.

CHAPTER TWENTY-SIX

Elizabeth spent the better part of her early morning in a fruitless search on the Internet for Henry Gesler. The curriculum vitae proclaimed that Gesler earned a medical degree in Vienna, Austria, and spent several years dedicating his life to the research of various bacteria-driven illnesses, which the doctor believed were responsible for much of the world's illnesses, including those traditionally believed to be genetic. It sounded good, but she could neither confirm nor dismiss Dr. Gesler's proclamations in his CV from her Internet research. If Dr. Gesler's claims were true, it went unnoticed in the Internet world.

Frustrated at her lack of progress, she decided to check in with Grace, figuring her morning was already unproductive, so why not call the cranky detective to add to it.

Grace answered the phone on the first ring and growled, "Donovan here."

"My, are you always this charming?" she asked in a singsong voice. She could almost hear Grace grind her teeth.

"What do you need?"

She was unperturbed by Grace's foul mood, accepting it as part of her demeanor. "What did you find out on David Collins?"

"Hold on a sec." She could hear the background noise fade and guessed Grace was moving to a more private location before she came back on the line. "I didn't get much. David was placed at the home that you gave me, but there's no record of anything after that."

"Have you spoken to the foster parents?"

"They're both deceased, but they have a daughter. She owns the house. I tracked her down, and she works at a bar in the same town."

"Are you going to see her?" Elizabeth asked.

Grace blew out a breath. "Yeeesss, and no, you can't come."

"Oh, come on," she whined. "You only have this lead because of me."

Grace remained mute for a moment, then finally spoke. "You're probably going to follow me anyway. For all I know, you're watching me right now."

"You have a coffee stain on your shirt." After a brief silence, Elizabeth laughed. "You looked, didn't you?"

"I'm heading over at four. That's when her shift starts. Meet me at the precinct if you want to come."

"Will do. Thanks." Elizabeth hung up feeling better.

In furtherance of her quest to learn who Henry Gesler was, Elizabeth decided to track down the information on his curriculum vitae the old-fashioned way, and she walked up the cement steps of the central library. The city boasted that its library contained the largest collection of books, documents, and research material in the state, and she was about to test it out. As she entered the front door and walked past metal detectors standing guard at the inside of the door, she was flooded with memories of law school. She shivered at the thought of the countless hours hunched over a stack of books meticulously cross-checking citations for law review. "Never again," she vowed.

She approached a teenager with a slight acne problem standing behind a central desk staring at his phone. She knew that she should be annoyed when he didn't acknowledge her immediately, but she felt for the kid stuck in a library all day. "Excuse me," she said, announcing her presence.

"Can I help you?" the teenager responded with his eyes still fixed on his phone.

"Can you point me in the direction where I can find published papers on medical research?"

"Medical research?" he echoed.

She pulled out a copy of Henry Gesler's curriculum vitae and pointed to the page that listed his professional research publications. "I would like to find these publications or any other information about this man."

The teenager moved to a computer behind the desk and rapidly typed, and after a moment, said, "In aisle forty-seven, you can find a collection of medical journals. The journals are organized by title and then date of publication. It's on your left."

"Thank you." She turned and headed deeper into the library.

The teenager softly called out after her, "Your other left."

After changing course, she started counting up as she passed each aisle until she reached forty-seven. She perused the books and felt overwhelmed and took a deep breath, "Okay, let's start with the first one on the list." She read the title of the first journal and found it on the shelf; it was in alphabetical order as the teenager had promised. Her research from her law review days came in handy, and she soon got the hang of it and selected several bound volumes of journals and dropped them on a table at the end of the aisle, which earned her a few shushes from fellow patrons.

After reviewing several of the journals, she found that Dr. Gesler's CV was fictitious. His name was not credited on any of the research papers he cited as his work; however, the articles she reviewed were based on the subject matter that Gesler discussed in his CV, so he clearly had an intimate knowledge of the research. On a hunch, she started cross-checking the citations on each of the research papers on Gesler's CV and found that each of the papers included a citation to the same unpublished research paper that originated from Germany, but didn't include an author. Gesler claimed to have gone to medical school in Vienna. *Austria, Germany, that's pretty close.*

She inspected the shelves and pulled down several more volumes of journals in an attempt to locate additional information on the German research paper, but with no success. She sat back down and laid her head on the table. "Damn, damn, damn."

Defeated, she stood and groaned at the cramp in her neck and shoulders, then guiltily looked at the stack of books in front of her and debated re-shelving them. She quickly dispensed with that idea and placed the books on a cart labeled "re-shelving," envisioning a certain teenager creating a voodoo doll of her replica when he saw the cart.

❖

Elizabeth headed to the precinct a little early, fearful that Grace might try to leave without her, and dialed her number as she sat in the parking lot. "Are you ready?" she asked before Grace could announce herself on the phone. She was learning a bit from her curt style. A loud knock sounded on her window, causing Elizabeth to jump and drop the phone.

She turned to see Grace next to her car, leaning into her half-rolled-down window. "Scare you?" she asked, pleased with herself.

Elizabeth didn't answer but instead pushed the release for the car lock and then bent to retrieve her phone that fell. She contorted her body trying to dig under her seat and her skirt rode up in the struggle, exposing her thigh. When she finally came back up triumphantly grasping her phone, Grace quickly turned away. Elizabeth popped a piece of gum in her mouth from a stray pack she found hiding under the seat. "Wanna come?"

"What?" Grace quickly asked with a slight edge to her voice.

"Do you want some gum?" Elizabeth annunciated more clearly through the wad of gum.

"No, let's get going," Grace said abruptly and rattled off their intended location.

As they drove, she explained all that she had learned about the mill, the Spiedel Trust, and Henry Gesler. The conversation seemed to help settle Grace, who loosened her arms, which had been tightly folded across her chest. Elizabeth slowed her car as they approached a litter strewn parking lot with a neon sign that was only half illuminated, announcing the "Purring Kitten."

"Is this a bar or a strip club?" she asked, pulling her car into the driveway.

"God help me," Grace mumbled as she pushed open the car door, not waiting for Elizabeth to bring the car to a full stop.

Elizabeth walked a step behind her as they approached the front door. The inside was dimly lit, tables were scattered haphazardly about the room, and a long bar stretched across the wall. The air was filled with a stench of stale cigarettes, even though it was illegal to smoke inside, but somehow Elizabeth thought the patrons paid no mind to that rule.

Two men were perched on stools at the end of the bar nursing their drinks of choice, and she was conscious that they were watching them. Grace walked up to the middle of the bar, and Elizabeth pulled up beside her.

"Hey, little lady," one of the men leaned over and slurred out. "How about you come sit a little closer and keep us company."

Grace opened her mouth, but Elizabeth beat her to it. "I would, but my girlfriend here might get a little jealous." She slung her arm around Grace. "She's strapped and dangerous."

The man looked at them confused. "Just can't tell the dykes nowadays," he said, and the two men picked up their drinks and moved to a table.

Grace paid little attention to the departing men and instead continued to glare at Elizabeth, who still sat with an arm around her shoulder.

"What?" Elizabeth asked, feigning innocence. "I was referring to your gun. What did you think I meant?"

Grace made a show of removing Elizabeth's arm from her shoulder when the bartender approached, cutting off any retort.

"What can I get ya?" she asked, slinging a towel over her shoulder and leaning an arm on the bar.

"Are you Ellen Myers?"

"What's it to you?"

Grace pulled out her badge. "I'm looking into the disappearance of a boy named David Collins. He was a foster child who lived with your parents. He went missing in 1981."

"Well, aren't you a bit slow?" the woman asked in a gravelly voice, clearly a partaker in the bar's indoor smoking.

Grace ignored the remark. "What can you tell me about his disappearance?"

"I don't know if it was a disappearance. They came and took him and—"

"Who came and took him?" Elizabeth interjected.

The bartender looked at her with a slight scowl. "I don't know. The people that brought him there, I guess."

"Where did they take him?"

"I overheard them tell my parents something about moving him to a group home or reform school or something like that."

"Was he having problems, getting into trouble?" Elizabeth asked, just as Grace was about to do the same.

"Nope, just kept to himself."

"So, why did they take him, then?" she asked. Grace had given up trying to take the lead on the questioning.

"How the hell am I supposed to know? You're the government people. Don't you know everything?"

Elizabeth ignored the retort. "Do you remember anything about these people or anything else they said?"

"Nooope," the bartender popped with her lips.

Grace looked to her to see if she was done, and Elizabeth gave her a nod. She tucked her badge back into her jacket. "Well, thank you for your time."

Elizabeth wasted no time getting out of there. "You sure know how to show a girl a good time," she said as they walked to her car.

"You should see what I do for a second date," Grace replied with a straight face.

"Oh my God, did you just make a joke? There may be hope yet."

Elizabeth waited until they were seated in the car before she spoke again. "There's no record of David being placed in a group home, reform school, or anywhere else. His record stopped after he was placed in the foster home."

"It could simply be faulty recordkeeping. We're talking pre-digital age. Paperwork falls through the cracks."

"Or..." she countered, "perhaps children fall through the cracks. Who would notice? He had no family."

"So, what, you think kids were being stolen?" Grace asked doubtfully.

Elizabeth's reply was cut off when Grace's phone rang. She snatched it off of her waist and growled, "Donovan."

At least she doesn't just save her charm for me.

After snapping her phone shut, Grace sat quietly, and Elizabeth waited for her to speak, none too patiently. "Well?"

"Well what?"

"The call," she said. "Who was it?"

"None of your damn business."

She arched her eyebrows in response.

"Not everything is about this case," Grace replied, irritation evident in her voice.

Elizabeth stayed silent and kept her eyes on the road but surreptitiously watched Grace out of the corner of her eye, who sat with her arms crossed and a scowl on her face.

"All right, fine," Grace said. "That was a call from the archdiocese. They need to talk; they said it's urgent. And how the hell did you know?"

"I can read you like a book. So where do they want to meet?"

"Oh no, you're not going."

Elizabeth pulled the car over to the side of the road and turned off the engine. "I hope you enjoy walking."

"You can't be serious," Grace said incredulously. "This is blackmail."

"Technically, no. This is simply me kicking you out of my car. My car, my way," she stated reasonably.

"I swear I've aged since I met you. You know, I woke up with a gray hair the day after we met."

She smiled. "So, where to?"

Grace released a breath and pulled out her phone. "It's at the office of the archdiocese. Hold on. I'll get the address."

Elizabeth started the car and pulled back into traffic. "No need. I know where it is."

"Now, why am I not surprised?"

Grace grabbed the handle of the glass door of the office building but didn't pull it open. She turned to Elizabeth. "I'll do the talking. You stay quiet."

Elizabeth offered a demure smile, and Grace pulled open the door, allowing Elizabeth to enter in front of her. As they approached the imposing security desk, Elizabeth slowed her pace so that Grace could step ahead, pulling out her badge to show to the security officer. Unlike Elizabeth's prior experience, the security officer submissively dialed the archdiocese office and announced their arrival, and Elizabeth looked at Grace's badge still clutched in her hand. *I'm going to have to get me one of those things.*

A middle-aged man dressed in a business suit came down and greeted them. Somehow, Elizabeth expected to see a bishop or a priest or at least a choirboy come down from the archdiocese offices, not a businessman. As they were escorted to the top floor, she thought about it and surmised that the Catholic Church was a well-organized business with the Pope as the CEO.

Elizabeth didn't have an opportunity to carry that thought further as they were greeted by a man wearing a formal black cassock when the elevator door opened. "Detective Donovan, I'm Father Eric Casas, Vicar General for the Archdiocese. We spoke on the phone. Please follow me."

The priest didn't acknowledge Elizabeth in his greeting, so she mutely followed Grace, who in turn followed the priest. They were led to a conference room with a large glossy table and well-padded chairs that swiveled. Elizabeth waited until the vicar general and Grace sat before she selected her seat, which was to the right of Grace and across from the priest. She resisted the urge to turn her chair in a circle to test its swivel power.

"Thank you for coming, Detective. It seems we have another problem."

"What is that?" Grace asked.

"It seems that Bishop Pallone is missing."

"What do you mean by 'missing'?"

"He was last seen yesterday afternoon in the cathedral garden. There's been no sign of him since."

"What can you tell me about him?" Grace asked.

The priest looked thoughtful for a moment. "It was expected that Bishop Pallone would be appointed the archbishop of this archdiocese in light of Cardinal Ryan's passing."

Grace leaned forward on the table. "Bishop Pallone was also poisoned along with the cardinal, is that correct?"

"Yes, but fortunately he didn't consume much of the tainted tea."

"That is fortunate," Elizabeth responded, surprising herself that she said it out loud. Grace gave her a sideways glance, but the vicar general didn't acknowledge her comment.

"Did he see anyone, talk to anyone?" Grace asked.

"There was a note," the priest replied.

"A note?"

"Yes, according to the bishop's personal assistant, on the weekend, the bishop received a note that was left for him in the garden."

"What did this note say?"

"I don't know. According to the assistant, the bishop opened the note in private."

"Is there anything more?"

"Yes, I'm afraid."

Elizabeth sat quietly, more careful to keep her thoughts in her head, but she wanted to jump in and speed up the pace.

"There is money missing," the priest said.

"How much money?" Grace asked cautiously.

"Fifty thousand is unaccounted for. If the bishop hadn't

disappeared, it would have gone unnoticed. He handles much of the finances for the archdiocese. This missing money led us to a deeper investigation into the Church's finances. Although we cannot confirm it yet, as it is a bit early, but…" The vicar general paused and blew out a breath. He grabbed the pitcher of water from the center of the table and poured a glass. He took several sips before setting the glass down.

Grace remained motionless, her face void of any expression; Elizabeth, on the other hand, did everything she could not to fidget.

After long last, the vicar general resumed speaking. "It seems we may be short another one hundred thousand. It would have gone missing within the last few months."

Grace pulled out a small notebook and began writing. "Is there anything else?"

"I think that covers it."

Grace instructed the vicar general to send over the documents relating to the missing money as well as the name of the bishop's assistant. He nodded, and as quickly as he escorted them in, he escorted them out.

Elizabeth waited until they were outside the building before she spoke. "You think blackmail?"

"Why would you say that?" Grace asked while keeping a brisk pace toward the car.

Elizabeth had to do a double step to keep up. "Well, you think being kicked out of my car is blackmail, so why not this? Think about it, a secret note, missing money. Someone was blackmailing the bishop. Maybe this time he wanted a bigger payoff than the bishop could give."

"So then this has nothing to do with your case?"

"Of course it does."

Grace stopped and threw up her hands. "Okay, I give. How?"

Elizabeth stopped even with Grace and faced her. "I think that the bishop poisoned the cardinal."

"This is starting to sound like Clue," Grace said.

"The bishop had everything to gain from his death. He would be the top dog of the archdiocese. Maybe the cardinal found out about the missing money."

Grace nodded in silent agreement that the theory was plausible. "But I don't see how this links to your case?"

Elizabeth wondered how the serial killer case suddenly became her case. "Maybe it doesn't. Maybe it's all a coincidence, but Sullivan's body was left in the same garden where the bishop was last seen. The archdiocese owned the school. I just think you should keep an open mind."

Grace smiled. "I have been forced to keep an open mind since the moment I met you."

CHAPTER TWENTY-SEVEN

Elizabeth pointed her car in the direction of the clinic and navigated the morning traffic on autopilot. After she parked her car in her usual spot, she realized that her routine of the last four and a half years would soon be no more. As she walked through the front door, a sense of dread washed over her. The clinic was once a place where she felt a sense of pride and accomplishment; now, it felt oppressive. She decided that there was no need to stretch out the inevitable another day and spent her morning completing case notes and packing up the files. She had already completed all that she could in the short time that she was given, and the rest would be Dan's burden. Before she headed back out the door, she stopped at Dan's office and knocked on the door frame. Dan momentarily looked surprised to see her, but quickly covered it with a neutral look of indifference. He gestured her in, and she stepped forward just short of the seat, grasping her hands on the back.

"Just wanted to let you know that the files are completed. I finished what I could. For the rest, I left detailed notes. They're stacked in order in my office. I don't see any need to drag this out to tomorrow. I'll come by on the weekend when it's quieter to clear out my personal stuff, if that's okay with you."

"That's fine."

She stared quietly for a moment, waiting to see if he had anything more to say, but when nothing came, she said, "I guess this is it, then." With that, she turned and walked out of Dan's office and out the front door of the clinic.

She numbly began the journey to her car when she was stopped by someone calling her name from behind her and turned to see Amy jogging toward her. She came to a halt in front of Elizabeth and pulled her into a hug.

"I'm going to miss you. It won't be the same."

Elizabeth held back tears. "Thank you," was all she could choke out.

Amy thrust a paper into Elizabeth's hand. "Here is my address and number. You better keep in touch or I'll hunt you down."

Elizabeth knew she would make good on her threat. She wrapped her fingers around the paper and simply nodded; her voice failed her.

"Oh, and here, this came for you. Thought you would want it." Amy handed over an envelope, and she mindlessly accepted it and looked at Amy through blurry eyes. "Thank you, Amy, for everything."

Amy gave her another hug and quickly turned and walked back. Elizabeth suspected that her eyes were blurry too.

When she returned to her car, she just sat. *Now what?* Unsure where to go or what to do, she closed her eyes and leaned her head back, and several moments later, snorted and jerked her head forward. She looked around to see if anyone had seen her fall asleep and, more importantly, her less-than-graceful way of waking up. Convinced she was alone, she glanced around her car to get her bearings and spotted the letter Amy gave her.

She read the lettering on the envelope, and when the words *Executive Office for Immigration Review* came into focus, she ripped it open. She quickly read the pages and let out a squeal. Elizabeth started her car and quickly made her way to Father Parker's church.

She wasted little time parking and making her way inside and ran down the center aisle with her bag banging against her side, not caring if it was proper decorum to run in a church. As she bounded through the side door, she nearly bowled over Rosa, who was just on the other side. Elizabeth grabbed her by the shoulders, and Rosa began to tremble.

"What is it?" Rosa asked.

"The court reopened your asylum case." Elizabeth couldn't contain her excitement. "The deportation order has been lifted. We have a chance now."

Rosa leaned back against the wall, sank to the ground, and rested her forehead on her knees and wept openly. Elizabeth sank down beside her, wrapped an arm around her, and let her cry. She knew these weren't tears of sorrow. Rosa let years of grief and anxiety flow out of her.

Father Parker came out of his office. He sat on the floor directly in front of Rosa and put his hand on the top of her head as though blessing her and turned questioning eyes on Elizabeth.

"This is a good thing," Elizabeth said. She explained the court's order, and Father Parker patted her on the hand.

"Very good work, Elizabeth."

She absorbed the praise from the father and reveled in it for a moment.

Mary soon joined them and sat on the floor. Father Parker filled her in, and Mary leaned over and hugged Rosa, who still had tears streaming down her cheeks.

Elizabeth looked around the misfit group sitting in a circle on the floor that fate or other divine force brought together and reminisced about nestling around a fire at summer camp. Everyone started out strangers, but went home family.

"All we need are marshmallows," she said.

Father Parker cocked his head but didn't say anything.

"Did I say that out loud?"

"Yes, and I don't bother asking anymore. I am way past that," he responded.

"Good, because it would be too hard to explain."

Within a few minutes, they dispersed, with Rosa and Mary walking arm in arm toward the kitchen. Elizabeth followed Father Parker to his office.

"So how goes the Raymond Miller case?" he asked.

She brought him up to date as he listened with rapt attention, sitting quietly and not interrupting. Elizabeth realized she could use some of his skills.

When she finished, Father Parker asked, "So now what do we do?"

"We? I thought I had lost you after our visit to the social services office."

"True, I didn't favor your scheme or my role in it, but I do realize the greater importance of what you're doing. The information you obtained will only help Mr. Collins, and possibly Raymond."

Father Parker never ceased to amaze her. He was the most reasonable and patient person she knew and her counterbalance. As she sat lost in thought, the father broke in, "So what's the next step, Sherlock?"

She expelled a breath. "I'm not really sure. I'd like to track down the German research paper. I have a gut feeling there's something there."

"So then, where do we find this paper?"

"The citations in the articles note that a copy of the paper is at the Science and Technology University."

Father Parker opened a book resting on his desk and bowed his head, trailing his finger across the page. "How about tomorrow morning?"

She cocked her head and smiled.

"What?"

"Nothing. Tomorrow it is. I'll pick you up around nine."

She started for the door, but stopped and turned. "Thank you."

Father Parker smiled.

As Elizabeth walked to her car, she realized that without a job, she had no place to be. *Well, let's go see what Mom and Raymond are up to.*

Elizabeth found her mother and Raymond in the library huddled behind a computer screen laughing uncontrollably. Charlie, her cat, or at least she thought it was her cat, was curled into a ball at the corner of the desk wearing a sweater. Elizabeth nudged the cat. "Seriously, a sweater? Your friends would so be laughing at you back home." Charlie ignored her and rolled over.

Unable to resist, she joined Raymond and her mother behind the desk, and a cat in a Santa hat was dancing across the screen. Elizabeth looked at the two of them with tears in their eyes hysterical over the asinine sight and wondered which one was the child. Something about it made Elizabeth start laughing with them or possibly at them; either way, it was cathartic, and for that, she was grateful.

❖

Dressed in his dark cloak, Salvator dragged a wrapped lump up the steps as he kicked at a rat that scurried across the cement trying to keep up with him. The curious rat refused to be dissuaded and remained at his side and watched as a naked body was revealed. With effort, Salvator lifted the motionless body and latched the first arm to the metal grate followed by the second. The body sagged as the legs were fastened. Last, the head was raised and tied to the grate across the forehead. The lifeless eyes stared ahead as though mesmerized by an imaginary sight. His mouth hung agape. The skin and hair on the left side of his head hung down in a bloody clump. A pool of blood began forming below.

Satisfied with his display, Salvator stepped back and watched as the rat crept forward. It cautiously approached the hanging flesh, drawn by the sticky substance that oozed and dripped from the body, and latched its razor teeth on a bloodied toe. He smiled at the sight and turned and silently slipped back into the night.

CHAPTER TWENTY-EIGHT

Elizabeth shielded her eyes from the morning sun as she and Father Parker approached the imposing stone building with carved columns flanking the sides of a large set of red doors. Father Parker pulled open the door that stood in stark contrast to the otherwise bleak building. Once inside, Elizabeth's eyes were drawn upward to the angels flying above her head. The ornate painting filled the top of the cavernous room.

"Let's find the reference desk," she whispered, leading the way, and delved into the room in search of the desk. After five minutes of weaving through bookshelves and occasional tables, she stopped, and Father Parker ran into the back of her.

"Really? We're back to this?" she said with her hands on her hips.

"Well, you should have brake lights or beeping sounds or something."

Father Parker waited a beat before he spoke again. "I think we're lost."

"We're in a library. We can't be lost," she said, exasperated, and began walking again.

"Well, use your flare gun."

Elizabeth stopped and turned. "A flare gun?"

"You pack bolt cutters and crowbars, so why not a flare gun, oh mighty Boy Scout? Shouldn't you always be prepared?"

She turned without a word and continued on as Father Parker obediently followed, until they passed the same bookshelf again.

"I do hate to state the obvious, but I believe we're going in circles, oh wise pathfinder."

"You're not helping," she said.

"Oh wait, I see land! Oh no, it's just a mirage."

"What are you two doing?"

Elizabeth turned to find a stocky woman approaching, who wore her graying hair back in a severe bun and a solid gray dress to match. A frown was etched on her face.

"I'm sorry. We're lost. We were looking for the reference desk," Elizabeth answered meekly, avoiding eye contact as though addressing the alpha of the pack.

"It's by the front door," the woman said sharply. "Follow me." She clearly had no issue with disciplining a priest.

Once at the desk, Elizabeth looked to her right and saw the front door. They had walked right past the reference desk when they entered, and she wondered how she could lead them out of a forest at night but get them lost in a fully lit library.

The stern woman broke Elizabeth from her musing. "State your business."

Elizabeth looked to Father Parker, who stood next to her mutely, clearly willing to let her handle the woman, and then she pulled out one of the articles and pointed to the highlighted citation to the unpublished paper. "We're looking for this paper."

The woman took the paper from her none too gently and pulled on her glasses that were hanging on a chain around her neck. After reviewing the citation, she removed her glasses and squinted at Elizabeth.

"Why, may I ask, do you need to see this document?"

"Well, uh, Father here has sort of a bucket list. Viewing this document is next in line. Can't say it would be on my list, but then again he has a fetish for flare guns," she rambled.

The woman cut her off. "Enough. The document is in the archive. It cannot be removed from the room. I will take you to it." Elizabeth didn't doubt that the woman would stay and watch as well.

After being led to a cramped room with a wooden table in the center and filing cabinets lining the circumference of the room, Elizabeth and Father Parker stood in the corner, motionless and afraid to move and offend the temperamental librarian. As the woman searched through a filing cabinet on the opposite side of the room, her movements became more frantic.

"It's not here."

Elizabeth just stared at her. The woman opened additional drawers, riffling through them, until she resigned herself to the absence of the document.

"It's gone. It never should have left this room. None of these documents should ever leave this room."

Unsure of how to console the woman in her time of grief and afraid that the woman's head might start to spin around, Elizabeth slowly backed out of the room and thanked the woman for her time.

"That was creepy. At least now I can cross off getting lost in the library from my bucket list," Father Parker said once they cleared the library.

"Oh, he speaks."

"What?"

"You were no help in there."

"I'm not afraid to admit it. She scared me."

"So now you're afraid of rats and librarians." Elizabeth shook her head and started walking in search of the campus directory.

"So what's the plan now?" he asked, walking beside her.

"The librarian isn't very trusting of strangers. Only someone she knew would have been left alone and could have taken the paper out of there."

"You have an idea who?"

She stopped and pulled out the same research article that she showed the librarian. "Him," she said, pointing to one of the names credited for the research. "Horace Pratt. He was a graduate student and is now a professor at this very university. Me thinks he had motive. He used the unpublished paper in his article, and he had opportunity."

"Very wise deduction."

As they found their way to Professor Pratt's office, Father Parker only offered one quip on the route, which Elizabeth chose to ignore. "Do you think we should mark the trees to help find our way back?"

Elizabeth approached the professor's door, and a corkboard on the wall provided a list of assignment due dates and office hours.

"I guess we'll have to come back," the father said.

"Why?"

"We missed his office hours."

"Right," she drew out.

Father Parker started to walk away, but she stayed put and firmly knocked on the door. The father quickly turned and threw his arms in the air in resignation.

"Come in."

She opened the door and entered with Father Parker right behind her. Professor Pratt was lounging back in his chair, his short-sleeved shirt half unbuttoned, exposing a stark white undershirt, and he sat upright when he saw them. The professor had a thin, wiry frame with dark hair carefully slicked back, and prominently displayed on his chest was the proverbial plastic pocket protector.

"I thought you were someone else. Who are you?" the professor asked in an annoyed tone.

"I'm Elizabeth Campbell. This is Father Parker. We were hoping to talk to you about an article you helped write."

The professor then registered the father's presence and quickly began buttoning his shirt, but stopped midway to grasp the article that Elizabeth was holding out. "Yes, well, I don't have much time. I have an early lunch engagement."

"We won't take much of your time. What we're interested in is this citation." She came around the desk, flipped through the pages, and pointed to the highlighted section.

The professor gestured for her and the father to have a seat as he looked at the page.

After taking a seat, she resumed. "You see, we just came from the library, and it seems that the paper is missing. The librarian was quite upset, as you can imagine."

The professor's pronounced Adam's apple moved as he swallowed. "Ms. Hatchet?" he asked.

She wondered if that was the librarian's real name or one he bestowed upon her; either way, it fit. "Yes, Ms. Hatchet was terribly upset." She fought the urge to speak with a British accent.

"Does she know who took it?" he stuttered. Elizabeth didn't blame him for stuttering. She wouldn't want to face the wrath of Ms. Hatchet coming down on her.

"No, she doesn't know...yet." She smiled.

The professor cradled his head in his hands. "I knew it was only a matter of time. I've had it for nearly a year. I needed it for my newest research project, but she was so..." He searched for a word.

"Dominating. Scary," Elizabeth and Father Parker offered respectively.

"Well, I was looking for 'protective.' Anyway, I never got the opportunity to put it back." Professor Pratt focused back in on them. "What do you want?"

"Just some information. The citation, all the citations to this paper, in fact, do not include the author's name. Who wrote it?"

"Heinrich Geizler," the professor answered and stood to retrieve the German research paper, which he placed in front of her.

Elizabeth flipped through the paper, but it was meaningless to her in German. "I don't read German."

The professor removed the paper from her hands and laid it on the desk in front of him, smoothing the pages down with his hands as though she had offended the document. "I'm fluent in German. My mother is German," the professor boasted. "Heinrich Geizler's work was quite impressive."

Elizabeth noted the similarities of the names, Heinrich Geizler and Henry Gesler. "What can you tell me about Heinrich Geizler?"

Professor Pratt released a breath and started in on a lengthy and technical explanation beyond Elizabeth's and Father Parker's understanding, and after several moments, the professor looked at them and realized that he had lost them. "In simple terms, Geizler's theory was that the body could be trained to fight and destroy malformed or defective cells at their inception before the cells developed and multiplied, thereby eradicating diseases before they start."

"How would this work?" Elizabeth asked.

"Through a series of inoculations, something like a smallpox or measles vaccination. Geizler's theory was that a synthetic gene code or DNA for an antigen of a harmful substance could be introduced into the body and some of the cells would take up this DNA. The synthetic DNA in turn would instruct those cells to make antigen molecules. Essentially, the body would be creating its own vaccine by creating its own antigens in response."

"So basically it's a vaccination?" she said, unimpressed.

"In oversimplified terms, yes."

"Maybe I'm missing it, but what's so special about that?"

"With traditional vaccines, the actual virus is introduced into the body, although the virus has been weakened or killed. However, there is a risk of infecting the body with the disease. When you're talking about diseases such as HIV or cancer, introducing the virus or cancerous cells into the body can be very dangerous, thus making vaccinations very difficult."

She nodded in understanding, and the professor continued. "With a synthetic vaccine, there is no danger of causing the disease because there is no microbe of the cell, only synthetic copies of the genes, but it's enough for the body to recognize it when it sees the real thing and create an immune response. This whole theory of synthetic vaccines was revolutionary. At that time, there was no talk of stem cells, and even vaccinations were at the early stage."

"So why wasn't his work published?"

"His work was never completed."

"Why not?" Elizabeth asked.

"Geizler crossed the boundaries of ethics. It was discovered that he was testing on human subjects, children."

Elizabeth shook her head in disapproval.

"You see, this was Germany in the early fifties. The physical scars of World War Two were still very evident; diseases were common. Many people were destitute and struggling. Medical care was out of reach for many in the poorer class. Medical testing without knowledge or consent on the poor, incarcerated, and mentally disabled was not an uncommon thing. Even here, the polio vaccine was being tested on mentally disabled children in New York in the early fifties. Geizler offered poor families what they believed to be medical care and vaccinations."

"But he wasn't," Father Parker stated bitterly, which surprised Elizabeth.

"No, he wasn't," the professor responded. "He was inoculating the children with his serum. They were his test subjects."

"Why children?" she asked.

"According to Geizler's theory, these synthetic vaccinations were most effective in the young before the immune system became more developed. A strong immune system could reject or fight the synthetically created DNA as it would any foreign bacteria, and not allow the body's cells to take up the DNA."

"So what became of Geizler's work?" she asked.

"The children began to get sick and eventually died. Geizler was once a renowned medical researcher credited with identifying and isolating bacteria in the bloodstream of animals in Europe. However, when the word spread that Dr. Geizler's test subjects were no longer animals, but children, and these children became ill and died, the scientific community turned its back on him. He was ostracized from the European medical community. This forced him to leave Germany, and he went to El Salvador."

"El Salvador?" she asked.

"Yes, San Salvador, the capital city, I believe. He continued his work there. There was less scrutiny. He believed if he could finish his work, prove his theory, he would be vindicated. This paper," the professor pointed to the document in front of him, "was a culmination of his work in Germany and El Salvador."

"The children in El Salvador? How did he get the children?" Father Parker asked, clearly concerned.

"I don't know," Professor Pratt answered.

"I think I do," Elizabeth responded, but offered no more explanation. "He didn't finish his work in El Salvador, did he?"

"No. As in Germany, the children started to die. The government finally caught on and put a stop to it."

"Why didn't anyone put a stop to him, not just his work?" Father Parker barked.

"I don't know," the professor responded meekly.

"I'm sorry. I didn't mean to raise my voice. I just find this upsetting."

Professor Pratt offered an uncomfortable smile.

"So what happened after El Salvador?" she asked.

"I don't know. He seemed to have dropped out. I assume he went back to Europe."

"Just curious, how did the school get Dr. Geizler's paper, if it wasn't published?" Elizabeth asked.

"No reputable journal would publish his work, but not for the lack of trying. Geizler sent out copies of the paper to several medical and scientific journals in Europe, North America, and Asia. Not one was interested. He had crossed the line. The university landed a copy from a former professor. He wasn't a scientist, but he collected rare and unusual manuscripts and other documents. When he passed, he bequeathed his entire collection to the school, and this was in it."

Before Elizabeth could ask her next question, the office door was pushed ajar, and a bare leg was extended through the opening. She and the father froze as the rest of the woman's body came through the door with cleavage spilling out of the open blouse. When the woman registered the presence of Elizabeth and Father Parker, she pulled her shirt closed and began stuttering nonsensical words before bounding out the door.

Elizabeth turned to the professor, who had his face buried in his hands. "Your early lunch engagement?"

"Not anymore," responded the professor.

Elizabeth quickly packed her belongings, expressed her gratitude, and exited. The father was one step ahead of her and was already out the door. Through their expedient departure, the professor remained mute and kept his eyes trained on the desk in front of him.

"Well, that was, um, different," she said as they walked down the hall.

The father didn't respond, and she assumed he was hoping to burn it from his brain.

"So what do you think?"

"It's not my place to judge. They're consenting adults."

"Not that!" she said. "About Heinrich Geizler?"

"Oh yes, of course."

"It's obvious that Geizler and Gesler are the same person. Geizler got booted out of El Salvador and set up shop here. I think I know why."

As they passed a bench in the courtyard, Father Parker took a seat and asked absently, "Why?"

"When I was visiting Father Samuel Rossi's church, in the office, there were photos on the wall. That's where I saw him posed in front of the school gate."

The father stared at her, providing his undivided attention.

"There was also an earlier photo of Father Rossi in front of an orphanage in San Salvador."

The connection visibly clicked on Father Parker's face. "So Father Rossi and Gesler or Geizler knew each other. Geizler followed Rossi here, and Father Rossi let him use the school. But why?"

"That I don't know."

Elizabeth sat in her car and pulled her phone from her bag and realized that she had forgotten to take it off silence mode when she visited the university library, and her phone urgently announced that she had several missed calls, all from Grace. Instead of listening to her voice mails, she opted to call and speak to her.

"Where the hell have you been?" Grace asked as soon as she answered the phone.

Elizabeth considered hanging up just to piss her off even more, but decided it was too juvenile. "I was at the university library, but hell is a close second."

"The bishop is dead. His body was left hanging on the metal grate outside the back door of city hall. It's the same as the others. He had the three triangles, just like the rest."

Elizabeth digested the information. "Where can we meet? We need to compare notes."

After agreeing to meet at a diner near the police station, Elizabeth sat thoughtfully, processing the wealth of information she had received that morning. Father Parker sat quietly in the passenger seat, and she momentarily forgot he was there. Finally registering his presence, she filled him in on the few details she learned and offered to bring him along.

"I'm sorry. I have to get back. I have a Mass to prepare for this evening."

"Oh that's right, you have a job."

She couldn't imagine Father Parker in a sermon or preaching. Although he wore the clothes, she had long stopped seeing him as a priest.

"Maybe I'll catch one of your shows sometime," she said.

"Maybe you should."

❖

Grace sat impatiently in the booth and stared down Elizabeth as she approached. "You're late."

"Sorry," was all Elizabeth offered. She decided not to tell her about Father Parker when the father declined to be a part of the meeting.

Grace wasn't able to provide much more detail than what she had already given on the phone. "So how does this fit?"

"The archdiocese owned the school, and there might be a deeper link between the bishop and the school, but I think there's something else."

Grace raised her hands in a questioning gesture. "What?"

"Sullivan's body was left in the cathedral garden. Then the bishop is dead."

Grace leaned her head on her closed fist. "Yeah, so?"

"It's a pattern. The killer is telling us who is next. He left Sullivan's body at the bishop's doorstep, and the next victim was the bishop. Now he leaves the bishop's body on the city hall doorstep."

Grace cocked her head. "So you think the next victim is who?"

"The mayor," Elizabeth responded without missing a beat.

"The mayor? How could that—" She cut herself off before she

dismissed Elizabeth's theory as absurd and pushed herself back against the seat.

"What is it?"

"Father Samuel Rossi's body was in the garden."

"Right, I remember," Elizabeth said. "What's the connection?"

"Sullivan lived in the building next to the garden."

Elizabeth blew out a breath. "So, the killer has been leading us all along. I think going back to the first killing. He led us to the school. Now he's leading us to the players. He wants us to put it together."

Grace absorbed the information. "So, why do you think the mayor's next?"

"Mayor Reynosa warned me off the Raymond Miller case."

"The mayor has protection. How could the killer kidnap him and carve him up?"

"He got the bishop, didn't he?"

Grace had to give her that one. "This could be a political nightmare. I can't just walk up to the mayor and say, 'Hey, I think you're next on the list of the serial killer. Do you mind not talking to strangers?'"

"If you say nothing and something happens, then what?"

"Shit!" Grace ran her hands through her hair in frustration.

CHAPTER TWENTY-NINE

The mayor will see you now." A conservatively dressed woman approached Grace. She rose and straightened her jacket as she followed the woman into the office. She noted a man with a crooked bow tie sitting at a desk, who kept his eyes to the floor as she passed, looking like a scolded puppy.

"Detective, please have a seat." The mayor remained seated and gestured to the chair across his desk. "What can I do for our city's finest?"

"Thank you for taking the time to see me, sir. I'm investigating the murder of Bishop Pallone."

"That is a travesty. What kind of monster would kill a man of God?"

"That's what I'm trying to find out, sir. I was hoping to ask you a few questions."

"I'm not sure what help I will be."

"Well, sir, there's a possibility that the killer may be forming a pattern, announcing his next victim."

"How so?"

Grace went through Elizabeth's theory, but wisely left her name out during the explanation of the placement of the bodies of Father Rossi, Sullivan, and the bishop.

The mayor turned his chair sideways, so that he could see out the window, and Grace only had a view of his profile. "So you believe that the next victim is who exactly?"

"You, sir."

He turned back to face her and raised his eyebrows. "Me? Why me?"

"That's what I'm trying to figure out, sir, your connection to all of this. Did you know the other victims?"

Mayor Reynosa leaned forward and steepled his hands on the desk. "A man is left dead on the doorstep of city hall, and you think that is a sign that I'm the next victim? Do you know how many people work in this building? How do you know this monster's message isn't a message of anti-establishment, whether it's a church or a city?"

It wasn't lost on Grace that the mayor didn't answer her question. "Yes, sir, but we must look at all possibilities. Sir, where did you go to high school?"

"How is that relevant?" the mayor asked, clearly annoyed.

Before Grace could respond, the man that was seated outside entered, urgently announcing the mayor's next meeting. Offering his apologies, the mayor rose and walked her to the door with a request that she keep him posted of any developments personally.

Elizabeth stood in front of the old mill building as Grace used her bolt cutters to break the lock. She was surprised when Grace called and said that she wanted to search the mill. She would rather have broken in with Father Parker because she would have more freedom to do as she wanted, but didn't hesitate when Grace made the offer.

"So this is what it feels like to enter a building with a warrant," Elizabeth teased as she watched the now defunct lock and chain fall to the ground. "It's a bit anticlimactic."

Grace didn't respond, but instead jerked opened one of the double doors, and the hinges squealed in protest as evidence of the years that the building stood abandoned. Elizabeth retrieved her bolt cutters from the ground, hefted her backpack on her shoulder, and entered, while Grace hesitated at the entryway. The building was an open room with iron beams crisscrossing the high ceiling. Large windows that ringed the walls were boarded up; however, a series of smaller windows near the top of the room were left uncovered. Dust particles seemed to effortlessly float on the light beams that streamed through the dirty and cracked glass, making a checkered pattern on the cement floor.

Other than a thick layer of dust that coated the floor, along with a few discarded boxes and newspaper refuse, the room appeared vacant. There was no furniture, machinery, or other evidence that this was once a working mill.

"This place has been cleared out," Elizabeth said.

Grace remained near the door looking up, taking in the structure of the windows and ceiling. In response to Elizabeth's voice, she moved forward and began inspecting the interior of the building.

Elizabeth circled the inside and kicked the few remaining boxes that proved to be empty and picked up one of the discarded newspapers dated July 1982. "I'd say this place has been vacant for a while. It looks like they cleared it out around the same time the school closed."

When she didn't respond, she turned to find Grace standing in the far corner staring at the ground. "What is it?" Elizabeth asked, approaching her.

Grace didn't answer, but instead crouched down to stare at a wooden trap door in the floor. "It looks like a cellar door," Elizabeth said. She reached over her and yanked on the frayed rope, and the door gave way to reveal a set of wooden steps. She dropped her backpack, removed her flashlight, and started down the steps, which led directly into a dirt tunnel, and she could smell the dank earth around her. The tunnel was smaller and more crudely formed.

"I think this tunnel was more recently dug, probably to join up with the other tunnel at the school," she said and was startled to find Grace standing directly behind her. Elizabeth found a sense of comfort in her close proximity and moved forward following the narrow tunnel, its shape or size never changing, which affirmed her belief that it was a fairly recent addition, more hastily constructed. It appeared that it was built for the sole purpose of acting as a passageway.

After nearly fifty yards, it came to an abrupt end, and a large mound of earth blocked her way. "This must be the cave-in I saw on the other side." Grace remained silent, but Elizabeth could hear her soft breathing. She knew Grace was uncomfortable in confined spaces.

Elizabeth shined her light through the small cavern, assuring herself that there was no other way through, and then ran her palm over the packed dirt that blocked the egress to the remainder of the tunnel. The dirt was cool and dry, unlike the moist earth wall on the other end. With nowhere else to go, she started to turn, but stumbled when she stepped on a loose rock. Grace reached out to catch her and wrapped her arm around Elizabeth's waist to steady her. Elizabeth allowed herself to fall into the embrace, closing her eyes, and for a short moment, relished the warmth that traveled through her before Grace released her hold.

"Are you all right?" Grace asked with true concern.

"Yes," Elizabeth responded in barely more than a whisper. "My foot just got caught up. Thank you."

The conversation suddenly strained between them.

"So, umm, I guess, we should head back up," Grace suggested.

Elizabeth turned to exit the tunnel with a sudden sense of urgency, while Grace lingered behind for a moment.

Carrying the recent imprint of Grace's warmth on her body, Elizabeth quickly ascended the stairs, snatched up her backpack, and walked toward the center of the vacated room, craving the open space to clear her suddenly cluttered thoughts. With a need to focus her mind elsewhere, she turned in a slow circle, taking in the large room once again, training her eyes to take in the finer details of the construction.

After several moments, Grace approached. "So, ready to head out?"

"Door," Elizabeth exclaimed.

"I closed it," Grace said, gesturing to the wooden door in the floor.

"No, that's a door." She pointed to a far wall and moved to it. She could hear Grace's footsteps following behind her and knew that if she made an unexpected stop, she would probably run into the back of her. As tempting as it was, she stayed on course and walked to the door. "See, it's flush with the wall."

Grace ran her hand over the door and came to a small metal latch that popped out when she pressed in. The latch served as a handle, and she pushed down on it, but the door didn't move. After a few more attempts, she sighed in defeat. "Damn, it's stuck or something."

"Let me try." Elizabeth pulled up on the latch, the lock released, and she slid the door open. Before Grace could ask, she responded, "Always strive for up," and walked into the windowless room.

The stark room with white walls and a white tile floor stood bare but for a single light that hung in the center of the room and a small white built-in counter against the far wall. Elizabeth moved to the counter and opened the drawers and found them all empty. The room was left much tidier than the rest of the mill.

"It looks like they spent more time cleaning up in here," Grace said.

"This was Geizler's room."

They both remained still. Elizabeth looked up and watched a spider creep along near the top of the wall above the counter, toward an air-conditioning vent. The color of the spider stood in contrast to the bleak room, and its movement seemed jarring in the suffocating stillness. It was as though the spider wouldn't be defined by its surroundings. She carefully observed the spider's actions as it circled around the vent cover looking for entry. After traveling the perimeter of the vent cover, the spider victoriously found its entrance at the top through the upward-pointing slats. She didn't begrudge the spider for wanting to leave the white room. She felt the same need to escape it.

Feeling the loss of the spider, she turned to Grace. "Let's go. There's nothing here."

Grace followed her out of the room and slid the door closed behind her. Elizabeth didn't wait for her and exited out of the mill. Her body felt much heavier than when she first entered. The white room burdened her.

Grace meticulously closed the outside mill doors and wrapped the chain through the door handles to give the appearance that the building hadn't been disturbed. Although Elizabeth glanced at her as she walked to Grace's government-issued car, her mind paid little attention to what she was doing. She yanked open the passenger door and tossed her backpack into the backseat before climbing in. She was slightly startled to find that Grace had already reached the car and was settling in behind the wheel.

Before Elizabeth could put on her seat belt, Grace started the ignition and put the car into reverse, and Elizabeth was assaulted by air blasting through the car vent, forcing her to let go of the seat belt to push the vent up. Elizabeth yanked again on the seat belt to stretch it across her body, but released it and let the buckle slap against the top of the seat when it retracted.

"Stop the car," she commanded.

"What?" Grace asked without looking at her.

"We have to go back," she said as she opened the car door while the car was still going in reverse.

Grace hit the brakes, and Elizabeth jumped out and slammed the car door shut. She opened the back door, pulled out her backpack, and trotted back to the mill door, then unceremoniously pulled off the broken chain. Grace was behind her and helped pull open the door.

"What are you doing?" she asked as she followed Elizabeth, trying to keep up.

Elizabeth stayed focused on her thoughts and remained silent. She pulled open the sliding door and stepped in.

"Are you going to tell me what we are doing?"

Elizabeth pointed up to the air-conditioning vent. "See the cover?"

Grace looked up. "Yeah, so?"

"It's upside down."

Grace stared at her, and Elizabeth blew out a breath. "See the slats on the vent cover? They should be pointing down, so that the air blows down into the room. The way the cover is put on, the slats are pointing up, blowing the air to the ceiling." She watched Grace, waiting for it to sink in.

"You think someone took the cover off and put it back on upside down?"

"Exactly. The question is why?"

"I guess this is where one of us crawls up there and takes off the cover?" Grace asked.

"Considering I'm wearing a skirt and you're not, you're the better candidate."

Grace trailed her eyes down Elizabeth's skirt. "Fine, I'll go up."

Elizabeth dug into her backpack and pulled out a screwdriver.

"Of course you walk around with a screwdriver. You walk around with bolt cutters, why not a screwdriver?" She spoke more to herself than to Elizabeth as she hopped onto the counter and reached down for the screwdriver.

She released the hold the four screws had on the cover and passed them down to Elizabeth along with the cover and screwdriver. She reached into the vent. "I got something here." She pulled her arm back out, holding an object wrapped in a plastic bag, and passed it down to Elizabeth, who handed her a flashlight in exchange.

"Make sure there's nothing else in there."

Grace dutifully scanned the inside of the vent with the light. "That's it. Nothing else here." Just as she handed the light back and hopped down, she screeched and swatted at her arm. A spider fell to the floor and started scurrying away, and she moved to step on it.

"Don't!" Elizabeth scolded. "Leave it be."

"You're defending a spider. Why does that not surprise me?"

Grace quickly forgot about the spider as Elizabeth opened the clear plastic bag and pulled out a light brown leather book. The book was stuffed full of papers, and a thin rope was tied around it to keep its contents from spilling out. The plastic bag kept the book well preserved.

Elizabeth reached for the thin rope that was tied into a neat bow.

"No, not here," Grace said. "Let's get out of here first."

Elizabeth clutched the book to her chest, making her way once again back outside the mill. Grace again pulled the mill door closed and began the task of replacing the chain.

"You know, we should dig up under the tree." Grace jumped at her voice, clearly unaware that Elizabeth was standing behind her.

"What?" she asked without taking her eyes off the chain.

"The lovers' tree behind the school. You should get a warrant to dig that up. You can tell them what we found here," Elizabeth stated, watching Grace's hand movements slow.

Grace didn't look at her.

"Oh my God, you really didn't have a warrant to go in there. We broke in," Elizabeth exclaimed. "There's hope for you yet."

Grace finally completed fiddling with the chain and looked at her. "No, I didn't have a warrant. Trust me, no one but you and me are interested in finding out about this case. The mayor, my supervisor, they all want this to go away."

Elizabeth now understood her earlier hesitation to enter the mill and her compulsive disorder to meticulously replace the chain. Grace's defiance of her superiors surprised her; maybe she had misjudged her.

❖

Grace and Elizabeth sat in the parking lot of Starbucks, each gripping their cups of expensive coffee and staring down at the book that rested in Elizabeth's lap.

"We shouldn't open it. I should put it back in the bag, take it to the station, and log the book into evidence," Grace said.

"What good will that do? It's fruit of the poisonous tree. You didn't have a warrant to go into the mill, so the seizure of this book was illegal. It's not admissible. If you turn it in, we will probably never see it again. You said yourself that no one wants this case investigated. It's much more useful to us if we open it." Elizabeth suspected that Grace knew all this, but needed to hear her say it.

When Grace offered no further protest, Elizabeth set her cup in the center holder and slowly and carefully untied the rope bow as though cutting the proverbial red wire.

"Here goes nothing," she breathed out with her stomach in knots. She didn't know what secrets the book held, but assumed it was important if it had been left hidden. She could feel Grace leaning in for a better view.

She opened the front cover, and the spine of the book made a slight cracking sound as it was bent back. A neat script covered the first page of lined paper, and she drew in a breath and starting flipping through the pages. Each page contained similar script.

Elizabeth closed her eyes. "It's all in German."

Grace sat back in her seat. "Of course it is."

Elizabeth began pulling out the extraneous papers that were shoved inside. "These look like German newspaper articles." She pulled out a few black-and-white photographs that depicted men posing together, but were otherwise nondescript. Each picture contained the same neat script on the back as though memorializing the occasion.

"This is a bit anticlimactic." Grace sighed in defeat.

"Don't give up so easily."

"Well, my German is as good as my Mandarin. I don't suppose you have a German translator stuffed in your backpack?"

"No, but I do know someone who's fluent in German and can help us out."

She pulled out her phone and dialed Professor Horace Pratt.

Chapter Thirty

So who would have thought to combine a coffee shop with a book and music store?" Father Parker asked as he browsed a selection of CDs.

"Add dry cleaning and I'm golden." Elizabeth smiled, standing at his side.

Some might have thought it strange to ask a priest to go shopping, but she missed his friendship. She had been on edge since she left the journal with Professor Pratt and needed a distraction, and she found comfort in his company. She thought of calling Grace, but that only tied her stomach in knots.

"I'm sorry you missed the mill."

"Oh yes, me too," Father Parker said, doing his best to feign sincerity.

"Hey, you just lied!"

"Doesn't count. I had my fingers crossed." He lifted his hand to show the *X* he formed with his fingers.

"Are you sure that collar is real?"

"It was when I paid for it."

"Admit it, you miss the thrill of it." She nudged the father with her shoulder.

"You got me. Once the life of crime gets a hold of you, you're hooked. It was just this morning that I was eyeing Hector's lunchbox on the table and contemplated picking the lock just to see what was inside."

She pointed her coffee swivel stick at him. "You know, you're funny when you want to be."

"You mean when I'm not in danger or in the midst of committing a felony."

Talking to Father Parker was cathartic, like a confession, at least the closest to confession that she would ever get.

"Is this it?" he asked, holding up a Barbra Streisand CD.

"No, my mom has that one."

"So why the gift? Is it her birthday?"

"No, it's sort of a peace offering."

"What did you do?" he asked.

"It wasn't me. It was my cat, Charlie. My mom has, um, had an exotic fish…"

"Spare me the gory details," he said, chuckling.

"In Charlie's defense, it was an ugly fish."

"Excuse me, ma'am," a man dressed in a T-shirt with the store's logo interrupted. He pointed to a sign on the wall. "You can't bring drinks on this side of the store."

"What's the point of having a coffee shop if you can't drink the coffee while you shop?" she asked.

"I'm sorry, ma'am. That's the rule," the clerk said.

"You wouldn't want to break the rules, now would you?" Father Parker asked.

She pointed her coffee stick at the father. "This is not over." She put the stick in her mouth and raised her hand in defeat to the clerk. As she passed the clerk, she gestured her head toward Father Parker. "You might want to keep an eye on him. He's a master criminal. He plots against kids' lunchboxes."

She made it out of the music section and turned the corner around an aisle of books but was forced to pull up short to avoid a fellow customer standing on the other side.

"Sorry about that. Didn't see you."

The customer nodded but didn't raise his head from his book.

She looked at him closely. "Jeff?"

The SILC intern lifted his head to make eye contact.

"What brings you so far north on a workday?"

Jeff stared at her as though he did not understand the question.

"SILC's on the other side of town," she said, unsure why she had to explain the obvious.

"Oh, right. I'm not with SILC anymore. I'm interning at city hall." Jeff closed the book and inspected the cover, and she stared at him, digesting this new information.

"So looking for some new Heart?" he asked.

"What?"

He motioned his head toward the music section. "I know how you like to listen to Heart."

She stared at him. "How would you know that?"

"Huh?" He held the book tight to his chest.

"How would you know that I listen to Heart?"

"You played it at work," he stated matter-of-factly.

"No, Jeff, I didn't play it at work. I never played it at work, unless I was alone...or thought I was alone."

He diverted his eyes and tried to swallow. It was the only answer she needed.

"Did you list 'noose tying' as one of your skill sets on your résumé with the mayor?"

Jeff squirmed.

"So what, the mayor offered you a cushy internship in exchange for playing a Halloween trick?" She puffed out a breath and crossed her arms.

"I don't know what you're talking about."

"Are you following me? Is that what he has you doing? You make one hell of an intern. Do me a favor. Tell your boss I think he's a coward."

Elizabeth didn't wait for a response and turned to continue on her course. Although she was incensed that a little weasel like Jeff scared the hell out of her with such a juvenile prank, a sense of relief washed over her that Dan was cleared. She didn't realize until then how much the thought weighed on her that Dan, a person she once trusted and admired, would have been involved in something so hurtful. No longer interested in her coffee, she tossed it into a trash can and went in search of Father Parker.

Chapter Thirty-one

So how exactly do you know this professor, and are you sure he can be trusted?" Grace asked as she and Elizabeth approached Professor Horace Pratt's office door.

"We sort of crossed paths when I was tracking down Geizler's research paper. He was a research assistant on one of the academic articles that cited Geizler's unpublished paper. He's fluent in German and has a vested interest in helping us out."

"A vested interest?" Grace asked.

"Long story that leads back to a cantankerous librarian." She left it at that as she stood in front of the professor's door and knocked. Although the professor was expecting them, she was still hoping not to stumble upon one of the professor's lunch dates.

The professor pulled open the door just after Elizabeth knocked. "Come in," he said and gestured toward the visitor chairs opposite his desk.

"Professor Pratt, this is Detective Grace Donovan."

Grace reached out her hand, and the professor hastily took it. "Yes, of course, Detective."

The professor rounded the desk and sat at the edge of his chair.

"Professor, is everything all right?" Elizabeth asked, watching the professor run his hand over the brown journal that took center stage on his desk.

"Fine, fine. Everything is fine. I just haven't slept much since you gave me this book," he said, caressing the book. "I've been sitting here for the last two hours waiting for you."

"Okay, now you have me curious. What is it?" Grace asked.

"You know whose book this is?"

"Heinrich Geizler's," Elizabeth and Grace answered in unison.

The professor looked deflated as though someone stole the punch line from his joke. "You knew that?" he asked.

Elizabeth looked to Grace as though asking for permission to let the professor in on their find, and she gave a slight nod. Elizabeth clasped her hands in her lap. "We found that book in a deserted mill. Near the mill was a private school, which closed down around the same time as the mill. We believe that Geizler continued his work at the mill, somehow using the school to get the children for his research."

"Geizler's here?"

"Well, we're not sure where he is now, assuming he's still alive. The mill closed down about thirty years ago."

"Thirty years tracks with what I found in this book, but he wouldn't have left this behind," the professor said.

"Why's that?" asked Grace.

"This is Geizler's personal journal. It dates back before World War Two when he was a student. His last entry was in 1982. There are gaps of several years where he made no entries, but it pretty much tracks his life."

Grace gestured her hand with thinly veiled impatience when the professor stopped there. "Go on. Tell us what the journal says."

"Much of the entries discuss his frustration at his failures. He really believed what he was doing was right. He saw his subjects as sacrifices for the greater good, that they had little to offer in life, but he was giving them a chance to offer great things to humanity by being a part of his work."

Grace and Elizabeth sat quietly listening.

"Geizler discussed how difficult it was to find a suitable place to conduct his research. He felt most people misunderstood him and the importance of his work and expressed sincere disappointment at the academic world for failing to acknowledge him. He believed if the public could just understand his work, they would see how important it was, how important he was. Although having the opportunity to get inside his head is truly interesting from both a clinical and ethical point of view, what's more fascinating is the history that this journal chronicles."

"What do you mean?" Elizabeth asked.

"I told you this journal goes back before World War Two. We all know about the Nazi medical experiments on the Jews and others held in the camps, but he was there."

"You mean Geizler was there?" she clarified.

"Yes, he was a medical student and then an intern, and he described firsthand some of the horrific events that took place."

The professor opened the book and pulled out some black-and-white photos and newspaper articles and lined up the aging photographs on his desk in front of them as he spoke. "This is Dr. Klaus Schilling." The professor pointed to a man standing in the center of three smiling men. "Dr. Schilling operated a malaria research station at Dachau's concentration camp. There, prisoners were exposed to the disease and then injected with synthetic drugs, often in lethal doses, in an attempt to find a cure for malaria."

He pointed to the man on the left. "This is Geizler." Elizabeth was surprised; he appeared normal. Since learning about Geizler and his work, her mind depicted an unattractive man with grotesque features because only a monster could do something so wrong. The man in the picture appeared to be a congenial, good-looking young man, someone a person wouldn't think twice about when passing on the street, but then again, so did Dr. Schilling.

"Looks can be deceiving. Who is this man?" she asked, pointing to the third man in the photo.

"Dr. Giovanni Rossi," replied Professor Pratt.

Grace sat up. "Wait a minute. Rossi? Are you sure?"

"Quite sure, see here." The professor picked up the photo and turned it over. "Here on the back, Geizler wrote who was in the photo. Giovanni Rossi. Says it right here."

Grace turned to Elizabeth. "What's the connection?"

"Samuel Rossi's father," Professor Pratt answered.

Both Grace and Elizabeth snapped their attention to the professor. "How did you know?" Elizabeth asked.

"You think I didn't look you and the detective up after I realized whose journal I had?" He pointed to Elizabeth. "You're defending the boy accused of murdering the first Catholic priest a few years back, and the new murder of Samuel Rossi casts doubt on his guilt." The professor then pointed to Grace. "You're the detective investigating Rossi's murder as well as the police officer that arrested the boy in the first place for the first murder. I must say that seeing the two of you working together is a bit unusual."

"Sooo, what exactly does this mean?" Grace asked Elizabeth.

Before she could offer an explanation, Professor Pratt jumped in again. "It means that Heinrich Geizler was blackmailing Samuel Rossi."

"How do you know that?" Grace asked.

"Well, besides the obvious, Geizler says as much in his journal." The professor picked up the journal and opened to a page that he had saved with a slip of paper. "He first goes on a long rant about the hypocrisy of the medical community and his colleagues for criticizing his work in Germany." After flipping pages in the book, he read, "*With my credibility stripped by the cowards who believe themselves to be scientists, I cannot continue my research alone. Rossi's son is the key.*" Professor Pratt looked up from the page. "His next entry in the journal explains how he tracked down Samuel Rossi and essentially blackmailed him into helping him."

"So Samuel Rossi's father wasn't the simple Italian country doctor that he wanted others to believe," Elizabeth said.

"No, definitely not," Professor Pratt answered and trailed his finger down the page, reading to himself. "It seems Giovanni Rossi met Schilling in Italy. Dr. Schilling started his malaria vaccination experiments on inmates in psychiatric asylums there. When Schilling moved to Dachau, he persuaded Giovanni Rossi to join him."

"And what, Geizler was holding this over Samuel Rossi's head?" Grace asked.

"Perhaps. Klaus Schilling was convicted at the Dachau trials in Germany. He was executed in 1946 for his crimes. Before he was hung, he pleaded to have the results of his experiments published."

"It says that there?" Elizabeth asked, pointing to the journal.

"No, that's from my own research," the professor replied. "What I also found interesting from my research is what I didn't find."

"Is that a paradox?" Grace asked.

"I went through all the German medical trials, and there was no mention of Giovanni Rossi. Somehow Rossi went under the radar. He probably slipped back into Italy and took up his country doctor profession, and no one was the wiser, except Geizler, who had this." Professor Pratt lifted the journal for emphasis.

"I guess we know why Samuel Rossi helped Geizler. He was protecting himself from the sins of his father," Elizabeth said, understanding the deeper meaning of the poem.

"As interesting as this all is, it doesn't put us any closer to what we really need to know. Who the hell is torturing and killing people?

It sure as hell isn't Schilling, Geizler, or Rossi," Grace said, with her voice elevating in volume at the end.

Professor Pratt shrunk back into his chair. "I thought it was fascinating," he sulked.

"Don't worry about her. She's always cranky. We appreciate the time you have taken to help us with this." Elizabeth started collecting the photos and newspapers that were strewn on her side of the desk and stood to collect the journal. Professor Pratt looked at it longingly.

"Must you take it?" he asked.

She looked to Grace, who had her phone in her hand and was immersed in her messages. "I'm afraid so. It's part of the investigation, but I will see what I can do to get it back to you when this is all over."

The professor brightened at the possibility of being reunited with the journal, and she expressed her gratitude to him once again as Grace had her phone pressed to her ear and had completely tuned them out.

"So, if you find the other book, you'll let me know?" Professor Pratt asked hopefully when Elizabeth reached the doorway.

She turned. "The other book?" She yanked on Grace's sleeve to get her attention.

Professor Pratt pointed to the book cradled in Elizabeth's arms. "That's his personal journal. There's another book with research notes of his work. In his last entry, he wrote that he thought he found it, the synthetic vaccine that is. He had a significant breakthrough. He overcame the impediment."

"What impediment?" Grace asked, tuning back into the conversation.

"I don't know. He doesn't say. You need the other book."

"What could someone do with the research book?" Grace asked.

"You mean other than patent Geizler's lifelong work and reap all the credit and rewards?" Professor Pratt asked.

Elizabeth rather enjoyed the professor's feisty comeback, but held back her snicker. "If a start-up pharmaceutical company got a hold of Geizler's research, would it be possible for it to streamline through clinical trials on a new drug?" Elizabeth asked.

"This isn't my area, but it seems possible. The pharmaceutical giants have been working on this for decades with no success. But if a company had Geizler's research notes, they had a big head start."

She shook Professor Pratt's hand. "Thank you so much. You've been extremely helpful."

Elizabeth turned to Grace, who stood quietly by through the entire exchange. "Come on. Let's go." Grace gave her a confused look. "I'll explain in the car," she said over her shoulder as she walked out of the professor's office.

Chapter Thirty-two

Elizabeth sat impatiently thumbing through the current edition of a gossip magazine. She didn't bother reading the articles, but scanned the pictures. *Don't know him, or him, or her.* She wondered if it meant she was getting old if she was out of touch with the current celebrities getting their fifteen minutes of fame.

"Ms. Campbell, Mr. Iverson will see you now," a petite woman in a well-tailored suit announced.

She dropped the magazine on the table and quickly rose to follow the woman. As her visit was unannounced, she expected to wait, but she had been sitting for the better part of an hour.

"Ms. Campbell, it's a pleasure to see you again. I'm sorry to have kept you waiting." Bradley Iverson strolled across the room, hand outstretched to greet her, and she could sense the insincerity in that statement.

"Thank you for seeing me," she said with an equally insincere smile.

Iverson gestured her to the same chair she occupied on her last visit and settled himself behind his desk, but she noticed his rigid posture.

"So what can I do for you?" No drinks were offered with this visit. It was straight to the point, which she appreciated.

"The mill, it was owned by Spiedel Trust," she stated.

"Yes, we covered that in our last visit," he replied with a flat tone.

"What I don't understand is why Spiedel Trust held the mill through a series of holding companies."

After her visit with Professor Pratt, she reviewed the notes Rich gave her on the mill, and although she thought little of it at the time, she now found the holding companies curious.

"I can't really say," was all Iverson said, but she wasn't perturbed. She was only getting started.

"Correct me if I'm wrong, but holding companies, especially a series of them, are useful in keeping the ownership of a company, shall we say, less than public."

Iverson offered no response. "So, I got to thinking, why? Why would Spiedel Trust go through such effort to bury its ownership interest in the mill?" She paused for a moment, more for dramatic effect than to wait for an answer, and no answer came, as she expected.

"I think that Pieter Spiedel knew exactly who Henry Gesler was and what he would do in that mill. As you said, your uncle was a desperate man searching for a cure. But he was also a smart businessman, so he buried his involvement in Gesler's work through holding companies."

"Ms. Campbell, I can't comment on what my uncle did or didn't know. This was a long time ago; it's history. I suggest you move on."

"I would have to agree with you, except...there's IPR. Infinity Pharmaceutical Research." She put more emphasis on the word "Infinity." After leaving Professor Pratt, she researched the pharmaceutical company that she had heard much about recently and was not overly surprised to learn its full name.

"I found it curious how this start-up pharmaceutical company could be in the final phase of clinical trials on a brand-new drug; a drug that will revolutionize the medical community; a drug that longstanding pharmaceutical companies have been striving to create for decades, but failed."

She was in her element, and although she wasn't in the courtroom, she felt the rush of an impending checkmate. "You see, I did my research. These companies continued to fail because they lacked adequate real life data to take it to trials for testing on humans. But IPR did have the real life data. Quoting someone else I know, 'IPR had a big head start.'"

"This is all very interesting, I'm sure, but I fail to see what this has to do with the trust or me. So, if you don't mind, I have other matters to get to."

"But I think you do see. IPR acquired Henry Gesler's, or should I say Heinrich Geizler's life's work. His decades of testing and research on children, it was all done for them. IPR only needed to step in and take the credit."

"I don't appreciate where this conversation is going. I'm going to have to ask you to leave," he said.

"But I'm just getting to the good part." She noted that Iverson remained quiet and made no move to have her removed and knew she had his interest.

"IPR is a closed corporation with private funding. Funding channeled through a series of holding companies. IPR's CEO, Seth Lowry, is merely a puppet. I think if we pierced the veil, we'd find that IPR is owned by you, but..." She rubbed her chin in mock consternation. "You couldn't have gotten Geizler's research without someone else...someone that was there." She crossed her arms over her chest, but Iverson didn't flinch. "Bishop Pallone went through great efforts to hide a secret, and IPR has been Mayor Reynosa's poster child for his economic reform. Iverson, Pallone, and Reynosa—IPR. Not very clever." She had to credit her father's law firm, CRAK, for putting together the true acronym.

Bradley Iverson leaned back in his chair and slowly clapped his hands in mocking appreciation. "Give the lady a gold star. All this from a single CV of Henry Gesler. Who would have thought? Of course, you can't prove this. Sure, you can connect the dots of IPR, but you can never prove the connection of Heinrich Geizler and IPR. But nice try. Now if you don't mind, I really do have more interesting things to do."

Elizabeth didn't need to be asked again and exited without another word. She got what she came for, confirmation of what she already knew.

As Elizabeth strode out of the building, a hand reached out and grabbed her arm, causing her to jump. She quickly turned and grabbed the hand, twisting the fingers until a familiar voice cried for mercy.

"God damn it, Grace, you scared me. What are you doing grabbing at me like that?"

"I was only trying to catch up with you. I called your name, but you didn't answer," Grace said as she made a show of flexing her fingers.

"Sorry. I didn't hear you. I was lost in thought. What are you doing here?"

"Probably the same thing you are. You want to fill me in?"

Elizabeth leaned against a low brick wall that lined the building walkway and crossed her arms, and Grace perched beside her, matching her stance. After Elizabeth provided a rundown of her meeting with Bradley Iverson, Grace snapped, "Why did you go in there alone?"

"I don't need your permission."

"Permission? This isn't about permission. This is about common sense. You corner him and God knows what he'll do."

"I can take care of myself. I don't need a babysitter!" Elizabeth stormed off, unsure why she was so angry. She knew Grace made a good point, and she should have at least consulted her before she went to meet Iverson. She did think of it, but told herself that she would extract more information from Iverson without a detective at her side. Although she did believe that to be true, that wasn't the reason she didn't call; she didn't call because Grace confused her. Technically, Grace didn't confuse her, but her own feelings about Grace confused her, and she thought it best to leave that emotional baggage out of the conversation with Iverson.

Chapter Thirty-three

Raymond played with the button on the side of the passenger seat, pushing the back of his chair up and down. The buzzing of the seat lowering and raising began to grate on Elizabeth's nerves.

"Raymond, will you please leave the seat alone? It's getting tired," she said.

He patted the seat next to his leg, and she smiled at his act of endearment, but it wasn't long before Raymond became bored and searched for something else to occupy him. He popped open the center compartment and began riffling through it; however, she found this less annoying and left him to it.

They spent a fruitless afternoon in court. The prosecution announced its position to pursue a new trial against Raymond, and a new date for jury selection was set. She had hoped that Robert Burke would reconsider his hard stance on Raymond's case, but time hadn't softened the prosecutor's resolve, and she suspected it was as much for his bruised ego as for justice.

Elizabeth's mother was conspicuously absent for both Raymond and Elizabeth. She had become a mainstay for Raymond and a silent source of strength for Elizabeth during the hearings, but a debilitating migraine forced her to stay home.

"Raymond, what are you doing!"

Elizabeth quickly pulled the car to the side of the road and snatched a matchbook from his hands. The sulfur tip on the match still in Raymond's hand didn't ignite, and he lowered his head in shame.

"Where did you get these?"

He pointed to the open center console without lifting his head, and she turned the matchbook over in her hand, trying to recall how it got there. Then it came to her. She found it in the church basement during one of her excursions with Grace. She paid little attention to it at the time, assuming the matches were left behind by an occupant of the homeless camp seeking refuge, but as she studied the matchbook, she realized she was wrong.

The front cover of the matchbook displayed a four-leaf clover and the backside, the name *O'Shays Pub*. She closed her eyes and swallowed hard. "Oh God."

Raymond mistook her distress as a sign of anger toward him and apologized with tears in his eyes.

"Oh no, Raymond, it's not you." She went on to gently reprimand him for playing with matches, but relieved him of the burden of thinking he was in trouble.

She felt an overwhelming urge to drive to the school for another look, but realized Raymond posed a problem. After convincing herself that she couldn't take him home and return before dark, she changed course and headed toward the school.

"Raymond, I need to make a quick stop. You'll have to stay in the car and be a big boy." He nodded vigorously.

On the drive, she called Grace. They hadn't spoken since their argument, instead both sulking in their stubbornness. Now she had a reason to reach out, but had to settle for her voice mail when she didn't answer. "It's Elizabeth. Look, I found Sullivan's matches. I mean, I found them in the church basement the last time we were there, and I just came across them."

She realized that she was rambling and took a breath. "Never mind. It's too hard to explain. Meet me at the school. I'm heading there now."

She disconnected the call and dialed Father Parker, figuring extra backup wouldn't hurt, even if it was a priest. She was disheartened when Mary answered and told her that Father Parker was out visiting a parishioner.

"Mary, please tell him to meet me at the church behind the school. It's very important. He'll understand."

She pulled the Roadster into the decrepit parking lot in front of the school and tried to patiently wait for Grace, knowing Grace would want that, but patience wasn't her strong suit. She reasoned that she only needed to take a look around, and if she waited, she could lose the light. Grace would see her car and catch up with her. Now that she had worked it out in her head, she opened the car door with a purpose.

"Where are we going?" Raymond asked.

His voice pulled her back, and she closed the door. She momentarily forgot about him. She explained her need to go look into one of the buildings, and he looked warily at the abandoned property, biting his bottom lip. He shook his head. "It's too scary."

Elizabeth explained that she wanted him to wait in the car, and she handed him her cell phone and opened up a game app to occupy him while she was gone. "Stay in the car," she said before shutting the door, but he was already too immersed in the game to acknowledge her.

She pulled her backpack from the trunk, an accessory she now seemed to never leave home without, and walked toward the church. She was grateful she had chosen to wear a pantsuit to court. It was slightly better attire to be trekking through a basement than a skirt and hose.

She noted the deafening silence. Only the sound of her boots bearing down on the soil could be heard. *Weren't there birds and other critters scurrying around before?* She wondered if they knew something she didn't and considered waiting for Grace. She stopped and imagined Grace coming to her rescue and chastised herself for being foolish. She was letting her absurd thoughts get the best of her. She hefted the backpack higher on her shoulder and carried on.

When she reached the church entrance, she pulled the chain wrapped around the door handles and let it fall to ground, then pulled out her flashlight, moving the light around the circumference of the room before she entered. Convinced it was empty, she moved to the basement door and slowly opened it and stood motionless, cocking her head to the side to angle her ear toward the opening. After several moments of silence, she turned off the light and crept down the stairs on the tips of her toes, being careful not to allow the heel of her boot to touch down. At the bottom, she stopped again and waited. When no sound came other than her own breathing, she turned on the light and shined it toward the metal cellar door, which appeared securely closed. Several footprints were impressed into the dusty floor, but she couldn't tell if they were new or prints left behind by her prior visits.

Reasonably certain that she was alone, she walked toward the concrete door and set down the flashlight to turn the handle and push with both hands. As the door began to give, a loud creak came from behind her, and she wheeled around.

"I have a weapon," she yelled, not recognizing her own voice as it shook. She dropped the backpack and pulled out the crowbar. The creaking sound stopped, and she and her unwelcome visitor were in a silent standoff. Her arm began to tremble at the weight of the crowbar hefted above her head. She slowly bent her knees and lifted the flashlight, which had been trained on the ceiling, and directed it toward the stairs. A set of hands hurriedly covered a set of eyes as the light pointed accusingly.

"Raymond, God damn it! You scared me. You were supposed to stay in the car."

Raymond stood motionless and continued to cover his face with his hands, and she realized that he must have been equally scared. She moved to him and pulled his hand away from his face and led him down the last step.

"I'm sorry, Raymond. I didn't mean to scare you." She could see the tracks of tears down his face and pulled him into her and held him tightly. He melted into her and wrapped his arms around her as though he was afraid she would leave him again.

"Raymond why didn't you stay in the car?"

"I was scared. I don't like to be alone."

She mentally kicked herself for bringing him. She had become so obsessed with the matchbook find that she didn't stop to really think about his well-being. "I'm sorry, Raymond. Let's go home."

He didn't respond, but stared over her shoulder. "Raymond, what is it?" She turned toward the concrete door and saw light spilling out of the crack of the slightly open door.

"Stand right here. I'm just going to peek in the door," she whispered, handing the flashlight to him, and held the crowbar out in front of her. She poked her head in the door and waited for her eyes to adjust to the light. Although a lantern hanging from the middle of the ceiling offered a modest amount of light, it was a stark contrast to the nearly black basement.

"What the hell?" she breathed out. A naked man stood against the wall with his arms and legs pulled apart by chains and secured to the wall. The man remained motionless with his head slumped down, and she turned to escape the sight, when a groan emanated from the man.

"Who's there? Please don't go."

She stood torn between Raymond and the chained man.

"Raymond, there's a man in here. I think he's hurt. I'm going to help him."

He nodded, causing the flashlight to bounce with his movement.

She scooped up her backpack and slowly pushed the door open the rest of the way and looked around the room. It seemed no different from her prior visits but for the light and a naked man chained to the wall.

She approached the man to survey his injuries. Dried blood trailed down the side of his face, but no other injuries were visible, and she stared at him in vague recognition. "I know you."

The man lifted his head and stared directly at her. "Simon Fisher," he croaked out. She failed to recognize the name and shook her head slightly.

"We met at the mayor's party. I'm his personal assistant."

As he said it, she recalled their meeting outside the restaurant where she assaulted the swan.

"I'm Elizabeth." She felt very foolish for having casual introductions when the man was naked, bleeding, and chained to a wall. With her senses returning, she dropped her backpack and yanked out the bolt cutters. She carried on their conversation as she clamped the cutter down on the chain. "So what happened?"

"I don't know. I was in the parking lot, leaving work. It was dark. Someone hit me from behind. I woke up like this."

She was so sure that the signs pointed to Mayor Reynosa as the next victim. "You attended St. John's."

Simon tried to nod yes, but the movement caused more pain, and he groaned. His sounds of misery focused her back on the task of cutting the chain, and she squeezed the bolt cutters as hard as she could, but it barely made an indentation on the metal chain. The locks on the doors were much easier in comparison, and she began to doubt that she would be able to cut the chains.

She kept up the conversation with Simon, in part to keep him calm as she continued to work at it, but also to finally get some answers. "Father Rossi ran the school. I'm guessing the first priest, Father Portillo, worked here too."

"Yes, but Father Portillo had nothing to do with what was happened here. It was Father Rossi. Nobody else knew but us."

"Who is us?" she asked.

"I think you know—Detective Sullivan, Bishop Pallone, the mayor, and me."

"I knew Mayor Reynosa was connected to this somehow," she said more to herself. She flexed her fingers, which were aching from the force of the bolt cutters, and sighed. She had made little progress, as the indentation was only slightly deeper.

"The four of us attended the school. The other three liked to sneak out of our dorm and go to the woods to smoke. The woods were supposed to be off-limits. I went along to prove that I was like them, but I wasn't. I'm not like them," he stated emphatically.

She resumed cutting. "And?"

"One night, we were wandering through the woods, and we came across some kind of old mining tunnel. We followed it, and that's when we saw Father Rossi with the other man, Gesler, and a kid. The kid was crying. I wanted to tell, to help the kid, but not the other three. They saw it as an opportunity to help themselves. We got special favors in school—homework done for us, skipping class, grades changed, all that kind of stuff, all sanctioned by Father Rossi. In return, we kept our mouths shut, but soon, that wasn't enough. The others wanted more. They wanted to be a part of it for money. We started helping Gesler with the children."

"With his testing, you mean."

"Yes," he confirmed softly. "Rossi would get the kids. I think they were runaways or had no families. He promised them food and a warm place to sleep." His voice cracked, and he paused to swallow.

She looked around the room. "This is where they kept the children. How many children?"

"I don't know." She eyed him with disbelief. "I really don't know. We only discovered this," he slightly gestured his head to the room, "about a year before the school closed. There were only three children during that year. I don't know how many before."

"What happened to the children?" she asked.

"They would just disappear. I don't know where."

"What are you not telling me?"

"The power over the children, it went to their heads..." Simon's voice trailed off.

Simon covertly watched the boy through the small opening of the tunnel door. Unlike the others, he volunteered to bring the boy's food, so he could check on him. He had even spoken with him and learned that his name was David Collins. It was important to him to know their names.

He knew that most days David spent his time in the dark, but some days, like today, he was privileged to have light from the lantern that hung in the middle of the room. As Simon watched him, David stared up at the design painted on the ceiling, something he had seen him do before. When he asked him why, David said that it was its color that drew him to it. It stood out from the cold concrete, and he found the curves and symmetry beautiful. It was his constellation.

Simon was reluctant to interrupt him as David tore his attention away from the ceiling, and began using the small rock held between his thumb and index finger to scrape a design on the cement. The floor had become his canvas, and several etchings surrounded him.

A chain holding his ankle restricted his movement, and Simon could see that his skin was raw and peeling where the metal band dug into his flesh. His hair, matted and greasy, hung in his eyes. He was afforded the luxury of a wet towel to clean himself twice a week, and a bucket that served as his bathroom was left within his reach.

David clutched his rock and surveyed his latest work. Simon knew that the small stone had become his sole possession in his barren world. Absorbed in David's world, Simon was unaware that Pallone, Reynosa, and Sullivan had snuck behind him, until they pushed him forward, and he tumbled into the room. David jumped at the commotion, and Simon quickly scrambled to his feet as the other boys mocked him. The scent of beer invaded the room, telling Simon all he needed to know about what the others had been doing.

Pallone, who was nearly twice the size of Simon, moved to David and kicked at him. "Get up."

David pushed himself back against the wall, clawing at it and trying to find a hold. "No, leave me be." Normally, the drugs made him seem less physically coordinated, but today he looked stronger. Despite the renewed strength, he was still too small to put up a serious fight.

Incensed at David's rebellion, Pallone pulled him down to his knees and held him by his hair. "Now, that isn't proper behavior. Is it?"

David involuntarily released the rock that was still gripped in his hand.

"What's this?" Pallone watched the rock come to a rest and then stomped on it. David rammed his shoulder into Pallone's leg in an attempt to defend his one possession, but it was too late, and Simon could hear the soft crack as it was broken into pieces.

David slumped in defeat, mourning his loss, while Simon stood by watching. He didn't want to cross Pallone, who was bending to tend to his leg. "I think you bruised me." He pulled back David's hair, forcing his head to tip up. David struggled to turn his head away, and a set of dog tags that encircled his neck came loose from under his shirt. Pallone snatched at it, snapping the chain. David struggled in an effort to take back the necklace, and Pallone tossed it at Reynosa. David lunged forward, attempting to intercept it, but the heavy metal chain had a hold of his leg and yanked him back. He fell to the ground and looked longingly at the necklace. Reynosa laughed at David's grief and then threw the necklace at Simon as though it were a game of keep-away. Simon grasped it as it struck him in the chest, but he was unwilling to continue the taunting and shoved the necklace into his pocket.

"Get up," Pallone ordered, but David ignored him. Pallone reached down and grabbed the front of his shirt, but before he could pull him up, David bit his arm. "Ow, fuck, he bit me." Pallone stared down at him with vengeance in his eyes. "Chain him up!"

Reynosa and Sullivan snickered and complied, forcefully pulling David up and securing his wrists to the chains that were dangling from the ceiling. "Get his other leg too," Pallone said.

David hung with his legs and arms pulled apart, and squirming became futile, as it only dug the metal cuffs deeper into his skin.

"Useful little things, aren't they?" Pallone asked, pointing to the chains. "They say that this used to be where they brought the boys that had 'disciplinary problems.'" He emphasized the words by forming quotation marks with his fingers. "After a few days, those problem students were new men. No more disciplinary problems. That was before Gesler came along and found a new use for this room."

Pallone walked over to the side wall and pulled down a coiled flat whip hanging on a nail. "Want to see how they cured those behavior problems?" He brought the whip down on David's body, and he screamed as the leather traveled across his skin. After a few more strikes, David settled into a soft whimper, but Pallone continued in his delight in delivering suffering as the whip fluidly rose and fell like a wave.

"Pallone, that's enough," Reynosa said.

David hung sagging on the chains, and Pallone stepped back to observe his work. Red angry welts were visible on his arms and stomach where his shirt was pulled up. Reynosa and Sullivan unchained him, and Simon turned toward the concrete door leading to the tunnel, unable to watch as David allowed himself to be pulled along. "Now that's more like it," Pallone stated in approval.

As they dragged him through the tunnel, Simon trailed behind, and they passed the inner cavern, where a soft glow spilled out. Simon noticed several small white candles that circled the outskirts of the room, and Pallone changed course and directed them into the small room. A panic rose in him when he realized that they had never brought the children outside the cement room without either Rossi or Gesler present, and certainly never into this room.

"I want him first," said Pallone. They dropped David onto a tattered couch resting against the side wall, causing an empty beer can to rattle against the floor, and Pallone began unbuckling his pants.

David lay motionless until he was roughly pulled up and pushed against a long table in the back corner. He stared up at a wooden cross hanging upside down. Simon stared at it too, sure it was a sign that God had forgotten him.

"You like that, don't you? It's my creation. It's sort of a 'fuck you,'" Pallone said with a slur more evident in his voice.

As he pressed his weight against David, Reynosa interrupted, "Shut up, Pallone, and be done with it." He began fumbling with his own pants in anticipation.

With a sudden rage over the violation that was occurring, David reeled back his head and slammed it into Pallone's face, causing him to stumble back at the unexpected blow. Turning quickly, a silver disc came free from beneath Pallone's shirt, and David viciously ripped at the chain, and Simon watched the St. Christopher pendant catapult through the air.

David swung his arms and kicked at the boys as Simon meekly attempted to step in and help restrain him, but he was too concerned with getting hurt to be effective. After an intense struggle, David's knuckles were bloody, and to Simon's amazement, the others were on the ground nursing wounds. Simon remained frozen, and they momentarily locked eyes before David seized the opportunity and ran down the tunnel, but soon his strength ran out, and the other boys descended upon him and knocked him over. He fell and rolled before he popped up and began swinging again, but the others were better prepared this time. Fists rained down on him, and he covered his head and fell to his knees.

After nearly a minute of continuous blows, Pallone ordered them to halt. "I think he'll be more obedient now." Blood was dripping from Pallone's nose, evidence of where David's head hit him. The group, panting slightly from the exertion, backed up, giving David room to rise, but he lay still on the dirt tunnel floor and turned his head to see the dim light filter out of the open door to the cement room, and Simon thought he saw a calm resolve in his eyes.

David rose unsteadily, and when he pulled himself up to his full height, he looked directly at Pallone and released a screech that ripped through the tunnel. They flinched when David threw himself on top of Pallone, and Simon remained motionless and watched as Pallone pulled David off of him like a doll and threw him to the ground. A dull thud could be heard as David's head struck a small boulder, and his body went limp.

"Oh crap, I think you killed him!" screamed Sullivan.

Panicked, Simon turned and ran out the tunnel, and he could hear the others following, but didn't look back. The only thought in his mind was to get Father Rossi because this mess was too big for them to clean up alone. In a matter of minutes, he was on his return trek with the other boys and Father Rossi in tow. Cutting through the church, Simon and the other boys ran bunched together down the aisle. When they reached the basement door, Pallone shoved him out of the way to pull on the door only to find that it was locked. Father Rossi came up from behind, panting heavily, and pushed his way through the boys and pulled a key from his pocket. Unwilling to let the father take the lead, Pallone forced himself past the priest once the door opened, and Father Rossi followed, with Simon trailing behind Reynosa and Sullivan.

They only stopped once they passed through the concrete door and were inside the tunnel. Turning in a slow circle, Father Rossi scanned the passageway. "Well, where is he?"

Pallone opened his mouth, but no sound came out.

"He was right there," Sullivan exclaimed, pointing to the rock on the ground.

"He's not here now, is he?" Father Rossi condemned.

"He wasn't moving. We thought he was dead," Reynosa defended.

"Well, as I see it, either he ascended or he escaped. I am betting he is not with the Lord right now."

Father Rossi swung around at a sound, and Simon's eyes followed to see a flashlight in the distance moving toward them, and they waited wordlessly.

"What the hell is going on," came a disembodied German accent from the dark.

Father Rossi pointed to the boys. "They let the boy escape."

Simon did not need to see him to know that Henry Gesler was clamping down his jaw. He had seen him angry before.

Gesler pulled himself just short of Father Rossi and spat out,

"You're incompetent, you fool." He pushed Father Rossi back, who lost his footing and fell. Simon backed up, unsure whether to stay and watch the altercation or run. Filled with fear and indecision, he stood frozen with the others.

From the ground, Father Rossi looked up. "No more."

"You pathetic fool, get up," Gesler commanded.

Father Rossi rolled to his hands and knees in an effort to rise. As he got his feet under him and pulled himself up, he yelled, "No more." The priest swung the heavy rock that was laden with David's blood and hit Gesler across the head. A crack sounded and Gesler stood still, his mouth gaping as blood began spilling out of the corners. A large trail of blood made its way down his face from the large indentation in the side of his skull. Eyes wide in disbelief, Gesler continued to open his mouth, but no words came out, and he finally succumbed to the blow, collapsing to the ground.

Father Rossi kicked at the prone body, but no movement came. He bent to feel for a pulse and slowly rose and made eye contact with each of the boys. "There is a plastic sheet in the basement. Wrap him in it, take the shovel and bury him in the woods." Without a word, Simon and the boys turned to follow the priest's command. Before they disappeared into the cement room, Father Rossi called them back. "Boys." Each of them turned to face the father. "We will never speak of this again."

❖

Elizabeth stopped her efforts with the bolt cutters, fully engaged in Simon's story. "Dear God, what did you do?"

He began sobbing, "I'm sorry. Just leave me here. This is my indemnity."

She actually considered leaving him for a moment, but realized that it would make her no better than him.

A noise from the corner of the room caused Elizabeth to snap her head to the side to find the source. Raymond stood just inside the door holding the flashlight, and she cursed herself for once again forgetting about him. She had no idea how long he'd been standing there or how much he had heard.

"Raymond, are you okay?"

He had a strange look on his face as he stared at Simon.

She beckoned him over and showed him how to work the bolt cutters. "Squeeze it together as hard as you can." As Raymond awkwardly worked the cutters, Elizabeth resumed pumping information from Simon.

"So the letter on my car, you wrote it. Then you sent the letter to the judge?"

"Yes."

"Why?" she asked. "Why the anonymous letters? Why not come forward? And sooner?"

"I was a coward." Simon sniffled. "The symbol carved on Father Portillo, we had seen it before." He stared at the cement floor as though searching, before he finally spoke again. "The others feared that it would all come out, but I hoped it would. But...then he was arrested." He gestured his head toward Raymond. "The others were relieved. They thought it was over, and there was no attention on the school."

"You set Raymond up, all of you." Elizabeth's mouth twisted in disgust as she emphasized the last word. "You torture children, abuse them. Why not target a mentally retarded man to round out your list of good deeds?" Her voice grew in volume as she spoke, and Raymond stilled his hands and approached her with concern. He knew she was upset, but the conversation was too difficult for him to follow.

"It's okay, Raymond." She patted his hand that held the bolt cutters and looked at his work, realizing that he had cut through the chain, and Simon's hand was free. "You did it. That's great," she said with more enthusiasm than she felt, for Raymond's sake. "Can you keep going and cut this side?" She pointed to the chain holding Simon's other hand, and Raymond nodded.

Simon tilted his head to the side to get a look at Raymond. "We didn't set him up."

"The hell you didn't. The anonymous phone call, the Bible, the cross, the confession." She delineated each one carefully.

Simon shook his head vigorously. "No, no, you have it wrong. We've done bad things. I've done bad things. Reynosa, Pallone, Sullivan, they did things to stop the new investigation to protect themselves, but the arrest and confession, that was all him," he said, looking at Raymond.

"Bullshit!"

"Look, you have no reason to believe me, but I swear the others and I had nothing to do with him being arrested or the confession. I put his case on the list to be reviewed. The mayor gave me the final list to distribute, and I added his case on it, even though I believed he did it."

"If you thought he was guilty, then why add it to the list?" she asked, crossing her arms.

"I'm not really sure exactly; it was an impulse. The mayor was being his usual asshole self, and I wanted to get back at him, so I added the case to the list. I knew it would piss him off, but I had no idea all of this would happen." He used his free hand to gesture to the room.

She had no reason to believe the man, but at the same time, at this point, he had no reason to lie. "So if you and your merry gang of thugs had nothing to do with Raymond's arrest and confession, then who did?"

He remained silent, but his silence was all she needed to hear, and she looked at Raymond. His face was red with exertion as he used all his force on the bolt cutters. She and Simon watched him together in a shared moment, and she could see a small portion of the angry scar on Raymond's hand that he had never explained.

In her moment of doubt, Elizabeth wondered how much she really knew about Raymond. In all the time she had worked on this case, he never claimed his innocence. She just assumed it because the pieces didn't seem to fit, but neither did the confession nor the cross in his pocket.

She shook off the chill that ran down her. Regardless of the confession and the cross, Raymond didn't commit the last three murders, at least not himself. While staring at Raymond, she heard the chain snap, and Simon's other hand was released from its hold against the wall.

"Good work, Raymond. Now just work on these last two," she said, devoid of any emotion, and pointed at the chains holding Simon's feet.

Before Raymond could settle in to work on the next chain, Simon grabbed the bolt cutters from him. "Let me do it."

Raymond looked hurt at the rough treatment, but Simon ignored him and bent over to clamp down on the chain, and Raymond backed away to take up his earlier position by the door. With Simon now working on his own freedom, Elizabeth contemplated returning to the car with Raymond to wait for Grace. She bent to retrieve her backpack and jumped when she stood up and faced a new figure standing near the door.

"Father Parker, you scared me. You got my message. Thank God," she blurted out rapidly.

"What's going on here?" he asked with his eyes fixed on the bent figure with the bolt cutters.

"This is Simon Fisher. He works for the mayor. It seems he was the next target. We've been trying to cut him free."

"I see. What can I do?"

"Maybe you could help him cut those a little faster," she said and turned to watch Simon's progress.

"Of course." Father Parker moved to step around Raymond, who turned slightly and broke into a smile, recognizing the priest.

"Pappy!" Raymond exclaimed.

Father Parker smiled at him. "Raymond, you're a good boy."

Raymond beamed with pride. "Pappy is happy."

Elizabeth snapped her head toward him. "What did you say?"

Raymond's smile faded at her serious tone, and he pointed to Father Parker. "Pappy is happy."

Her eyes grew wide as Father Parker stepped behind Raymond and removed a knife and casually put one arm around his chest. He pulled Raymond back against him, holding the knife in his other hand below his throat. Raymond stood oblivious to the knife and the threat, and he snuggled back into Father Parker's hold, relishing the attention.

"No," she choked out.

Simon stopped his movements and stared at the priest, holding the bolt cutters in front of him defensively.

"I-I don't understand," she stumbled out. "You're a priest. You helped me."

Father Parker smiled. "This suit is but a costume, as you know very well. As for helping you, I think it was mutual. The first one, I traced him to the school, but he was the wrong one, a mistake I truly regret. I almost gave up, a failure, but then I met you."

She scrunched her brows together in confusion.

"You gave me this." Father Parker reached into his pocket and pulled out a worn card. She squinted to read it and recognized it immediately. It was her business card with her cell phone number written on the bottom. She remembered giving him the card on their first meeting.

"My card?" she asked.

He turned the card over, and on the back was a drawing of the circle with the three triangles that Raymond drew during her first visit to the prison. "As time went on, I guess I became complacent. Lost sight of my purpose, but then you gave me the sign to begin again."

Elizabeth's head was reeling with the knowledge that she had awoken the slumbering beast and unwittingly set the recent series of murders in motion.

"And I got it right this time with Rossi, and he was a tough old man. He wouldn't talk...at first. But I can be very persuasive." A maniacal grin formed on his face. "He told me everything, gave me the names of the others."

She stood suspended with the weight of Father Parker's words sinking in. "You, you killed those men. You brutalized them," she spat out.

He shook his head and spoke with more force. "No, don't make them martyrs. You know what monsters they were."

She looked at Raymond, who was still standing in the father's grip, blissfully unaware of the danger. "What about Raymond? You set him up?" she asked with a bit of hope for Raymond's innocence.

She thought she saw a look of sadness momentarily cross the father's face as he glanced down at Raymond in his grasp. "He is an innocent in this, like the first one, which I also regret. But as I have learned in this journey, there must be innocent sacrifices for the greater good."

Elizabeth realized that she could have had a similar conversation with Heinrich Geizler. "Why Raymond?"

"Because he was there," the father answered. "I wanted to make a statement by leaving the body at the school, but it proved to make things more..." he searched for the word, "complicated, being that this is where I do my work and all." He gestured to Simon for emphasis. "Having Raymond step up and take responsibility took the pressure off and allowed me time to begin again. A fresh start," he said in an upbeat tone as though he were discussing a New Year's resolution.

Elizabeth felt sickened, but chose to stay quiet to hear the rest of the father's story. He patted Raymond's chest. "I would see Raymond here around the neighborhood. We became friends, didn't we?"

Raymond nodded with a grin.

"He didn't have any friends until he met me. I taught him things. Gave him gifts."

"Like a cross and a Bible?" she asked, not trying to hold back the venom in her voice.

"What other gifts would a priest give? Raymond understood that the gifts were our special secret because only he got gifts from God." He spoke in a childlike manner and rubbed Raymond's chest soothingly, which made him smile.

"The Bible was for safekeeping for the nights when he was lonely. He could look at the pages and remember our friendship and God's love. And the cross would protect him, and I told him to carry it everywhere. He was a good boy and he listened very well. We read Bible stories and I explained how God would punish the bad and reward those who followed His command with eternal life in His kingdom."

Father Parker paused for a moment and looked directly at Elizabeth. "Raymond understood that taking responsibility for killing that man was a good thing because it was what God wanted. For that, he would be rewarded with eternal life in His kingdom. Raymond wants this eternal life, don't you?"

Raymond nodded with a smile still on his face.

She realized that Raymond's drawings that hung in the shed were not of Raymond and his mother, but of Raymond and Father Parker. "You continued to visit him in prison, not to save his soul, but to ensure that he would continue to stick to the story," she said with disgust.

Father Parker had fooled her. She had been traipsing through the basement, the tunnel, the woods with him, all areas he knew well. She could easily see how he could dupe Raymond into confessing to his murder. He was a master manipulator.

Simon shifted his position, pulling Father Parker's attention to him, and she looked back and forth between the two and settled her glare back on Father Parker. "Who are you, really?"

He nudged Raymond to move forward, and when they reached Father Parker's intended destination a few feet in front of them, he swept at the floor with the bottom of his shoe, clearing a spot. She could see several scratches in the cement and moved a little closer for a better view. She could make out several circles with the three triangles etched into the floor.

"So, you're David Collins," Elizabeth stated.

"I am not David, not anymore. He died in that tunnel, and Salvator was born." He gestured to himself and smiled. "Salvator means savior, in case you are interested in learning any new Latin."

"But..." Simon spoke up, which surprised her, as he had been mute since Father Parker arrived. "Father Rossi said that you would be...dead. He said Gesler's kids...they all died."

She realized that David was Geizler's breakthrough, just as he claimed in his journal.

"Lucky me then," Father Parker snorted derisively with Raymond still nestled in his grip. Father Parker turned his head upward and pointed to the ceiling for Raymond's benefit. "See? There it is."

Raymond followed his finger and smiled at the faded picture painted on the ceiling. "The falling star. It's just like you said," he stated in childlike wonder.

She looked up to see an antique painted sign on the concrete ceiling that was probably once vibrant, but was now a faded black and sickly yellow. With only a flashlight, Elizabeth had missed it on her prior visits.

Its design resembled the carvings on the bodies. It was a black circle containing three congruent yellow triangles with their points joining in the center, an image with which she had become very familiar. Below the circle with the triangles, some of the original letters remained. *Fall S t r.* Even with the missing letters that had been erased with time, she knew what it once read.

"This room used to be a fallout shelter," she said, hoping to rain on Father Parker's romantic notions about a sign that was a reminder of the country's darkest fear.

He was unfazed. "I spent hours staring at this. I memorized every detail, so that when they took away the lantern, I could still see it. It was my constellation." Father Parker jumped and abruptly turned his head to the corner. The arrogance from his face drained. "I haven't done anything—but I, I didn't bring them here," he said meekly to the empty space and continued to hold on to Raymond, but now more for comfort. "They—they just came."

Elizabeth followed Father Parker's stare into the dark corner. "Who are you talking to?"

"Shhh, quiet, you'll only upset him more," he said.

She fixed her eyes on Father Parker. "Who?"

He ignored her and stared at the corner and nodded to keep up his end of the conversation that only he could hear.

"Father." After a moment of silence, she tried again. "Father, please. There is nobody there."

He tore his gaze away from the corner and looked at her in disbelief. "He's there," he whispered. "I can't protect you from him."

She shuddered as she watched Father Parker engage in a one-sided conversation. She was spooked, but realized that keeping him focused on his ghost was her best option for getting Raymond and her out of there.

"Who is he?" she asked.

"It is David."

"You said that he died in the tunnel."

"He did, but he continues to live here. I can't stop. He won't let me stop."

She considered arguing the logic of Father Parker's sociopathic reasoning, but thought the better of it. She knew she had to confront his demon and turned to face the dark corner. "Please let me help you. We can stop them all, the mayor, IPR. The truth can be told, but I need your help. Please."

Father Parker turned to face the corner to hear the response to Elizabeth's emphatic plea, and his face contorted, but she couldn't read it. He was lost in a world only he could see, and from that distant place he spoke. "She can help us." After a moment of silence, he pointed accusingly to the corner. "It wasn't me. You killed them."

Father Parker released his grip on Raymond and shifted his stance to square off against the corner. She stared at his profile and wondered whether it was the childhood trauma that led him to this or if it was an unknown side effect of Geizler's breakthrough. She pushed the thought away and refocused. She crept forward and yanked on Raymond's sleeve, pulling him toward her. Raymond turned his face toward Father Parker, but shuffled his feet to her as though he was on a line being reeled in. Raymond's foot knocked into the abandoned flashlight on the floor and toppled it, and she jumped at the jarring noise, then quickly bent to retrieve it before it rolled.

"You're the weak one!" Father Parker yelled to the corner. "You let them have you!"

Raymond flinched at the father's angry voice, and she covered his mouth with her finger to silence him, then handed him the flashlight. Father Parker continued to stare at his ghost as though taking in the reply to his harsh accusation.

With this distraction, Elizabeth made small steps back and slowly lowered herself to grab the crowbar that she had left resting near Simon. She made eye contact with Simon to assure him that she hadn't forgotten him, but she knew that the only way to save him was to save Raymond and herself.

She crept back to Raymond and tugged at his free hand, pulling him toward the concrete door leading to the tunnel. With the crowbar tucked under her arm, she reached for the handle and pulled with both hands.

"No!" came a scream from Father Parker.

She jerked her hands back, causing the crowbar to fall from under her arm, and she turned around, only to find Father Parker still locked into a heated argument with the corner.

She resumed pulling on the handle and flinched when Raymond placed his hand on her shoulder, but quickly realized that it wasn't Raymond when the hand changed from slight pressure to pain of fingers digging into her clavicle. She deftly twisted and swung her fist, catching Father Parker across the side of the head. He stumbled back at the unexpected blow, and she followed with a second punch, but missed when he moved out of striking distance. With her hit missing its target, Elizabeth lost her balance and fell forward onto her knees, and Father Parker approached her with the knife.

"I told you, I couldn't protect you," he said without remorse.

He was stopped when Raymond stepped between them with the crowbar raised above his head, hovering over Elizabeth.

Father Parker smiled. "That's my boy."

"Raymond, please. You can't do this," she pleaded.

Raymond stood suspended, caught between the two forces.

A tear rolled down Elizabeth's cheek as she squeezed her eyes shut.

A dull thump sounded, and she opened her eyes to see Father Parker drop to the ground and Raymond standing above him poised to deliver another blow.

"No, Raymond. That's enough."

He released the crowbar from his trembling hands and let it fall, and she popped up and frantically yanked on the door and freed it open. She pushed Raymond through, but he stopped just inside the tunnel, and she ran into the back of him. Raymond's eyes stared in wild fear into the blackness in front of him.

"Run, Raymond!"

Elizabeth knew he shook his head in refusal by the bouncing of the flashlight in his hand. "Please, Raymond. Run. There's danger behind us. Use your flashlight." She began pushing him with what strength she had, and he began to move. The danger and urgency of the situation finally set in with him, and he picked up speed. His flashlight bounced wildly about the tunnel walls as they ran.

Raymond's legs moved effortlessly through the darkness, but

Elizabeth stumbled and fell to one knee. He hauled her up with one hand and began pulling her along, but she didn't have time to analyze the irony. She could only concentrate on the pounding of her heart in her ears.

"Stop," came a screech that seemed to be magnified by the echo bouncing off the walls, and she could hear the labored breathing behind them.

She knew they were closing in on the end when the light passed across the metal grate guarding the door to the forest. "There's the end," she yelled breathlessly to Raymond, just as an unseen force rammed into her back, causing her to fall into Raymond. Elizabeth and Raymond toppled into a heap onto the unforgiving dirt floor. Father Parker threw himself on top, and she rolled, sending Father Parker to the side. Raymond scrambled to his feet with the flashlight still clutched in his grip, and Father Parker rose, lunging for him, the knife still in his hand.

Elizabeth felt movement under her hand as she pushed herself up. She closed her fist and threw herself at Father Parker and wrapped her arms around him. Before he could break free from her hold, she jammed her hand into the top of his shirt and released. Father Parker let out a bloodcurdling scream as he was bitten by a frantic rat trapped in his shirt.

She didn't have to prompt Raymond to run this time; he was already at the metal grate, shaking it violently. She pulled the grate away from the side. "Raymond, over here."

He quickly covered the short space between them, and Elizabeth began pushing him through the small space. He squealed when he became lodged between the grate and the wall. His stomach was pushed tight against the side of the metal frame, and he began to flail his arms in panic. "Raymond, relax. You can do this. Suck in your stomach." He pulled in a deep breath and she pushed. "More, Raymond, suck in more." He popped free to the other side, and she followed through in a fraction of the time.

Raymond yanked on the door handle. "Raymond, pull the handle up."

The door flung open under the excessive force, and Raymond flew backward and fell. She helped pick him up, and they ran into the woods. The warm, stale air of the tunnel was replaced with crisp fall air, and she relished it and took in a lung full. The light was nearly gone as the sun approached the horizon.

Elizabeth took a moment to study the direction of the school. She knew that Father Parker would be behind them and could easily catch them if they ran the predicted route directly to the school, so she opted to run a path parallel to the school and hoped to cut to the parking lot from the far end. Raymond had a difficult time making his way through the underbrush and stumbled several times. To his credit, he kept himself quiet despite the urge to yell out with each near tumble, and she held his hand to guide him and whispered words of encouragement to keep him moving.

Because of Raymond's slow motor skills through the undergrowth, it took several minutes before they reached a distance that she believed equaled the opposite end of the school property. She redirected Raymond to cut toward the school and stopped just short of the property. They followed the circumference of the school just inside the tree line, and Elizabeth could see the hollowed structure of where the main school building once stood. She paused and took shallow breaths in hopes to make it easier to hear any subtle noise, but it was futile because Raymond was panting.

After neither sight nor sound of Father Parker, she turned to Raymond and gestured with a shushing finger to her mouth for him to remain quiet. She tugged on his hand to follow, and they crept past the demolished building and out to the parking lot. Father Parker was still nowhere to be seen, but a blue Toyota Camry sat adjacent to her Roadster.

When she reached her car, she motioned for Raymond to go to the passenger side and pulled on her door handle. It was locked.

"Raymond, where are the keys?"

He pointed to the keys lying on the passenger seat next to her phone.

"You locked the keys in the car?" she whispered harshly.

"Always lock the car," he recited.

"But not with the keys in the car."

Raymond relayed how he dutifully pushed the lock button on the key fob and then tossed the keys on the seat before he closed the door.

"You're supposed to take the keys with you."

"But I might lose them," he explained rationally.

She ran her hands through her hair in frustration, but knew it was useless to argue with him at this point. She backed away from the car and noticed that the tires had been slashed.

"I'm getting good at that," Father Parker said from behind her.

She jumped and ran to Raymond's side of the car.

Father Parker started to circle the car toward them, and Elizabeth and Raymond moved the opposite way, trying to keep the car between them. She searched her brain for options, but she could think of no good choice.

"Raymond, run." She grabbed his hand and pulled him along.

Father Parker easily caught up to them and pulled her to the ground and straddled her, pinning her arms at her side. He held the knife mockingly over her. Raymond stood at her side, tears streaming down his face, and started pushing Father Parker in an effort to free her. With the knife handle gripped firmly in his palm, Father Parker swiped at Raymond and cut him across the abdomen. Raymond fell to the ground cradling his stomach, blood saturating his shirt.

"Fuck you, asshole." Elizabeth swung a fist that she had worked free and connected with Father Parker's face. His head jerked back, and she bucked her body, tossing him to the side. She jumped on him and began pounding him with her closed fists.

Father Parker raised the knife to lunge it at Elizabeth, and she grabbed his hand holding the knife. Despite the dominant position on top of Father Parker, she was losing the battle for the knife, and it moved closer to her chest.

Elizabeth closed her eyes, unwilling to watch, when Father Parker suddenly yelped and jerked his leg, allowing her to gain control of the knife. Using her body weight, she jammed it into his chest, and Father Parker's eyes widened with surprise at the turn of events. In one swift motion, she rolled off him and saw Raymond locked on to Father Parker's leg with his mouth. She pulled Raymond away, blood dripping down his chin, and crawled toward her car. She settled Raymond against the car and went in search of a large rock to break her window and free her phone.

Just as she crashed the rock through her passenger window, Grace raced into the parking lot and pulled up next to her. "Seriously, you waited until after I threw the rock?"

Grace ignored the remark and rushed to her and pulled her into a tight embrace. Elizabeth allowed herself to be held, enveloped in the warmth, prior arguments and personal boundaries no longer relevant, and she could feel Grace's body shivering.

"Are you all right?" Elizabeth asked.

Grace pushed her back, just enough to see her face. "Am *I* all right? Are you all right? I was scared to death when I got your message and then you didn't answer my calls. Are you hurt?" She brushed the hair out of Elizabeth's face and caressed her cheek. Elizabeth closed her eyes and leaned into her touch.

Grace softly traced her finger over her lips. "God, you're beaut—"

"I don't feel so good," Raymond interrupted from the other side of the car, still propped up against the tire.

"Oh, Raymond, I'm so sorry." Elizabeth pulled away and ran to him, cradling him in her arms.

CHAPTER THIRTY-FOUR

Elizabeth stopped to admire the fresh window sign of the Southern Indigent Legal Center. The new storefront, as well as SILC's other upgrades, were compliments of Elizabeth's father and CRAK. She smiled in approval and walked through the glass door. Amy sat at her usual post with a phone to her ear and eagerly waved to her as she passed.

SILC was the same, but very different, and Elizabeth's stomach churned at the thought. It didn't take long for the missing one hundred thousand dollars from the archdiocese to be traced to the clinic. Although Dan couldn't be implicated in any impropriety, he resigned in the best interest of the clinic and named Elizabeth as his successor as supervising attorney before he departed.

Rosa Sanchez walked past with a file box in her arms and deposited it into a cubicle. "Morning, Ms. Campbell." She beamed. "All the files have been put in alphabetical order in the cabinets."

"Thank you, Rosa."

"No, thank you, Ms. Campbell. You have done so much for me and Hector. Giving me this job was more than I could ever dream." Tears welled in her eyes.

Elizabeth offered a tight smile, afraid to speak for fear that her voice would betray her. She and Rosa shared a silent bond—Father Parker. He had been a generous soul, a trusted confidant, and a betrayer. With nothing more that they could say, Rosa turned to finish her task.

Elizabeth moved to her old office and paused to look at three new filing cabinets that were efficiently lined up against the wall. A worker dressed in paint-splotched clothes had his back to her, and he reached for one of the framed inspirational posters.

"That's okay, you can leave that."

The man looked at the poster once more before he made his exit. She wasn't sure why she decided to keep it, but she just knew she would feel its loss. It was too many changes at once.

She approached BD and stroked its worn black leather. "Hello, old friend."

BD reminded her of Grace—they were both cranky, didn't adjust well to new people, but once she got to really know them, they became a needed friend, both providing a source of comfort, although her relationship with BD was less confusing.

"Speaking of the devil." She smiled.

"What?" Grace asked as she walked in and settled into the worn black chair on the other side of the desk.

With no words to answer the simple question, Elizabeth shrugged it off and continued to caress the top of BD.

They remained in companionable silence for a moment, and she understood that Grace was working something through in her head. Grace finally spoke, but didn't look up. "They've been digging up behind the school."

Another moment passed in silence. Despite her usual impatience, she gave Grace the time she seemed to need.

"They found twelve bodies so far. Eleven of them were kids. The adult body was under the tree you showed me."

"The lovers' tree?"

Grace nodded. "I expect it's Geizler's body. There's still a lot more ground to cover. I'm certain there will be many more children before we're done."

A perverse sadness blanketed the room.

"What about Simon Fisher and the mayor?" Elizabeth asked.

"Simon Fisher is completely cooperating, and he's confirmed what we suspected. Reynosa and Pallone took Geizler's research journal when they were clearing out his lab in the mill. Sullivan and Simon were offered shares in IPR for their silence." She shifted in her chair before continuing. "Reynosa, on the other hand, the true politician, is categorically denying it all, but it's only a matter of time before he goes down. The feds raided IPR and seized all the research and records. The clinical trials and patent have been suspended."

"I'm glad, but..." Elizabeth paused.

"The children?"

"Yeah, I mean, how many children died for that research? Geizler might have actually found the cure," she emphasized the last words, "and it will probably be lost. It just seems wrong on so many levels."

Elizabeth turned to look out her window, needing a moment to process it. Fred, the rat, scurried across one of the trash cans in the alley. "What about Father Parker or, uh, David Collins?" She corrected, nearly choking on the name.

"Physically, he'll be fine. The knife missed any major organs." A wave of relief washed over Elizabeth. He was a monster, but she didn't want to be responsible for taking any life. "He's being held at a maximum security psychiatric hospital. It's doubtful he'll ever be deemed competent to stand trial."

Elizabeth wrapped her arms around herself in an attempt to thwart the chill that was growing inside her, and she could feel rather than hear Grace move behind her. "Grace," she whispered, her voice catching in her throat, and she turned to face her.

"I want…" Grace's voice trailed off, her usual confidence waning. Elizabeth assumed it was easier for her when she was filled with fear and could pull Elizabeth to her without thought, panic overruling reason; but now, Grace looked conflicted.

Elizabeth reached out and rested her open palm on Grace's chest and slowly and deliberately slid it up to her shoulder, her neck, and then the back of her head. Elizabeth watched her own hand in fascination as though it moved of its own accord, then tore her eyes away to watch Grace, who stood motionless with her stare never wavering. "I want to kiss you," Elizabeth breathed out, and Grace responded by ducking her head, meeting her halfway.

Elizabeth closed her eyes when she felt the soft warmth against her lips, and she craved more. She used her hand still perched behind Grace's head to pull her forward and pushed her lips harder, then groaned when she felt a warm silk tongue slip inside. She greedily pushed harder, wanting more.

Grace's hand traveled down her back, sliding over her bottom and gently massaging before she slipped her leg between Elizabeth's and held her tight as she continued to thrust her tongue inside her. Elizabeth felt an explosion of warmth emanate from her, and she pulled her lips away. "Oh God, Grace."

Grace held her as Elizabeth rested her head against her shoulder, not wanting to relinquish the moment. "I've wanted to do that since the first time we met. You were so smug and, God, so sexy," Grace panted out.

Elizabeth kissed her neck and reminisced about their first encounter when she approached the stout man by mistake. "Thank God, Detective Donovan, that you didn't turn out to be the other guy."

"Excuse me, Ms. Campbell. Mrs. Francis is on the phone, and she said it's an emergency?" Rosa interrupted as she entered with a stack of files before she realized their position.

Elizabeth slowly pushed herself back, in no hurry to lose Grace's contact.

Rosa turned away. "I'm sorry. I didn't know you had a visitor."

"That's okay, Rosa. What's the problem?" Elizabeth said with a false smile, her body still vibrating with the last bit of pleasure.

"Mrs. Francis's grandson has been arrested and charged with murder, but she says he didn't do it."

"Oh no, here we go again," Grace groaned out.

David Collins lay on his back with his wrists encased in leather straps that secured him to the metal bed frame, and his ankles were equally secured. He stared at the white ceiling. The room reminded him of a time long ago, and he closed his eyes searching his mind for the star that once comforted him in his dark times. He found it and smiled.

"We're not done."

David darted his head to the corner, straining his neck, and stared in disbelief. "How—how did you get here?" he stumbled.

The voice ignored the question and repeated even more firmly, "We're not done."

"It's over," he said, his voice quavering.

"It's over when I say it's over," boomed the voice. The streak of bravery that caused David's rebellion in the cement room was fleeting, and he once again found himself cowering to the dominant power.

"Our work is not complete. There is one more."

"Who?" David meekly asked.

"Elizabeth Campbell. She is why we're here, and for this, she must pay."

About the Author

A. Rose Mathieu has been an attorney in California for more than twenty years, finding her most rewarding work to be with underserved populations. By challenging laws and bringing suits for those with too small a voice, she has been able to change legislation. She writes as an outlet, crafting mysteries with a touch of comic relief. Her first try in writing began in fifth grade with a short story that won her the top award in California. To fulfill her mother's dream of her becoming an author, A. Rose picked up the pen again and began to write.

A. Rose lives with her wife of nearly twenty years and their two children, spending weekends conquering a very busy school and sports schedule. She is inspired by their wit and imagination every day, as they develop into writers off their own.

Books Available From Bold Strokes Books

The Sniper's Kiss by Justine Saracen. The power of a kiss: it can swell your heart with splendor, declare abject submission, and sometimes blow your brains out. (978-1-62639-839-9)

Divided Nation, United Hearts by Yolanda Wallace. In a nation torn in two by a most uncivil war, can love conquer the divide? (978-1-62639-847-4)

Fury's Bridge by Brey Willows. What if your life depended on someone who didn't believe in your existence? (978-1-62639-841-2)

Lightning Strikes by Cass Sellars. When Parker Duncan and Sydney Hyatt's one-night stand turns to more, both women must fight demons past and present to cling to the relationship neither of them thought she wanted. (978-1-62639-956-3)

Love in Disaster by Charlotte Greene. A professor and a celebrity chef are drawn together by chance, but can their attraction survive a natural disaster? (978-1-62639-885-6)

Secret Hearts by Radclyffe. Can two women from different worlds find common ground while fighting their secret desires? (978-1-62639-932-7)

Sins of Our Fathers by A. Rose Mathieu. Solving gruesome murder cases is only one of Elizabeth Campbell's challenges; another is her growing attraction to the female detective who is hell-bent on keeping her client in prison. (978-1-62639-873-3)

Troop 18 by Jessica L. Webb. Charged with uncovering the destructive secret that a troop of RCMP cadets has been hiding, Andy must put aside her worries about Kate and uncover the conspiracy before it's too late. (978-1-62639-934-1)

Worthy of Trust and Confidence by Kara A. McLeod. FBI Special Agent Ryan O'Connor is about to discover the hard way that when you can only handle one type of answer to a question, it really is better not to ask. (978-1-62639-889-4)

Amounting to Nothing by Karis Walsh. When mounted police officer Billie Mitchell steps in to save beautiful murder witness Merissa Karr, worlds collide on the rough city streets of Tacoma, Washington. (978-1-62639-728-6)

Becoming You by Michelle Grubb. Airlie Porter has a secret. A deep, dark, destructive secret that threatens to engulf her if she can't find the courage to face who she really is and who she really wants to be with. (978-1-62639-811-5)

Birthright by Missouri Vaun. When spies bring news that a swordswoman imprisoned in a neighboring kingdom bears the Royal mark, Princess Kathryn sets out to rescue Aiden, true heir to the Belstaff throne. (978-1-62639-485-8)

Crescent City Confidential by Aurora Rey. When romance and danger are in the air, writer Sam Torres learns the Big Easy is anything but. (978-1-62639-764-4)

Love Down Under by MJ Williamz. Wylie loves Amarina, but if Amarina isn't out, can their relationship last? (978-1-62639-726-2)

Privacy Glass by Missouri Vaun. Things heat up when Nash Wiley commandeers a limo and her best friend for a late drive out to the beach: Champagne on ice, seat belts optional, and privacy glass a must. (978-1-62639-705-7)

The Impasse by Franci McMahon. A horse-packing excursion into the Montana Wilderness becomes an adventure of terrifying proportions for Miles and ten women on an outfitter-led trip. (978-1-62639-781-1)

The Right Kind of Wrong by PJ Trebelhorn. Bartender Quinn Burke is happy with her life as a playgirl until she realizes she can't fight her feelings any longer for her best friend, bookstore owner Grace Everett. (978-1-62639-771-2)

Wishing on a Dream by Julie Cannon. Can two women change everything for the chance at love? (978-1-62639-762-0)

A Quiet Death by Cari Hunter. When the body of a young Pakistani girl is found out on the moors, the investigation leaves Detective Sanne Jensen facing an ordeal she may not survive. (978-1-62639-815-3)

Buried Heart by Laydin Michaels. When Drew Chambliss meets Cicely Jones, her buried past finds its way to the surface. Will they survive its discovery or will their chance at love turn to dust? (978-1-62639-801-6)

Escape: Exodus Book Three by Gun Brooke. Aboard the Exodus ship *Pathfinder*, President Thea Tylio still holds Caya Lindemay, a clairvoyant changer, in protective custody, which has devastating consequences endangering their relationship and the entire Exodus mission. (978-1-62639-635-7)

Genuine Gold by Ann Aptaker. New York, 1952. Outlaw Cantor Gold is thrown back into her honky-tonk Coney Island past, where crime and passion simmer in a neon glare. (978-1-62639-730-9)

Into Thin Air by Jeannie Levig. When her girlfriend disappears, Hannah Lewis discovers her world isn't as orderly as she thought it was. (978-1-62639-722-4)

Night Voice by CF Frizzell. When talk show host Sable finally acknowledges her risqué radio relationship with a mysterious caller, she welcomes a *real* relationship with local tradeswoman Riley Burke. (978-1-62639-813-9)

Raging at the Stars by Lesley Davis. When the unbelievable theories start revealing themselves as truths, can you trust in the ones who have conspired against you from the start? (978-1-62639-720-0)

She Wolf by Sheri Lewis Wohl. When the hunter becomes the hunted, more than love might be lost. (978-1-62639-741-5)

Smothered and Covered by Missouri Vaun. The last person Nash Wiley expects to bump into over a two a.m. breakfast at Waffle House is her college crush, decked out in a curve-hugging law enforcement uniform. (978-1-62639-704-0)

The Butterfly Whisperer by Lisa Moreau. Reunited after ten years, can Jordan and Sophie heal the past and rediscover love or will differing desires keep them apart? (978-1-62639-791-0)

The Devil's Due by Ali Vali. Cain and Emma Casey are awaiting the birth of their third child, but as always in Cain's world, there are new and old enemies to face in Katrina-ravaged New Orleans. (978-1-62639-591-6)

Widows of the Sun-Moon by Barbara Ann Wright. With immortality now out of their grasp, the gods of Calamity fight amongst themselves, egged on by the mad goddess they thought they'd left behind. (978-1-62639-777-4)

Arrested Hearts by Holly Stratimore. A reckless cop who hates her life and a health nut who is afraid to die might be a perfect combination for love. (978-1-62639-809-2)

Capturing Jessica by Jane Hardee. Hyperrealist sculptor Michael tries desperately to conceal the love she holds for best friend, Jess, unaware Jess's feelings for her are changing. (978-1-62639-836-8)

Counting to Zero by AJ Quinn. NSA agent Emma Thorpe and computer hacker Paxton James must learn to trust each other as they work to stop a threat clock that's rapidly counting down to zero. (978-1-62639-783-5)

Courageous Love by KC Richardson. Two women fight a devastating disease, and their own demons, while trying to fall in love. (978-1-62639-797-2)

One More Reason to Leave Orlando by Missouri Vaun. Nash Wiley thought a threesome sounded exotic and exciting, but as it turns out the reality of sleeping with two women at the same time is just really complicated. (978-1-62639-703-3)

Pathogen by Jessica L. Webb. Can Dr. Kate Morrison navigate a deadly virus and the threat of bioterrorism, as well as her new relationship with Sergeant Andy Wyles and her own troubled past? (978-1-62639-833-7)

Rainbow Gap by Lee Lynch. Jaudon Vickers and Berry Garland, polar opposites, dream and love in this tale of lesbian lives set in Central Florida against the tapestry of societal change and the Vietnam War. (978-1-62639-799-6)

Steel and Promise by Alexa Black. Lady Nivrai's cruel desires and modified body make most of the galaxy fear her, but courtesan Cailyn Derys soon discovers the real monsters are the ones without the claws. (978-1-62639-805-4)

Swelter by D. Jackson Leigh. Teal Giovanni's mistake shines an unwanted spotlight on a small Texas ranch where August Reese is secluded until she can testify against a powerful drug kingpin. (978-1-62639-795-8)

Without Justice by Carsen Taite. Cade Kelly and Emily Sinclair must battle each other in the pursuit of justice, but can they fight their undeniable attraction outside the walls of the courtroom? (978-1-62639-560-2)

21 Questions by Mason Dixon. To find love, start by asking the right questions. (978-1-62639-724-8)

A Palette for Love by Charlotte Greene. When newly minted Ph.D. Chloé Devereaux returns to New Orleans, she doesn't expect her new job and her powerful employer—Amelia Winters—to be so appealing. (978-1-62639-758-3)

By the Dark of Her Eyes by Cameron MacElvee. When Brenna Taylor inherits a decrepit property haunted by tormented ghosts, Alejandra Santana must not only restore Brenna's house and property but also save her soul. (978-1-62639-834-4)

Never Enough by Robyn Nyx. Can two women put aside their pasts to find love before it's too late? (978-1-62639-629-6)